Copyright 2022 Danielle Aimie
Published by Artalure
https://danielleaimie.com/index.html
mailto:danielle@danielleaimie.com

Edition 3 License Notes

This eBook is licensed for your personal enjoyment only. This eBook may not be re-sold or given away to other people. If you would like to share this book with another person, please purchase an additional copy for each recipient. If you're reading this book and did not purchase it, or it was not purchased for your enjoyment only, then please return to Artalure.com or your favourite retailer and purchase your own copy.

Thank you for respecting the hard work of this author

Contents

Prologue – The ultimate fantasy 4

Chapter 1 – Am I middle aged and boring? 6

Chapter 2 – Watching 15

Chapter 3 – Life goals 23

Chapter 4 – My first strip tease 32

Chapter 5 – The Rules 42

Chapter 6 – List of Fantasies 50

Chapter 7 – My Interview... 60

Chapter 8 – Underwear shopping 67

Chapter 9 – My First Photo Shoot.. 76

Chapter 10 – Sharing My Fun 83

Chapter 11 – A Bad Date.. 90

Chapter 12 – The Beautiful Couple 100

Chapter 13 – Dress Shopping 112

Chapter 14 – Sex 121

Chapter 15 – My First, Second Interview 130

Chapter 16 – Not Sleeping My Way to The Top....................... 138

Chapter 17 – Setting Up a Fantasy Situation............................. 145

Chapter 18 – My First Group Experience 151

Chapter 19 – Thanking the Cameraman 160

Chapter 20 – Sharing My Porn 165

Chapter 21 – My First Girl Experience 175

Chapter 22 – Sex on A Yacht 182

Chapter 23 – I'm A Hotwife! 192

Chapter 24 – Chance Encounter 201

Chapter 25 – My Ultimate Fantasy Fulfilled 213

Connect with Danielle Aimie 225

Prologue – The ultimate fantasy

"So, what is this plan that you need help with?" Jess said with her usual, bright, beaming, joyful smile. She had greeted me with a kiss on the cheek. She took off her light summer jacket and sat herself down opposite me in the restaurant booth. She looked intrigued as she leant forward from the padded bench chair.

"Should we order first?" I asked, avoiding her question temporarily. "I'm a little nervous about telling you. I hope some food will help with the butterflies."

Jess laughed and rolled her head back as she did. "It must be good if it makes you nervous around me, Sophie. Take your time." She seemed amused by my shyness. We had been intimating with each other a few times. I suppose it was pretty unnecessary for me to feel any awkwardness, but I did anyway. Maybe it was because I was asking a favour? I hadn't known her for more than a few weeks. That was a potential explanation for my slight insecurities.

We ordered salads and a glass of white wine each, catching up on the mundane events of our mornings. She looked radiant in her figure-hugging knit dress. Her smiling face, shining happiness at me from across the table.

"Come on, I can't wait any longer, Soph." She interjected into our small talk. What are we going to do? You were so vague on the phone. I've been wondering about it ever since we spoke".

"Well," I drew the word out slightly, with a hint of a smile arriving at my lips. "I actually need your help with something just for me."

"Ok, with what?" She was leaning forward in her seat again now. Instinctively drawing herself closer to find out what I was planning.

"I've had a fantasy for years about being with a group of guys," I began." I'd like to be the centre of attention, where they all focus on me." I paused for a second to gauge her reaction.

"Go on," she urged. "That sounds exciting. How can I help?"

"The fantasy is about being submissive, I think." I continued. "I've read about it, and it seems to be very common. The thrill of having several men desire you, doing with you whatever they want."

"Not to mention the fact that it would be loads of sex." Tess laughed. "I don't know many women who haven't fantasised about that."

"That's exactly it, I've read that it is a very common fantasy, but I worry about how it might play out in real life. Being submissive would leave a lot to chance, and that is my concern. In a fantasy everything happens exactly the way you want it to, because you are inventing it. In reality, submitting yourself to a group of guys could be an awful experience. I want men to lust over me, but I don't want it left to the choices and impulses of men. That's where you come in." I grinned.

"You'll have to explain." She looked at me quizzically, not quite sure of what I was asking of her yet.

"I'd like you to be there with me to make sure it goes well." I paused for a split second, but then continued before she had a chance to respond. "I want to experience being submissive, and having men focus on me, but I'd like to experience it under your control. You can make it happen as if you were playing it out in your own fantasy. I won't have to think or give out orders. I don't want to have to say stop at any point. I can maintain my position of being submissive, knowing that nothing will happen to me that I won't like. I will be able to relax and focus on enjoying it." I paused now, waiting to see how she would respond.

"Ok. So, I would be in charge? Will I be naked as well?" She smiled an even wider smile than normal at the second question. Her smile exposed her straight teeth. The white contrasted vividly against the gloss red of her lipstick.

"You would be completely in charge, but not naked." I answered, with a smile. "That's why it would be a favour. I want the attention to be on me. You are so beautiful that'd you'd definitely draw away some of my spotlight."

"I see." She relaxed back into the booth bench. "Would you return the favour another time?" Her smile continued.

"Of course. You've asked before I could offer. The guys I will invite are so nice. You can take their numbers, or I can set it up for you? Either way, of course I'll return the favour. I know that you and I have similar ideas about fantasies. I know that if you are there, organising things in a way that you would want them to be for you, I'll have an amazing time. I want to forget myself and have no worries or concerns. It can be relaxed and fun, I don't want to be thinking about anything other than pleasure. I want you to do my thinking for me. I suppose I'll be submissive to you, which I like the thought of."

"It sounds very erotic. I'll be charged up after watching that." Jess gave a mock worried look at the prospect. "Can I get naked with you afterwards?"

"Definitely." I gave her a slight wink as I nodded agreement. "Should we go somewhere else for a drink? We can talk more as we walk. Lunch was on me."

"Your nerves seem to have gone!" Jess chuckled. "Ok, let's go. We might even meet some more prospective candidates for your plan."

"My nerves are still there, but I'm more excited now. If you hadn't said yes, I don't know what I would have done."

"You knew I'd say yes." Jess gave me a look which suggested I hadn't been honest with myself. "It sounds like an amazing idea. As if I'd miss out on watching some live porn! When are we going to do it?"

I laughed as we got up and picked up our bags. Of course, she was always going to say yes. I don't know why I had worried. I was very relaxed now. Exactly how I wanted to feel. "How about this weekend." I replied. "Why wait?"

Chapter 1 – Am I middle aged and boring?

Three months earlier.

"What do you mean our sex is boring?" I said, hearing my voice prickle and raise in volume as I said it.

"I didn't say that Soph." Paul replied over his shoulder as he rinsed his coffee cup in the sink. "I said our routine is boring. I always enjoy our sex, it's intense. We're amazing together. It's just that it's always the same. That's all."

That was a very carefully worded answer. Paul could do that. He knew how to make a controversial point, but without upsetting people. In other circumstances I admired it. His thoughtfulness, but at the moment it was frustrating me. I didn't want anything to be sugar coated. What he'd said had worried me, and I wanted to get to the bottom of it. "What do you want to do that's different?" I asked, still with a raised, and not very friendly tone.

He turned and lent back against the worktop, wiping the cup with a cloth. "Whatever you want." It seemed to be a genuine response, but it wasn't helpful. It meant that I now felt bad because our sex life had been called into question, and there was no obvious way to fix it. I hated talking about this stuff.

"I'm going to be late for work!" I shut the conversation down. I gave Paul a rushed goodbye kiss on the cheek after I'd gathered my things.

I walked out into the cool morning. It felt immediately good to get some space. Not space from Paul, but space from the intensity of intimate conversation. Talking about anything to do with sex made me clam up straight away. I never had any idea what to say. I always felt awkward and under pressure. What a very English stereotype I seemed to have become. I didn't feel like that was who I was on the inside. I felt that I should be confident, brave, sexual and sexy. I didn't seem to be able to express it outwardly, or even talk about it. My parents had never mentioned sex when I was growing up. I had never talked about it with anyone. I had listened to conversations between friends at school, but I don't think that helped to prepare me for grown-up conversations.

As I turned out of our drive and started my walk to work, I glanced back at our suburban street. I loved our house. I had always felt love when I looked at it. It was home. Situated in the overpopulated, but beautiful countryside, on the outskirts of London. Was everything in my life so middle class and ordinary?

Even our geography seemed too normal for words. I loved where we lived. I loved Paul. But it felt like everything was becoming very predictable. The thrill of life seemed to be drifting away. Suburban mediocrity had infiltrated my days. My future looked like a very well-trodden path. I had always assumed that I would somehow avoid that road, and never succumb to the usual trudge. I had always wanted to live a life less ordinary. Now my mind was filled with worries about my life of metaphorical grey. Was it all as a result of one thirty second conversation about sex? My thoughts were finding a life of their own in my head.

It wasn't actually a thirty second conversation. The bit about sex had been thirty seconds, and that was the only bit that I was focussed on. We had been talking about what we had in the diary over the next few weeks. During the conversation it had become clear that we weren't going to see each other very much. Paul leads a busy life, with work and friends, and it always frustrates me when he doesn't make enough time for us. I think a stable job creates a stable circle of friends. Lifestyles often seem to be centred around peoples work. Paul seemed to be happy to immerse himself in all aspects of his job, and the interrelated lifestyle. I wasn't as busy. My work, on the reception desk at the gym, was a stop gap job. Temporary, until I found something that I really wanted to do. I had always wanted to work in events. Even though I'd had a lot of interviews I had never been offered a job. It seemed to be so competitive. I'd been in my temporary stop gap job for almost five years. This morning I'd complained to Paul that I wasn't happy that he was about to be away from home so much. I had also mentioned that we hadn't had sex for a while. I'd pushed him to find out why, and that's when he'd said that our routine was boring. It had been difficult for me to pluck up the courage to mention it. Now I wished I hadn't.

My thoughts raced as I paced the fifteen-minute walk to the gym. It was the start of what was going to be a beautiful day. As soon as I'd noticed how lovely it was, I ignored it. The weather wasn't important today. I needed to get a grip of my feelings and stabilise my emotions. I didn't notice much else as I walked, and I soon arrived at work. The gym was an unattractive building. The bright blue sky and sunshine seemed to highlight how dull the lump of concrete and glass was. No different to most gyms. On beautiful days it seemed so strange to be leaving the sunshine behind. To enter into an artificial, airconditioned world, created for people to exercise. Reception was pretty quiet when I arrived and settled in, so I carried on thinking. I was lost in my own head for most of the morning, only interrupting myself to welcome someone, or to hand over a towel. I seemed to be convincing myself that everything in my life was going wrong. I couldn't pull myself back from that thought spiral. Everything I went over seemed to be plain, and terrifyingly normal. It took a while, but I eventually managed to drag myself out of the negative downward spin. I knew that this was about sex. I didn't want to change everything in my life. As far as I could tell I was having a wonderful time and I wouldn't change much at all, other than my job. I didn't want to move house. I loved Paul and wouldn't change being with him for anything in the world. The issue was sex. I felt stupid because I was the one who had brought it up during the conversation this morning. Now I was the one who felt terrible. I had invited this awful feeling with open arms, and now I wished I'd repressed it. "We haven't made love for over a month," I had blurted out. It wasn't the right time. Not even close. I find it so difficult to talk about sex that, when I've managed to wind myself up enough, it explodes out. I suppose my frustration had boiled up and I felt that I had to say something. Paul was honest in his reply, but no sooner had I said something, I had run away. It hadn't been very productive.

    I enjoy sex with Paul. I've been deeply in love with him since we met. He is a good-looking guy, and funny, and kind. I love him in a slightly different way from when we first got together, but still completely. He exercises quite a bit and eats well so he isn't one of those men who will fall into middle age before their time. He doesn't use the gym here. He has a small one available at work which he uses a lot, and he often runs. He's in great shape. I'm still attracted to him, even though we've been together for eight years, married for four. I still desire him. He's all I've ever wanted, and I'm happy. Why does he think our sex is boring?

Before I met Paul, I'd had a couple of long-term relationships. One at the end of school which lasted until I was about twenty. Then a five-year relationship with an older guy that I met in a previous job. I suppose I was pretty inexperienced in relationships. I was inexperienced in sex as well, come to think of it, but I didn't feel like I should be. It felt like circumstances had led me to this point in my life, not choice or desire. I'd never had the opportunity to experiment, or to have one-night stands. I'd always been in a relationship with someone. Pauls previous life could have been full of all kinds of adventurous sex that I knew nothing about! This thought chain was making me feel worse again. I felt angry that things weren't right. It annoyed me that with Paul going away so much with work, that we'd have little chance to sort it out. It felt like things needed to change, but his priorities were on other things. Was I in the backseat of his life?

I was only working a short shift in the morning. As soon as the four hours were up, I went through into the gym to work out. The basic wage on reception was made up for, in part, by the free gym membership. I loved working out, it always made me feel more positive, virtuous even. I started on the tread mill and immediately drifted into my thoughts again. Paul was an architect, spending a lot of time away during the week, visiting projects. We don't make love very often. A couple of times a month, but I'd always assumed that was because we weren't together all the time. When we first met, we had sex a lot. Sometimes we lacked sleep because of it. We were always in bed. We couldn't get enough of each other. I looked at myself in the mirror as I ran. "Does he still fancy me? Am I desirable?" I thought I was, but this morning had made me doubt many things. I was happy that, at thirty-four, I looked younger. Although I'd never been signed up as a model and whisked away to the catwalks of Paris, I had always considered myself to be pretty enough. I was symmetrical, which seems to be deemed important, with big eyes. They were the favourite part of me, along with my hair. Hair is so feminine. I'd always been lucky to have thick, healthy hair. I kept it long and loved how it made me feel. I liked my feminine and curvy body. I wasn't one of those women who wanted to change things. I would never consider surgery of any kind. I'm not sure if that's because I was lucky that I looked ok as I was, or whether it was because I objected to it as a feminist. I'd like to think it was the second reason, but I expected that my feminist standpoint was a luxury of circumstance. It wasn't all down to luck and circumstance though. I did control some of it. I didn't have any input when it came to my symmetry, but I did work hard in the gym, and I always ate well. You could make your own luck to some extent. Guys looked at me in the gym all the time. I think some of them probably wanted me, but I didn't really know. There was a gym regular watching me now. He was working out in the weights area and was constantly sneaking glances at me as I ran. I knew him fairly well. His name was Craig. We chatted when he passed through reception. Did he fancy me? Did he desire me? How can one short conversation make me question so much. Did Paul look at other women? Younger women? I'd had enough, I wanted to stop thinking about it.

Paul was working from home all day. I didn't do my normal work out. I had been running for longer than I'd realised, or intended, so I didn't move onto anything else. I showered and then set off home. I wanted to talk to Paul. That was the only way to stop this. All I wanted to do was stop feeling bad.

Paul was in the office when I arrived. He smiled as I came through the front door and asked if I wanted a coffee. All was back to normal, it seemed. Why wasn't he worrying himself into an early grave like me? Why hadn't our conversation affected him to his core and given him a morning of doubt and anxiety? I didn't want things to go back to normal. I was wound up. I wanted to confront this whilst I was still worked up enough to be capable of doing it.

"What are we going to do?" I demanded.

"What about?" Paul looked up with a slight smile, indicating his confusion.

"Sex!" I replied, with the same unfriendly tone of voice I had adopted this morning.

"That's a bit dramatic Sophie." Paul got up from his desk and moved towards me. "I don't think this needs to be an argument."

It didn't, but the only way I seem to be able to deal with things that are difficult is with confrontation. It almost feels like I'm confronting my feelings. I know it comes across as confronting other people, which can seem very unfair, but that didn't matter at the moment. I needed to say this. I needed to confront my thoughts, so if that meant an argument with Paul, then so be it.

"We've gone stale!" I stated, almost categorically. "Our relationship has lost what we first had together, and we need to do something about it!"

"Christ", Paul looked shocked. "Where has this come from?"

"Our conversation this morning," I said. "I don't want to have boring sex. I want to be appreciated. I want passion in our relationship." I was being aggressive. I couldn't help it. I felt sad, and anger was a way that I was able express my frustration and sadness. I could see Paul was reacting badly. He didn't say anything for a couple of seconds. Probably trying to repress an instinctive retaliation to my confrontation. "Ok, well what are you going to do about it?" He asked, after a significant silence, turning to face me as he spoke.

That took me by surprise. I had no idea. I wanted the problem solved. This was Paul's fault. He was the one who had said things were boring. I wanted him to resolve the anxiety and worry that he'd caused. Now he had turned it around. It seemed like such a reasonable question, but it made me so angry. "Don't you care?" I was shouting now.

"Why are you shouting?" He asked. He was calm, but there was a hint of frustration creeping into his voice.

"I want more." I continued with a raised voice but being careful not to shout. "This isn't right. We're not right!" All my frustration was boiling now. "We can't go on like this!"

Paul turned his face away, visibly annoyed. "Why can't we just talk about it?" he asked. "I don't understand why you're so angry."

"I'm angry because you don't seem to care about this. Are you having an affair? Is that why you don't care about our sex life?"

"Fuck off." Paul's reply was blunt. He seemed hurt, and angry. I didn't know why I'd said that, and I didn't know what I was going to say next. I turned around and walked straight back out of the front door before anything else could come out of my mouth. I wasn't being rational, and I didn't want to say something awful that couldn't be unsaid.

My head was racing as I stormed away from the house. That hadn't worked at all. I felt so much worse than I had before. Tears rolled down my cheeks. Everything seemed so confusing. I couldn't focus on any individual thoughts. How had this happened. It all made me feel so upset. I had a burning in my gut, a desire to change things, but not the first understanding of what to change or how to change it. I was walking back to the gym. I needed some space. I had to somehow control the thoughts in my head and make some rational decisions.

I walked straight past reception and went to get a drink in the coffee shop. I ordered, then waited for the new girl behind the counter to prepare my coffee. It was a relief to break my thoughts and have some contact with someone else. I even managed to force a smile. The girl looked like she'd only left school a few weeks ago. She was wearing too much make up and had a blue streak in her blond hair. Girls care so much about what they look like at that age. How do they spend so much time on it and still get it so wrong? She wasn't a pretty girl, but the way she was presenting herself was highlighting that. I felt a little pang of sorrow for her. I imagined all the angst and self-doubt in her. I gave her another smile as she handed me my drink. I went and sat at a small table, to the side of the room, out of the way. What was I going to do now? I was still wound up too much to think clearly, so I ended up staring out of the window. I took a few deep breaths and tried to step back. I tried to put myself in the position I had been in last night. Paul and I had watched a movie together, with a glass of wine and the lights low. It had been lovely. Thinking about this immediately made me feel better. I knew that Paul wasn't the issue, nor was our life together. I'd been through that already. Why had I forgotten all that when I had spoken to Paul? Life doesn't change dramatically in less than twenty-four hours.

Not without some kind of unexpected outside influence at least. No revelation, or act of God had entered my life. What had made me feel this bad then? It became obvious as I gazed out of the window. It was the mediocrity that I was fearing. It was treading water in my stop gap job. It was the lack of any life built around my career. A career that didn't exist. The cherry on the bun was the boring sex. I was angry because I had become the person that I didn't want to be. In a situation that I never thought I'd be in. It was quite a moment of realisation, whilst looking out of that window. I just sat there and kept on looking.

Chapter 2 – Watching

After another coffee, I sent a text to Paul saying "sorry, I love you." For what seemed like hours of staring out of the window, but was probably only half an hour, I relaxed a bit. It seemed like most of the pressure that had built up had exploded out of me this morning. I felt better. As I sipped my third coffee, I carried on trying to stay objective about what was happening. I definitely needed to build my career. First priority, I needed to become the same confident, dynamic individual, that I wanted to be. I felt sure that if I could manage that, it would help me with my career. There were more pressing issues that I needed to deal with before these priorities kicked in. I needed to apply the same confidence to my situation with Paul, which was about sex. I needed to be brave and address the issue, without breaking anything else. As far as I could tell, everything else was fine.

I felt an immediate shift in my mood. The change from negative to positive felt good. I was going to take charge and make things better.

"Are you ok?" A concerned voice interrupted me from my gaze into the middle distance. It was Craig. He'd finished his workout and was heading to the exit with his gym bag over his shoulder.

"I'm fine, thank you." I managed enough of a smile to try to suggest that there was nothing wrong. Sitting alone, staring out of a window wasn't the best way to give the impression of everything being fine.

"How are you?" I asked before he could continue, trying to divert the conversation away from me.

"I'm ok thanks, working hard, training hard, the usual. I saw you running earlier, you seemed to be going for it today!"

"I had a lot on my mind", I replied. "I like to run when I need time to think." Is he flirting I wondered? Not that it mattered to me whether he was or wasn't. Is this a guy who fancies me, or is he a friend? It had been so long since I'd considered the motivations of others, that I'd forgotten how to understand these interactions at all. I'd known him for a couple of years, and yet I didn't know what he thought of me. I wanted to know. Why not take the opportunity to practice my ability to talk directly? They say practice makes perfect. Now was the time to start becoming the person I wanted to be. Here was a chance to be the new me in a situation that didn't matter. The trouble was, I didn't have the first idea how to start.

"Did you like watching?" I asked and focussed my gaze onto him. "I saw you looking." I could hardly believe the words had passed my lips. I hadn't flirted with anyone for years. I wasn't even sure if this was flirting, but now I wanted to know what he thought. It all seemed very relevant to my self-doubts and relationship problems. He looked quite shocked.

"I'm sorry, I wasn't……I didn't……." he looked mortified. That wasn't flirting, I'd made him feel like a pervert. Oh God, I felt bad for him. He was a nice guy.

"Don't worry" I said. "I liked that you looked". That seemed to soften the atmosphere. That might have been better than my opening effort. My initial flirtation had probably seemed about as sexy as a knock on the door from the police. He dropped his eyes as he tried to think of a response.

"You have a lovely body. I enjoy watching you. I hope that doesn't make you feel uncomfortable?"

"Not at all" I replied, not actually caring what he thought. "I didn't know you fancied me." I'd realised as soon as I'd said it that I'd assumed a lot. He hadn't said anything about fancying me, he only said that he was watching me. I wondered if I'd put him in another difficult position.

"Of course, who wouldn't?" He was looking straight at me now. "I bet you get attention all the time."

He was wrong about me getting attention. I felt like I didn't get any. This was a confidence boost that I hadn't expected. The new me needed this energy to take control.

"Do you want a coffee?" I asked. Talking to someone seemed to be making my mind slow down. Spending time on something other than my own thoughts felt good.

"I need a shower", he replied. "There is only one working in the changing room, and someone was using it."

"You can use the staff shower if you like?" I offered. "It hardly ever gets used."

"Ok". Craig seemed a bit hesitant. I had worked at the gym for a long time, I didn't think anyone would mind if I let a long-standing customer use the staff shower. Especially when there was a shower out of order. It wasn't something that needed management sign off.

"I'll show you where it is," I said, getting up from the table and moving towards the gym. The staff changing room was opposite the men's and women's changing rooms. It didn't have a sign on the door, but there was a keypad lock. There was a cupboard containing all the cleaning equipment as you entered. To the left was the changing room, laid out pretty much the same as the male and female changing rooms. There was a bench in the middle with some hooks above it, and another bench against the far wall. On the far side of the room was an open shower area, with two showers on the wall on the right-hand side. I picked up a towel from the worktop where the basin and mirrors were.

"Here you go," I said as I passed Craig a towel. "You can use one of these. Leave it in the basket afterwards." I nodded to a laundry basket next to the basin counter. Craig took the towel from me and put his bag down on the bench.

"Thank you", he said. "Should I meet you back in the coffee shop?"

"It's my turn." I replied folding my arms and leaning back against the counter.

"Your turn to what?" he glanced round at me, looking confused.

"Watch." I smiled. I had enjoyed the tiny bit of flirting from earlier, it had made me feel a bit lighter of mood. I thought I'd push things a bit further. This was definitely flirting now, and even though it could make life awkward for me, it felt good. I wanted to know how much he fancied me. I needed more of the confidence drug. A moments silence passed. I smiled again and continued. "You watch me whilst I'm running, it's only fair that I get to watch you."

"You want to watch me get undressed?" He still seemed confused. He hadn't moved from the centre of the room.

"And shower." I added. I hoped my smile would make this seem more like flirting, than blackmail. He looked down at the floor for a second, and then looked to the door as if in thought.

"What if someone comes in?" He asked.

"They won't. It's only staff who have the code and the only two staff in the gym today are busy with clients. Besides which, neither of them has ever used the staff changing room. They always go home in their gym kit."

As Craig took his t-shirt off it struck me that this wasn't flirting. There were definite consequences. Flirting was less definitive. His only options were to strip, or to leave. I suppose he could have carried on talking, and then left. Ultimately, leaving was still one of the only two outcomes available. I'd expected him to tell me he had a girlfriend, or to say that he wasn't comfortable. I expected him to make any kind of excuse and I was prepared to head back to the coffee shop and wait for him. What I wasn't expecting, was for him to do exactly as I'd asked.

He was half naked now. He looked good. He must have been still pumped up from his workout, as he had a bigger physique than I had expected. The lighting in the changing room was bright from above. It cut shadows into the areas of his body that enhanced the definition of his muscular frame. I liked it. He looked at me before sliding his tracksuit bottoms down and over his feet. He pulled his socks off as he removed his pants and stood in front of me in only his boxers. It felt so good to be in such a position of control. As I stood there, fully clothed, I knew that he desired me. He was prepared to put himself in such a vulnerable position in front of me. This was more than him being physically naked, he was exposed in so many ways, and I was not. He paused for a second, before removing his boxers and walking into the shower.

I watched for a few moments as he turned on the water and waited for it to run warm. His back was to me for a while giving me a chance to study the curve of his bottom for a few seconds. When he turned back to look at me, I smiled and turned to leave. "I'll see you in the café," I said as I headed for the door.

I was gazing out of the window again when Craig came back. He asked if I wanted anything, and then went to the counter to order. My racing thoughts were under control now. I had managed to pull myself out of the trap of my own head. I couldn't believe what I'd done, but it had been fun. I had felt very in control. I wasn't nervous at all about what I was going to say to Craig, which surprised me. I felt complete calm. Whatever I did, or said, was up to me. No one else had any influence. It seemed liberating not to care about what was going on in someone else's head. I was doing exactly what I wanted, and Craig could like it or lump it.

He sat down with his coffee, stirred it, and looked up at me. He was nervous. That made me feel even better. "Good shower?" I asked with a smile.

"Very, thank you." Some of the nervous tension seemed to be released from him as we began to talk.

"What are you doing with the rest of the day?" I continued.

"I've got to do some work at some point," he said, as if it was the last thing he wanted to do, or even think about. "I expect I'll put it off for a while by tidying up at home and watching some daytime TV. Then I'll do a couple of hours after lunch. I'm out with some friends this evening."

"Are you going anywhere nice?" I asked.

"Just for a few drinks, nothing out of the ordinary."

"What is your job?" I realised I didn't know much about him. It's amazing how you can say hello to someone for years, and make small talk about your surroundings, but not actually find out anything about them. I was sure some people's entire friendship circles were made up of people that they knew nothing about. It's a very hassle-free way of engaging with others.

"I'm an accountant", he responded. "I work for a small firm, it's almost like working for myself. It means I can work from home when I want. As long as my customers are happy. I can pretty much do what I like."

"Is it boring?" I wanted to know. I'd often heard people say accountants were boring.

"I wouldn't say it's boring. It's interesting to see how businesses work, or don't work. I get to be involved in some pretty good projects, without the pressures that come with owning a business. I just do the numbers. I don't make that much difference to whether anything succeeds or fails. That's down to the management and sales teams I suppose".

"Doesn't that ever seem a bit peripheral?" I pushed. "Don't you ever feel the need to be creative?"

"Not really," he seemed genuinely not to care. "As long as I can pay my bills and sleep at night, I don't worry. I've seen enough people stressed out by business, that I know it's not for me. I'm happy with what I do. What about you? Does working at the gym get your creative juices flowing?"

I smiled. That was a very fair question. It seemed that we were actually developing a conversation that was interesting to me. What had happened in the changing room hadn't made things awkward between us. "It's a stop gap job that I can't seem to move on from." I told him. My face scrunched to demonstrate my displeasure. "I'd love to work in events. Being creative and interacting with loads of interesting people, but I can't seem to get a foothold."

"You don't seem like the type", Craig said with a confused look on his face. He could see from the reaction in my face that he may be on the verge of offending me. He continued, "you seem very quiet, I mean."

"I wasn't quiet when I was telling you to strip for me in the shower!" I stated, to defend myself.

"Very true." he nodded. "That was a surprise. Is that the real you?"

"I don't know," I dropped my guard and answered honestly. "Maybe I am quiet. Maybe that's why I am stuck working here." The conversation seemed to be turning back in the direction of the thoughts that had plagued me earlier. This was more productive than my initial wild, spiralling thoughts. It seemed like I was able to articulate myself. Having to explain things to someone else seemed to help make sense of it.

"Do you have a girlfriend?" I changed the subject in spite of the potential upsides of opening up to someone. I'd done enough thinking for one day.

He hesitated for a split second, and then replied, "Sort of. We've been together for a couple of months. It's going ok." He definitely would have said no if I had been single. I could see the thoughts going through his mind. He wanted to keep his options open but didn't want to seem desperate. He was talking in a very non-comital way about his girlfriend so he would seem available somehow. The conversation was becoming interesting again.

"Do you think she would mind you showering in front of me?" I wanted to know.

"If she found out," he nodded. "I don't suspect she'll ever know though, so she'll never have the chance to mind. I wouldn't want to hurt her."

"Have you ever cheated on her?" I questioned him further. It was none of my business, but I found men fascinating on this subject.

"A snog here and there, but nothing more," he seemed to be speaking honestly. "We haven't been together long."

"Does that imply if you were together for longer you would cheat on her?" I pushed.

"That's a possibility." He nodded again. "It depends on the circumstance." It was clear that he was thinking about the opportunity he might have to cheat with me. It looked like a difficult balance for him to strike. Trying to be a nice guy, at the same time as trying to make sure I knew he would jump into bed with me, given the chance. He wasn't doing a bad job of it.

"I have to go." I picked up my bag. "Thanks for the chat, it's been nice to get to know you a bit more. Have a good afternoon." He looked a little bit shocked that I had ended the conversation so abruptly. I had stood up and begun the automatic ritual of straightening out my top after standing. "It's your turn to strip for me next time," his face softened, and he smiled as he said it.

"We'll see." I replied, smiling back. "Enjoy your night out." I touched him on the shoulder as I made my way past him and out towards the reception. I hadn't wanted to keep going down the route that the conversation was taking me. I had found out that he was attracted to me, I was in control of what happened next, so I decided to put it on pause. I didn't know what if anything, I wanted to happen, so I left it. I could pick the conversation up again if ever I wanted to or take him up on his suggestion and strip for him, I suppose.

    I decided to go back home again. My mind had cleared so much, and I was very aware that I needed to apologise to Paul. I had been very unfair. During the walk home, I decided that I was going to apologise for being so confrontational. I was definitely going to apologise for asking him if he was having an affair. I don't even know why I'd said that. Was I trying to create a sub conscious excuse for my anger? Had I needed a tangible reason for being so upset? I bet the poor bloke didn't know what had hit him. Beyond apologising, I needed to tell him that I was going to change things. I was going to let him know that I needed to do some more thinking before we discussed it further.

Chapter 3 – Life goals

When I got home, Paul wasn't in the office. I went into the kitchen. He wasn't there either. I shouted his name up the stairs, there was no response. I went back to the kitchen to pour a glass of water. I wondered if he had gone out, but where would he have gone, and why wasn't the door locked? I felt terrible. I bet he had been feeling awful about what had happened earlier and was trying to avoid me. As I sipped my water, I heard the TV. I followed the noise into the front room. Paul was on the sofa watching sport of some kind. He had a beer in his hand which was very unusual. It was lunchtime. He took his work seriously, and he wasn't a daytime drinker. "Sorry," I said as I entered the room.

"What for?" Paul didn't move, or even look round. That wasn't very gracious, I thought.

"For accusing you of having an affair."

"You're accusing me now? I thought you were just asking." He was angry, it was going to be difficult to avoid an argument.

"I didn't mean it," I needed to continue with my apology, and let him know why I had acted that way. "I was confused and upset, and I wasn't thinking straight. Sorry."

He softened, and I saw his shoulders relax in an involuntary demonstration of his mood change. He looked towards me for the first time. "It's ok. Do you want a beer?"

"It's a bit early. Don't you have things to do?"

Paul ignored the question. It seemed that there were more important things on his mind than work. He sat forward in his seat. "We've been together for eight years Soph, how can we end up having the conversation we had this morning?" I had caused him significant upset. I could see in the depth of his concentration and the sound of his voice that he had been shaken. He was staring straight ahead whilst he spoke. He looked like he was trying to piece things together. "In a moment you seemed not to trust me, and we seemed like two strangers arguing, not me and you," he continued. "How did that happen? Where did it come from?"

This must have been so out of the blue for him. Why was it possible to see it from his point of view in hindsight, but never in the moment? Let alone in advance. "Let's start again," I proposed. "I'll explain myself better this time, I promise. Let's start at the beginning and keep talking until it's all ok." He looked at me and nodded. I felt like that was the most grown-up thing I'd ever said. I felt a flush of pride. I also wondered if I'd actually be able to do it.

"It hurt me when you said our sex was boring," I began. "It made me feel distant from you I suppose, and I felt undesired, and old, and all sorts of things."

"That's awful," he looked even more hurt than he had before. "I hate the thought that I made you feel like that. You're the most beautiful woman in the world, I tell you that all the time, don't I? I never want you to feel like that."

He does say those things, damn him and his loving nature. "Why is our sex boring then?" I moved on.

"It's not. Stop saying that." I could sense anger creeping into his voice. "You can't hear what you want to hear so that feeling bad seems acceptable. I said our routine is boring, I distinctly remember saying that our sex was great."

He did say that. This was annoying. There should be a rule against remembering stuff during arguments. If I moved on quickly enough maybe I wouldn't have to admit that a lot of this had been entirely in my head. "What is boring about our routine then?" That ought to do it.

"We've been doing the same thing for months, or even years." His frustration was clear in his voice. "Our relationship is like a 1950's cartoon. We don't have kids, we can do whatever we want, yet we seem to have found a rut. A routine, where we go to work, come home, have dinner, and go to bed tired. If we're not careful another eight years will go past in the blink of an eye."

"What do you want to do that's different?"

"I don't want to do anything massively different. I love my job, and I love you. I just want things to be a bit more adventurous I suppose. I want to visit interesting places and meet interesting people. I want to have interesting and fun sex, the reason that this conversation started in the first place."

"I want all those things as well. What's the problem?" Why shouldn't we do those things? That solution seemed too simple. I wanted to see why Paul thought we weren't.

"The problem is that we don't seem to do those things very often. Not together." There was a pause. "I don't mean I have sex with anyone else," he clarified and looked a bit panicked. He moved on before I could pick him up on it. "I mean, I travel with work, and I meet interesting people through work, but you and I don't do those things together, for fun."

I had perched on the arm of the chair nearest the door. Paul leant forward in his chair and had muted the TV. I sat in silence for a moment, thinking about what he had said. On the face of it, it was true. I racked my brains to think of a different way of seeing things. I couldn't. I was aware that the silence was gaining momentum. I decided to buy some time. "Why don't we?" It seemed like an obvious question.

"I don't know. Why does it happen to anyone?" He shrugged. "A relationship slipping into the predictable and stale. It's a pretty well-worn path, isn't it? We're not the first Soph."

"But it shouldn't happen to us." I could feel myself getting upset and it showed through a wobble in my voice. "We have never been that couple, we are great."

"I bet everyone says that. You're right though, we are great. Don't worry, we can fix it. Don't be upset." He had picked up on the shake in my voice. "It's probably a mixture of familiarity, and our age, and a lack of communication."

That made sense and made me feel a bit better in some small way. "What should we do about it?" I knew that the confident new me would sort this out, but that would take some time. I needed to understand what I could do now, and make sure the next few days would be ok. Once we'd got back on track, the new me would make everything alright.

"What do you want from the world Soph?" He looked straight at me now. "What do you want from your life? What do you want to experience?"

"I don't know. The normal stuff." I didn't want to go into it now. I needed to do more thinking before talking it through.

"There is no normal stuff Soph. Some people want to spend all their time surfing or sky diving. Some people want to have children and devote themselves to that. Some people want to be rich. Some people want to save the whales. There are a million ways to go, and I don't know what you want. I'm not sure you do."

"Maybe I don't." I thought out loud. "What do you want?" Asking questions had worked so far, I wasn't going to walk away from that strategy now. I was also genuinely interested in the answer.

"I want to create a beautiful and meaningful building. One would be enough. I want the work I've done over the past years, together with the work I'm doing now and, in the future, to culminate in something that I can be proud of. I've worked and learnt and absorbed, and I feel like I could develop my skills to the point where I could create something of value. I hope that I can put all my collective growth and development into one building. A building that will change the world in some small way, or at least change a few people's lives. It might sound very self-important, or naive, but it's what I am aiming for in my career. Outside of that I want to spend time with you. I want us to be in love forever. I want to retire young and travel with you. I want to grow old with you, and for us to drink wine together. That's about it."

He looked down at his beer as he finished talking. "That's lovely." was all I could think of to say to express what I felt. "I want those things too. Not the building, or the growing old bit if I'm honest, but definitely the travelling and drinking wine." I smiled at him as he looked up when I spoke.

"So, what do you want from your life in the short term? What does Sophie's ideal next five years look like?" He paused and smiled at me. "You don't have to try and come up with an answer Soph, it's not something that you have to know today. Unless you know what, you want, you won't get it. Then you might end up with regrets, and I don't want that for you. When you know what you want, I will help you get it. I'd love to see you happy."

"Don't you think I'm happy?" I was concerned by the thought that I was miserable.

"Not happy like you could be. I don't think this morning's argument came from a happy place! I don't think you've been happy at all this morning."

I looked down at my hands. He was right. This morning's inner turmoil had been horrible. On top of that I now felt guilty about the Craig thing, which was making my insides churn. I didn't say anything, I just sat, thinking.

Paul interrupted the silence. "I think you're fairly happy Soph. I just think there are areas where you probably want more. I know you're not happy that your career isn't taking off. I don't know if you've decided on the career that is actually want you want. Otherwise, you'd be doing more to get somewhere with it. I know, because you raised it this morning, that you aren't happy with our sex life."

"I'm not sure about the career." I responded. It seemed like the easier of the two issues that were on the table. "I need to think about that a bit. I know I don't want children. I haven't changed my mind about that, but I'm not sure I'm a career woman either."

"You don't have to be one or the other!"

"What else could I be?" What other options were there?

"You could take up a hobby that matters to you. You could climb mount Everest. I don't know what it is Soph, but there has to be something that excites you in the world. You must aspire beyond what you do each day at the moment. It seems that sometimes you're a passenger in our relationship. I know that sounds terrible, and I don't mean it to. What I mean is that I don't want to take over and dominate our lives. I don't want it to be all about what I want. I've always wanted a real partnership, you know that. Fifty-fifty on everything. You need to bring something to us, a dream, or a goal. I don't want to feel alone. Like I'm controlling or leading you."

"You don't try and control me. I know that. I will think about it. What you say does make sense. I will need some time."

"There is plenty of time. No rush."

"I do want us to have sex more. I know that. I think about sex quite a lot, I'm quite a sexual person."

"Why don't you express that?" Paul asked.

"I do." I thought I did. "I ask if we can have sex quite a bit. You reject me."

"I don't think asking for sex counts as being expressive. I meant more why don't you communicate what you want? You've always been quick to say what you don't want, but you've never said what you do want. Is it the same as what you want from life? Have you not given it much thought, or is it that you want things, and you aren't telling me?"

I pondered the question. "Probably a bit of both," I said after a few seconds of silence. "I suppose I don't have much experience."

"Do you watch porn, when I'm away I mean?"

I was surprised by his question. Buy some time Sophie, I thought. "What do you mean?"

"You just said you are a sexual person. When I'm not here what do you fantasise about? Do you watch porn?" He repeated the question. I hadn't really made any use of the time I'd bought, but at least the shock of the turn in the conversation had worn off slightly. This was brand new for us, we'd never even acknowledged that porn existed before. We'd never acknowledged that we found other people attractive, even celebrities, we just didn't talk about sex in any way.

"Not often." I replied honestly. There was a silence which followed, a silence that I didn't know how to break. Changing the subject didn't seem to be an option at this point.

"What do you fantasise about then?" he continued. I liked it more when I was asking the questions. I felt prudish and shy and uncomfortable. This wasn't the new me at all.

"Don't worry", he seemed to read my mind. "Just say whatever you want. There is no right or wrong answer."

"Do you watch porn?" I'm going to get back to the asking questions approach.

"Of course," he answered with ease. "All men like porn. Men are visual, and I'm no different. It's probably why I'm an architect. I like the form of things, buildings, trees, landscapes. I love to see the form of an attractive naked woman. You know I love seeing your body."

"What about the sex?" I questioned. "Porn stars have sex, or do you watch women on their own?"

"Watching attractive women having sex is great. I suppose the fantasy of porn is seeing someone beautiful enjoying sex and being sexual. I haven't put too much thought to the why, but all men like porn, trust me. You avoided my question, what do you fantasise about?"

He seemed much more at ease talking about this than I felt. His relaxed state was making me feel more confident about saying things. Maybe there was no wrong answer. "All sorts." I answered honestly, without saying anything specific. I could see some frustration in his face, so I went on, "I fantasize about you." I expected that was what he wanted to hear.

"Are you telling me you don't have any other fantasies?" He questioned, looking a little incredulous. "If you think about me, what exactly do you think about?"

"I like the feeling of being desired." I revealed. "I fantasise that you want me so much you rip my clothes off, as if we were strangers and you wanted to see my body for the first time."

"What else?" He pushed.

I felt liberated by what I'd said. It was true. It was something that I fantasised about. Sometimes it wasn't Paul though, sometimes it was a stranger. They were actually seeing my body for the first time.

"Sometimes it's a stranger who desires me." I continued. "Sometimes two or three men who all want to see me naked. The fantasy is almost always about them desiring me and lusting after me." I couldn't believe the words were coming out of my mouth. How would he react to that? Had he not expected something quite so outrageous. Would he think I'm a pervert?

"That seems pretty normal" his manner gave the impression of someone deep in thought. "Everyone wants to be desired. I want to see you take your jeans off right now."

His face was serious. I felt a shiver of excitement at the thought of fulfilling the request. I stood up and moved into the middle of the room in front of where he sat. I unbuttoned my jeans and slid them down, flicking off my slip-on trainers as my jeans reached my ankles. "There you go", I acknowledged his request with open hands and a push of my hips to the right, as I stood in front of him.

"Come here," he said with a smile. He undid his belt and unzipped his trousers as I moved towards him. I put one knee either side of him on the sofa and leant forward and kissed him. He pulled his trousers down around his thighs. We kissed, with intense passion, and he pulled my panties to one side. He was desperate to be inside me. I could feel it in his movements and his kiss. Normally he would want to see my tits, he loves my tits, but it appeared that he wanted me so franticly that he left my hoody zipped up. I felt desired and horny. It was good to be on top of him and be able to give him what he wanted. I reached back, moved his cock into position and slowly sat down onto him. I gasped with pleasure as he immediately began thrusting into me. Now he unzipped up my top and grabbed at my tits through my vest as he continued to fuck me. I joined in with the motion and moved up and down on top of him, faster and harder. In only a few moments he gasped in pleasure and thrust deep into me as he orgasmed. His hands moved from my tits and pulled my hips down onto him as he shuddered to a stop underneath me. I leant forward on him, breathing heavily, grabbing his hair, and kissing him.

I hadn't orgasmed, but I didn't care. I felt exactly what I wanted to feel, desired. He couldn't have stopped himself from climaxing, even if he'd tried.

"That was fun" I breathed as I sat more upright.

"It was," he was breathless as well. It was a long time since we'd had daytime sex.

I climbed off him and nipped into the downstairs loo. I went back into the living room, put my jeans on and sat down on the chair. He was still sat in the same place. He had pulled his trousers back up, but not fastened his belt.

"Is that what you had in mind?" he asked.

"That was great," I answered. "We should do that more."

"It doesn't just happen Soph. We only had sex because we were talking about it, and you were honest with me. You seemed sexual and interesting. I don't often see you like that. I love it."

"How do we do that more then?"

"We keep communicating Soph. Tell me what you like and don't like. Tell me about your fantasies. Don't worry about being judged, be open and honest. Why don't you watch some porn whilst I'm away and see if it gives you some ideas?"

"Ok. I'll give it a try." I nodded. It couldn't hurt I suppose. "What do you want?" I asked. This wasn't an attempt to avoid answering questions anymore, I wanted to know.

"I like the thought of sex outdoors" he said. "In the forest, or by a river."

"That sounds pretty uncomfortable!" I spoke my thoughts.

"Typical." He pretended to be mildly narked by my response. "Women dream of Christopher Grey turning up, to take complete control and shove a pineapple up their arse, but they won't have sex outside with their husbands because it might not be comfortable. You're all impossible." I laughed and laughed at his mock indignation.

Chapter 4 – My first strip tease

The day was dragging at the gym. Paul had set off on his business trip the day before, and when he was away everything seemed to go a bit slower. I tried to find things to do in the evenings, when I was at home on my own, but for some reason work seemed to drag more when he was away. I had been half-heartedly working through a teach yourself German App on my phone. It was a token gesture. I was trying to convince myself that I was developing my skills. Preparing to launch my international career in events management. "I'm fluent in German and I have a working knowledge of all the major European languages." I heard myself saying in a daydreamed interview. Judging by the time it was taking this parrot to teach me colours and numbers, fluent German was a little way off. The Germans love porn, don't they? Is that only something the British say, or is it true? It had been two days since Paul, and I had spoken. I felt so much better in some ways. I had thought that it was the sex that had relaxed me. Now I was starting to think that it was the open conversation that had freed my mind. Being able to talk about sex, porn and fantasies was very liberating. It was only a five-minute conversation, but it felt somehow very powerful to me. I suppose it had allowed me to feel less isolated in my head, and much closer to Paul. I had persuaded myself that you have to be in a strong relationship to talk about such things. Sex is a topic which is avoided by most couples that I knew. I knew one thing for sure, the new confident me was definitely the way to go. I was going to address things head on from now on.

I hadn't watched any porn yet. I had always thought porn was for men. Anytime that I had watched it, I'd never found it a huge turn on. Perhaps in the past I had subconsciously resented the sexuality and confidence of the people involved. If I never watched it, I didn't have to acknowledge my own quiet, boring sex life. I wanted to have more conversations about sex with Paul, that was for sure, but I wouldn't have a clue about how to start one. There had been a pattern in my life over the past few years which, if followed, would now involve me going into my own head. This would continue until someone, namely Paul, brought me out of it again. Was I prepared to wait for another few months until another conversation happened to me? I decided that I wasn't. Even though the thought of closing up and waiting for the world to come to me was a very comfortable and tempting option. I was going to grab a hold of my life. By watching some porn I'd be able to tell Paul I'd done it. That would definitely set off another open and intimate conversation. It felt good to have a plan. I was going to make this happen, maybe.

I picked up my phone. It was a warm sunny day outside. The gym was dead. I hadn't seen anyone in the reception area for at least fifteen minutes. If I could sneak ten minutes for my German speaking parrot, I'm sure I could glance at some porn without getting caught.

Porn, I typed into Google. Then I deleted it straight away. Google will know forever that I've been looking at porn on my phone, I thought. When I'm the Prime minister my internet history will be trawled through, and I'll be exposed as a pervert. I put the phone back down on the desk. I looked up at the ceiling and tried to give myself a reality check. In the past Paul had tried to help me with indecision and worry, suggesting that I try and see my actions through someone else's eyes. I tried to look at what I was doing now, as if someone else was doing it. I would then be able to judge the imaginary person, and thus figure out how I would be judged if I did it myself. "She's never going to be Prime minister" was my first thought. A public figure of any kind? No. She doesn't even want to be. If she was a public figure and I found out she'd looked at porn on her phone, would I care? No, not in the slightest. I don't imagine anyone would. A flush of bravery swept through me, and I typed porn back into Google and this time I pressed enter.

A list of websites came up. I clicked on the second one. The site opened up and showed a series of pictures. There was a little caption under each picture, briefly describing the scene that the video depicted. I felt a flutter of excitement as I looked over the naked bodies in the images. What should I look at? I wondered. Should I click on the top one? The first one was a picture of an Arab woman in a headdress having her boobs fondled from behind. There was the caption, "Arab women rounded up". I decided to move on. The picture looked awful, the opposite of sexy. The premise seemed unsettling, and very odd indeed. There were young looking girls in several of the other images. They were titled "petite teens", or something similar. I didn't like the look of that either. I wasn't a petite teen, and I didn't want a man who wanted a petite teen. That didn't interest me in the slightest. "Stepmom is horny," was the next clip. Why was it all so perverted? Family sex can't be a turn on for anyone, can it? Surely not. "Big titted Brit with casting agent," that looked better. I'm British and have big tits. This could be a good place to start. The image was of a pretty, blonde woman. She had her hair tied up and was sat on a couch, wearing a pink blouse and black skirt with tights. She looked like she was going for a job interview. Had I picked the first picture where no one was naked? Was I a prude? Oh well, I hadn't looked at porn for ages, I had to start somewhere. There is no need to rush things. I clicked on the picture. The flutter of excitement that was bubbling within me, flickered a little more. The scene opened up with the image that had advertised the clip. The woman was on the couch and there were subtitles on the bottom of the screen. I'd turned the volume right down on the phone. I didn't think that the sound was going to be too important, or appropriate in the gym reception. The subtitles were coming from someone off camera, I assumed a man. He asked the woman if she had ever thought about doing porn. She had apparently thought about it but never made the leap into actually doing it. The subtitles told her that she had made a good decision to come to a reputable company. After a bit more chat she was asked if she would strip for the camera. The woman seemed keen to agree and smiled at the person behind the camera. She then got up and started to unbutton her blouse. The subtitles complimented her on her figure. She undid the buttons all the way down and removed her top to reveal a white bra. She dropped the blouse onto the sofa behind her and moved towards the camera. She was very sexual, her movements were deliberate, but graceful. She seemed so confident in revealing her body.

Completely sure that everyone wanted to see it. Not a trace of doubt. That's what made her seem sexy, I thought to myself. She slipped the straps of her bra down off her shoulders one by one. She then turned around so that her back was to the camera. She looked over her shoulder with a provocative glance as she unhooked her bra. There was no smiling now. This is where those odd words like smouldering and sultry are used to describe women. Mostly by men. The woman's confidence was captivating. She tilted forward as the unhooked bra fell into her hands. She threw it carelessly onto the sofa where her blouse lay. She looked back over her shoulder again and now the smile returned. A smile that said, I know you want me to turn around. She was moving a little all the time, never still. She did turn around after a few seconds with her arm across her chest covering her tits. She smiled again, as if to say look, I've turned around, but you still can't see what you want to see. She was showing a little bit more of herself. The curve of her tits under her arm, and flesh pushed up above her arm and hand. She did have big boobs. I was intrigued to see what they looked like. She'd even got me enthralled. I couldn't imagine how it would feel if I was a man watching this. She swayed more and moved ever so slightly closer to the camera as she took her arm away. Her tits fell into a natural position and looked magnificent. She was not thin, but not fat. Curvy and beautiful. Voluptuous, another one of those odd words which seemed to fit here. She lifted her hands to touch the back of her hair, exposing herself further. She then leant forward and moved from side to side so that her tits rocked gently in front of the camera. She smiled again as she straightened up, a knowing smile. Knowing that her audience had got some of what they wanted from her. She turned around, facing away from the camera again and bent forward a few degrees, with a small arch in her back. The arch in her back made her bum almost point at the camera. She looked back over her shoulder once more and started to ease her skirt down over her hips. Little by little, one side then the other, she slipped the material down so that the top of her panties. Her movement exposed a thong diving away into the curve of her arse cheeks. Then, in one slow movement she bent forward from the waist and slid her skirt down to her ankles.

She revealed black stockings that ended halfway up her thighs. Whilst looking back at the camera she caressed her legs. After a few moments she stood up to reveal the beauty of her bum, magnificently framed by her panties. The cheeks of her bottom forming perfect curves over the top of each thigh. It was wonderful. The knowing smile was back. She knew that revealing the curves of her buttocks were as desired by her audience as the curves of her breasts. She was now only wearing her panties, stockings, and a pair of heels. She turned around and presented her arms to the camera as if to say, there you go. She sat down, crossed her legs, and put her arm across her chest again. It was as if she'd shown what she wanted to show, and now it was going away again. Complete control.

    She was building the audience up for another tease. I hadn't been paying much attention to the subtilties. They had occasionally been popping up at the bottom of the screen as the woman had stripped. Now that she was sat down and covered up, I concentrated on the words a bit more. "Let's see if you're feeling horny?" The subtitles said. At this point a man came into view from the chest down. The camera had been static throughout the strip. It must have been mounted on a tripod or something. Before the man had entered the scene, the camera position had been moved to a lower angle, to focus on the couch where the woman sat. The subtitles had turned into a person. He stood to the left-hand side of the blonde lady, who was still sat down. She looked up at him as he stood parallel in between the couch and the camera. He undid his belt and dropped his trousers to the floor. He immediately pulled his boxer shorts down, careful not to get his face into the camera shot as he bent forward. Who was he, I thought? He was probably married. He was very erect, almost bursting. The woman smiled her knowing smile again. She understood that her tease had produced the arousal that was now on display in front of her. She slid forward on the couch and stood up. Her top third of her disappeared from view as the camera shot remained focussed on the couch. She had her arms up on the man's chest and I guessed they were kissing as a few seconds went by. Her hands then moved down over his chest and stomach and found their way onto his cock. You could see his legs buckle at the pleasure of being touched. The woman's knees bent, and she came back into view, as she squatted down in front of the man. She stroked him gently and looked up at him. The well-rehearsed smile was there as she knew the man wanted her to take him in her mouth. She knew the audience were desperate to see it. She glanced at the camera before moving her head forward and plunging his cock between her lips.

"Sophie," I heard a voice above me. "Do you have a moment?" Fuck, fuck, fuck. It was James, the shift manager. He was standing in front of me at the reception desk. "Can you come with me? Terry will cover the desk."

Oh fuck. Had he seen me? Was this going to be the most awkward conversation of my entire life. I put my phone in my pocket. I didn't want Terry picking it up and having a look whilst I was away. I stood up to follow, as James walked towards the manager's office.

When he entered the room, he smiled as he turned and sat down. My heartbeat eased at the sight of the warmth in his face. I felt the heat in my own face as I blushed uncontrollably. "Are you ok?" he asked. "You look concerned".

Concerned didn't even begin to cover it. "I was wondering why you wanted to see me?" I tried to calm my thoughts so that the flush would drain from my face.

"Nothing to worry about", he smiled again as if to reassure me. "Have a seat. I wanted to catch up with you to see if you can take on any more shifts. We've had one of the students go back to university. Rather than recruiting someone new I wanted to see if the current staff would make up the extra hours."

He hadn't seen my phone. Thank God. If he had seen it, then he was covering it brilliantly. I was so relieved. I was barely listening to what he had said. I was so relieved to have avoided embarrassment. Not to mention disciplinary procedures, or possibly the sack! I was thrilled at the lucky break that I'd had. I told him that I'd need to speak to Paul about the extra shifts and made my escape. There was only ten minutes left on my shift. Terry said he'd hang on at reception until cover arrived if I wanted to get away early. I thanked him and grabbed the opportunity. I was glad to be out of the door and on my way home. Terry was a sort of caretaker at the gym, cleaning, tidying, and fixing simple things. An older guy, always with a smile and a kind word. What he lacked in ambition he seemed to make up for in a calm, quiet, easy-going demeanour. He sometimes covered for us on reception, and today I was grateful for his help.

Thoughts of the porn clip came back to me as I walked home. I'd love to have the power over people that she had. I'm sure it would be ten times more intense for a man to watch. Or a lesbian, I supposed. Imagine having that power.

With Paul away, I for once felt I could enjoy having the house to myself. I poured a glass of white wine from an open bottle in the fridge and stood by the island in the kitchen with my phone. I resumed watching the video from where I had been interrupted earlier. The woman had moved from a squatting position onto her knees. She then proceeded to suck the man for a few minutes. Sometimes using her hands, sometimes only with her mouth. She appeared to be enjoying it. In what seemed to be a short time for a porn star, the man withdrew from her mouth and started to wank himself. She straightened up on her knees, bringing her tits up in front of his cock. She positioned her fits in front of him, in time for them to be completely covered with cum. It must have been a massive turn on for her, as she was able to command such a reaction from him. Within minutes of her alluring strip tease he was bursting at the site of her. I wanted to be able to do that.

I took my wine upstairs to the bedroom. I had a bit of a search through a couple of drawers and soon found a little flexible tripod. It was a freebee from a conference that Paul had taken me to. I didn't know if it was for a phone or a camera. As luck would have it the clamp held my phone pretty well once I'd worked out how to tighten it. I wrapped the little metal legs of the stand around the handle of the wardrobe and stood back. I could see myself in the mirror on the front of the wardrobe. The phone would film what I could see, as it was set to the right of the mirror. Perfect. I stepped back and considered getting changed into something sexy. The thought disappeared as quickly as it had arrived. I didn't have anything particularly sexy. Nice underwear was about as provocative as it got, and this film wasn't for anyone else to see. It wasn't worth the effort. This was an experiment to see if I could do it. A test to see if I could have the power and control that the woman in the porn video possessed. I opened the camera on the phone and started to record. As I stepped back, I tried to mimic exactly the strip I'd seen earlier. I had trousers on instead of a skirt, but other than that I could do the same things that the woman had done. I glanced at myself a few times in the mirror as I went but couldn't see as much as I'd hoped. I was too busy concentrating on undressing. Once I'd stripped to my panties, I went over to the phone and stopped the recording. I unclamped the legs from the wardrobe, sat on the bed and watched the results. It was good, and bad. The good thing was that my body looked ok. I wouldn't change much, and it gave me a boost to think that I had a body that people would want to see. The problem was my strip tease was not sexy. I was wooden and clumsy. My face almost expressionless, demonstrating my obvious concentration. I didn't seem to have the allure and confidence of the woman in the clip. I looked foolish. I stopped watching after only a few seconds. I threw on some comfortable clothes and went downstairs to get more wine.

Even though my strip had been disappointing, I realised I was still feeling very much more confident. The wine could have been helping, but I felt liberated by my recent freedom of thought. The desires that seemed to be resulting from that felt good. I thought of Paul, and suspected he'd be quite proud of me. I put the wine down on the counter and took my phone out of my pocket. I pulled up my t-shirt, and as I held the material up with one hand, I took a selfie with the other. I opened up the image to see the result. My confidence rose even more as I saw myself. You could only see my arm and my tits, but it was a provocative image. I liked how my body looked. The soft light from the kitchen, reflecting from the brushed steel of the fridge beside me, made my tits look lovely. You could see my chin, but nothing that would show that it was me. I know it was only for Paul, but I wasn't confident enough to be sending naughty pictures with my face in them. I messaged it to him, with a few kisses and a shocked emoji.

As I went up to bed a message came through from Paul. He was surprised and delighted to receive my picture and was very complimentary about my body. He asked for more. The thought of taking more pictures for him sent a little shiver of excitement through me. I messaged back and told him I was going to bed but promised him more soon. As I lay in bed, I checked the rest of my messages and set an alarm. My mind drifted back to my first attempt at stripping, and my topless picture for Paul. I wondered where people would go to post the kind of photos I'd taken online. I picked up my phone again and searched for "boobs selfie", I wasn't sure what else to write. A lot of the sites that came up seemed to be porn sites. I assumed that they would come up first on any search relating to sex of any kind. There was a site called "Rate my boobs" which looked different, so I opened it. It was a pretty amateurish website, with thumbnails of even more amateurish photos. The pictures were of women, of all ages, and all shapes and sizes. Under each picture was a score out of ten. I clicked on one of the first images I saw. It was of a blond woman with lovely tits, stood next to a balcony. The picture opened up to a larger size, with the caption underneath saying, "I want some attention." Below that was a rating out of ten. I assumed that the rating was voted for by blokes who'd been browsing through the site. They had the opportunity to give a score out of ten for the boobs on display. She had received an 8.3, which I thought was low, although I suppose it was an average and she might not be everyone's cup of tea. At the bottom of the page there were comments from men, and they adored her. Most of the comments were a variation on "great tits", or "I'd love to fuck you". Although these comments were unimaginative, they must have been good for her ego. Some of them were a bit more detailed. They described what they liked about her. "Perfect nipples on nice natural full tits," wrote one guy, almost as if he was critiquing a dish on a cooking show. Many men were asking if they could cum over her tits. Equally as many were sending her their e-mail addresses and asking for more pictures of her. She had replied to some of them, sometimes giving her e-mail address. Sometimes she informed them that she was available but expensive. She seemed to be in complete control. There were hundreds of comments.

I had a look through a few more pictures and found myself hooked on reading the comments. It was fascinating to see what men thought, and how they would try to stand out from the crowd. They wanted to somehow try and elicit contact from the girl. One guy had cut and pasted the same comment into all the profiles I saw, "You look amazing, I love your tits. Can you send more to me at...." and then he gave his e-mail address. The guys were desperate for these girls to interact with them. Did they believe anything would ever come of it? Did anything ever come of it? I opened up my selfie again and looked for anything that might be a giveaway that it was me. There was nothing in the background, no jewellery, no t-shirt logo visible. I gave myself a quick reality check. What are the chances of someone I know seeing this and taking the effort to work out it's me? Zero. There are women from all over the world on here. No one came to this site for any reason other than looking at boobs. I decided to create an account. I called myself "Natural Boobs." Judging from the comments being natural seemed to be the most important thing to the rating public. I couldn't think of anything more inspiring than "Do you want to see more?" for my strap line. It would do. I decided the words weren't very important. I uploaded my photo and clicked create. A message came up thanking me, letting me know that my photo would be verified and posted within a few days. I felt another little rush of excitement as I put the phone down again and switched off the light.

Chapter 5 – The Rules

I had taken the extra shifts at the gym without speaking to Paul about it. If I'd waited until he was back in the evening to speak to him, I wouldn't have been able to give my response to Mark until he was back at work after the weekend. I didn't think it would matter much to Paul if I took the opportunity.

It was a Friday, and I was working a long late shift covering the afternoon and evening. The evenings were always busy, which made the time pass. The afternoons were slow and boring. I'd been in for a couple of hours, and it had got to the slowest part of the day. It crossed my mind to watch some more porn, but the memory of my near miss last time removed those thoughts. I had watched a few more clips since then. Most of them were odd, or boring, but a couple of them had turned me on. Yesterday evening at home, I had found a clip that I liked. I pleasured myself to an intense orgasm whilst watching it. It featured a beautiful girl who was sunbathing by a pool. Nearby there were two black men relaxing, supposedly working on the house. It was set in America. They got talking to the girl, and within a very short space of time they'd gone from flirting with her, to fucking her. In the pool, all around the pool, and in the pool house. It seemed almost racist in its conception, but beyond that, the sex was amazing to watch. Such beautiful actors. It was a similar fantasy to one that I'd had before, but this seemed to play it out in a very erotic and sexy way. The girl got exactly what she wanted from the experience. At the same time, she was an object of desire and pleasure. I'm not sure I would tell Paul about that one yet.

In the absence of porn, I was busy learning how to introduce family members in German, when Craig arrived at the gym. My heart sank unexpectedly when I saw him. Not because I didn't want to see him, I feared for any awkwardness that there might be between us.

"Hello" he smiled as he caught my eye. "You look good today."

That wasn't awkward at all, I was relieved and felt immediately relaxed. "Thank you, why aren't you at work?"

"I'm working from home today, some boring reports, so I thought I'd break the day up with a workout."

"That sounds like a good idea" I smiled and passed him a towel.

"They have towels in the special shower, I won't need that." He seemed to almost wink as he said it, but not quite. It was a suggestive smile rather than a wink, but the meaning was the same.

"You owe me a strip!" He lowered his voice as he spoke and quickly looked over his shoulder to make sure we were alone as he said it.

I laughed. "Go and work out, don't get distracted."

He laughed as well, "see you in a bit." He tagged himself through the gate and disappeared into the gym.

For the next few minutes my mind was filled with thoughts. Was he serious? Did I want to strip for him? What was I going to do? I calmed myself down. This is the new, confident me. I'll do exactly as I please.

I had expected to have a bit more time to think, but Craig returned from the gym much earlier than I thought he would. He had cut his work out quite short. Was that because of me I wondered?

"That was quick," I smiled.

"I'm not feeling it today," he made his excuse. "I had other things on my mind."

"Your boring reports?" I asked, still interested by the day-to-day life of an accountant.

"No, the shower I'm about to have," he replied.

My stomach fluttered. I hadn't thought it through, no decision had been made. Judging by Thursday nights practice performance, I wasn't ready to strip for anyone. I wasn't even close. "You can use the shower," I smiled. That wasn't committing to anything. I got up and moved out from behind reception to open the door for him.

We always got cover for the reception if there was someone available. Break times were usually covered by a manager, or the caretaker. In the afternoons when there were fewer staff around, we used a sign saying, "back in ten minutes." We put it on the counter if we needed to nip away. I liked it because no one knew when the ten minutes started. Unless you were unlucky this could almost always give you fifteen or twenty minutes without it being noticed. I reached for the sign and placed it where it would be visible to anyone coming through the door. That sign could do my job for about seventy percent of my day, I thought. I led Craig over towards the staff changing rooms. Without thinking too much I followed him inside and pulled the door shut behind me. I made sure the latch had caught behind us, meaning only staff who knew the code could come in. It might only end up being a bit of flirting, but there was a slight thrill at the thought of being caught with a customer. Perhaps that's something I should put some thought to. Am I an exhibitionist?

"Let's see it then" Craig said with the eagerness of a schoolboy.

"Not so fast" I said, trying to calm him down. "You start your shower."

"That wasn't the deal", he looked disappointed.

"There is no deal." I smiled. "No promises have been made. If you play your cards right, you might get lucky. I'll see how I feel." This was going to be entirely on my terms. He wanted to see my body. His desire was almost tangible. I became aware in that moment that I held all the cards. My confidence improved at the realisation. I could almost feel myself standing taller and relaxing into the moment.

He started to take his gym kit off without complaint. He didn't seem as nervous as the last time. He was almost racing to get his clothes off. I suspected he thought that as soon as he'd finished, I would strip. He stood naked before me with an expectant look on his face. His body was tight from the exercise he'd done, and he was starting to get an erection. I hadn't focussed on his cock last time, it had all seemed like a bit of a blur, but this time things were clearer. I looked, and I liked what I saw. "Start your shower," I ordered. He moved into the shower area and turned on the water. He waited at the side for the water to warm up before getting underneath. His cock was bigger than I remembered. He was more relaxed than last time and aroused. He cut an impressive figure as he stood under the water and ran his hands through his short hair. He looked at me again, not sure of what to do or what was going to happen next. I leant against the wall of the shower entrance and pondered my next move.

"I want you to touch yourself," I suggested.

"What?" Came his surprised response.

"You heard me." I smiled. "I want to see you play with yourself. If you turn me on, I might give you something to look at."

He didn't move, he was rinsing himself under the water to get rid of any sweat from the exercise. He didn't immediately acknowledge my request. I slipped my hand under the back of my vest top, and he lifted his head to watch. I unhooked my bra and brought one of my arms inside the top so that I could slip out of the bra. I pulled it out of the other side of the vest. It was a white bra, a little bit lacy, but it could not be described as sexy underwear. I managed to squeeze it into the back pocket of my jeans, so that my hands were empty. My tits flied my top and I leant back against the wall. I had done enough to arouse Craig and let him know he had a chance of seeing more. He was now fully erect. He began to touch himself slowly whilst his eyes were focussed on my tits, pushing against the ribbed material of my white vest. It was exciting to watch. He was really turned on by me, and I was still fully clothed. The feeling of power increased, and my confidence grew with it. I felt sexy. I didn't even need to strip, and I had this guy hooked. His movement got faster and I the fluttering in my stomach increased as I saw him become more urgent.

"Show me," he requested. I stepped towards him as I watched.

"Show me your tits", he pleaded. This was a real turn on. I could see how excited he was getting. I was only about half a meter outside of the shower area. I pulled my top up with one hand and covered my boobs with the other. His eyes were on stalks.

"Will you touch me" he asked.

"No, I want to see you do it." I smiled.

"Can I cum on your tits?" His arousal had caused him to lose his inhibitions and he was being very open about what he wanted. It highlighted how much I was turning him on. It felt amazing.

"No, I have to go back to work". I stepped closer still, but out of reach of the water, and moved my arm away from my chest. "You can touch me if you're gentle."

He seemed now to be in a state of near ecstasy as he reached out and grabbed at my tits with his free left hand. Drops of water ran over my chest and nipples as he groped me. I gasped with pleasure at the feeling of being touched with such urgency. Within a few seconds he orgasmed, still holding my tits. I watched as cum leapt from him, and he gasped with pleasure. As his movements came to a stop, he let go of my chest and I looked down at my wet boobs.

"How was that?" I asked.

"You have amazing tits," he said, ignoring the question. Any tits are amazing when they're naked in front of you I thought. Men change completely the moment they orgasm. It's so odd to watch. All the sexual feelings, aggression, desire, seem to flood out of them along with their semen.

"Enjoy the rest of your shower," I suggested as I turned and moved out of the shower enclosure. I walked towards the counter and saw myself in the mirror. My tits exposed and glistening with water droplets. I felt really horny. I picked up a towel, dried myself off and put my bra back on. After a quick rearrange of my vest I tucked myself in and walked back out into reception. I tried to adopt as calm a look on my face as I could muster.

It was quite a while before Craig emerged from the changing rooms. He looked a bit sheepish as he moved over towards the reception.

"Refreshed?" I wanted to take away any uncomfortable feelings from him. I had enjoyed his show.

"I am, thanks." He nodded. "Back to the grindstone I suppose."

"It could be worse. You could be stuck in here," I consoled him.

"At least I'd be able to look at you all day."

I blushed a little. "You're kind. See you soon." I said with a smile.

"You will. Have a good afternoon." He said as he turned and walked towards the door.

I sighed, not with relief, but with a release of the tension of the experience. It was unexpected, but such good fun. I felt sexy, and alive. I was definitely going to practice my stripping. I wanted to feel like this more often.

I spent the rest of the shift thinking. It was easy to get lost in thought when there was no one around. I began to realise a few things about myself. I wanted to enjoy more sexual experiences and become sexier and more confident as a result. I felt like one thing would follow the other. No one is automatically good at anything. Practice and experience are what leads to success in any area of life. Why would sex be an exception? I wanted to become the real me, and the real me would definitely be confident and sexy. I thought through how I might go about becoming more experienced in practice. Being married meant that I couldn't broaden my experience as if I was single. I wondered if Paul only wanted to talk about fantasies, or whether we could fulfil some. I planned to talk to him about it tonight and gauge his reaction. I would let him know that I thought it would be ok for us to experiment from within our secure relationship. It was obvious that any fun that I was going to have should be completely outside of my normal life. People would judge me. They would then judge Paul as well. I promised myself two things. I would tell Paul about everything that I wanted to do and experience, if he didn't like it, I wouldn't do it. Also, I would never let anybody who knew me, or Paul know about my adventures. That meant no more flirting with people at the gym. I had felt all along that Craig was a mistake, but these thoughts clarified why. There was a chance that Craig thought that my marriage wasn't in a good place, and that upset me. It wasn't true. If I wanted to experiment and liberate my sexuality, I had to be confident enough to meet new people, if Paul was ok with that. I was not going to give the wrong impression of myself or my marriage to anyone that knew me.

I also had another, quite sobering thought. By asking Paul if I could experiment, that would mean Paul would have the same freedoms. That was only fair. I couldn't on one hand separate sex from love, but on the other tell him that he had to be faithful. I thought it through as if it was him asking me if he could experiment. I put myself in that position and worked it through being as honest with myself as I could. How would I cope? How would I react? How would it change my view of him? I was sure I could be happy with it, as long as he was honest with me. A lie would be devastating, as it always is when someone cheats. It would be even worse in a situation like I was imagining, because there would be no reason at all to lie. It was good to see it from another point of view. As usual it made things very clear. If Paul was thought it was a good idea, I had my rules. Number one, we couldn't flirt with or experiment with anyone either of us knew. Or where there was a reasonable chance that we would bump into in our normal lives. Second, it was just about sex. No relationships, no double lives. Sex for fun. Third, and most important, condoms are compulsory. I wasn't about to let my wonderful life and marriage be damaged by a sexually transmitted infection. No amount of sexual experimentation and fulfilment was worth contracting something awful.

My thoughts drifted throughout the afternoon as I planned what I wanted to say to Paul. I wondered about how I had got myself into the place that had made me so upset, only a few days ago. It was clear that my communication skills, or lack of them, had led to the difficulties in my life. If I had been open and talked to Paul, I could have avoided the fight, and the fireworks going off in my head.

All my life, my first instinct had always been to shy away from confrontation. Even if confrontation was avoidable, I think I always feared it. It led me to treat situations as if conflict was going to come. This would lead me to defend against something that wasn't necessarily going to materialize. In these situations, I would go quiet to avoid a fight. My silence made sure I had no chance of getting my point across or getting what I wanted. My silence in essence made sure that I wasn't going to be happy. I would then bristle because I felt ignored. By the time I had got to this point it would end with me exploding into confrontation. My plan moving forward was to talk openly, remove the anger, and make the best choices for my life. I knew this would take some work.

Chapter 6 – List of Fantasies

When Paul arrived home from work, I jumped on him almost before he was through the door. It was late in the evening. I'd got home from the gym about half an hour earlier and had been watching TV with a glass of wine whilst waiting for him. I dragged him into the kitchen as I kissed him. He dropped his bags and loosened his tie. Whilst he unbuttoned his shirt, I lifted the loose tie over his head and put it over mine. I lifted my white vest top to expose my boobs, his tie falling between them. He was wide eyed as he threw off his shirt and grabbed my tits and kissed me. Pushing against me I could feel his excitement through his suit trousers. I turned around and pulled my shorts down around my thighs as I leant forward. I didn't want to wait, I wanted to be fucked right there, over the breakfast bar. It was intense and frantic. Paul fucked me harder than normal, slapping into me as I leant further forward and held the countertop. It was exhilarating. My tits brushed against the cold granite as I rocked forward each time Paul pushed into me. I was in ecstasy. The build-up of sexual tension during the last couple of days was releasing from me. I orgasmed in less than a couple of minutes. That speed of orgasm hardly ever happened to me, it felt incredible. Paul was going faster and harder as I relaxed, I looked back over my shoulder and smiled.

"I want you to cum on my tits," I requested. He didn't say anything, he pushed into me a few more times, making me groan as he did, and then he pulled out. I turned around and dropped down in front of him. I made sure my tits were at the right height. I held his thighs in my hands as he grabbed his cock and exploded all over my chest. I loved seeing how turned on he was. Cum pooled on my tits and ran down over me and dripped onto my thighs. I leaned back and looked down at my dishevelled state. It was so exciting.

"That was unexpected," he was breathing heavily. He seemed surprised by what had happened.

"Didn't you enjoy it?" I asked, already knowing the answer.

"Oh God yes," he replied. "It's just that I didn't expect it."

I had stood up and leaned back against the counter. I picked up my phone and smiled. I stretched out my arm, leant my head to one side, and took a picture of my tits, still covered in cum. I put the phone down and went to get the kitchen roll to clean up.

"Did you just take a picture?" Paul asked, seeming confused.

"I did. I watched some porn whilst you were away. It made me a bit frisky. How was your trip?"

"I've completely forgotten all about it now, but it was fine thanks. What porn did you watch? Did you find things that you liked?"

"I'll tell you about it shortly. Get changed and then come back down. There is some dinner in the fridge."

Paul returned downstairs in less than five minutes and ate some of the same salad that I'd had a little earlier.

"I loved your picture. Why didn't you send more?" He looked puzzled.

"I suppose the right time to take some didn't arise. I picked up a selfie stick from town yesterday though. It'll make it a lot easier than trying to stretch my arms out. I put that picture of my tits on a website, do you want to see?"

"Wow!" Paul exclaimed. "What website? What has made you decide to be so adventurous?"

"I've been thinking a lot. It stemmed from our conversation the other day. I've explored a lot of things in my head. I suppose it feels a bit out of the blue to you, but I get so much time to think at the gym. I've analysed my life over the past few days.

I opened the link to the rating site on my phone and passed it to Paul. He looked at it and gave a nod. "It is a good picture!"

"Did you read the comments?" I asked.

He was silent for a few seconds as he scrolled down. "These guys like your boobs!" He carried on reading. "Is that why you asked me to cum on them? That seems to be what most of these guys want to do."

"It did turn me on reading them. It is a huge confidence boost to hear things like that written about you, even though some of it is a bit vulgar. It's best not to take it too seriously. They can only see my tits after all."

"They can see enough to be sure that you're beautiful, and that you have a lovely body," Paul observed. "Will you post more?"

"I hadn't thought about it," I lied. "At some point, if you're happy with it?" I corrected the needless lie straight away.

"If it makes you as confident and sexy as this, you should be doing it every day." Paul smiled.

I took the phone back and got up from the breakfast bar to top up our wine. As I moved to sit back down, I decided to push on with the conversation. This was going well. I was more relaxed than I had been for what felt like years. If I wasn't going to talk openly now, I never would.

"Whilst I was thinking, a few things occurred to me. General things I mean. Not specific to me, or to us."

"Go on." Said Paul, he seemed genuinely interested.

"People cheat all the time. It's a standard thing in relationships. Everywhere you look it's there, in Films and TV show story lines. In books, in conversations with friends. It seems to be so…what's the word?" I paused for a second as I tried to think. I knew there was a word that was exactly what I wanted to say, but I couldn't get to it.

"Pervasive?" Suggested Paul.

"That's not the one I was thinking of, but it'll do. The cheating is always with someone close by, usually someone at work. People seem to become tangled up with the people close to them to try to achieve sexual fulfilment." My thoughts turned to Craig and why I'd done what I'd done. I think I'd made sense of it, and I wanted to see if I was right. "The trouble is that this gets confused with everything else that connects the two people. All other aspects of their relationship change, and soon it isn't about sex anymore."

"I'd say that's undeniable," said Paul, looking deep in thought as he spoke. "I can't imagine anyone being able to argue with that appraisal of western society. Where did those thoughts take you?"

"Well, it made me think about relationships. People who are together always pretend to each other that they don't fancy anyone else. It's the first lie. It's a lie that's never articulated, but by the absence of admitting it, a lie is born. People would talk about finding someone attractive to almost anyone close to them, yet never to the person they're supposed to be closest to. On a subconscious level, everyone knows it's a lie, and lying then becomes subconsciously accepted. It makes all the other lies easier. To protect someone. Does that make sense?"

"It does." Paul responded immediately. "I've never thought about it in those terms, but everything you've said is true, and very interesting. It explains a lot."

I became more confident as Paul agreed with me. I hadn't been sure it would make sense out loud. I carried on. "The trouble is it always ends up in betrayal. That's what leads to divorce. Being a couple that stays together is rare these days. It's not the norm. I don't want us to go down that usual route. I don't want us to lie."

"That's brilliant," smiled Paul. "Who knew you were a philosopher? Ok, how does that affect us, in a practical way?"

"I'll try and explain. Say you met a super beautiful pornstar that you recognised in a pub, and she wanted to sleep with you. Would you want to?"

"Er, yes, but..."

"No buts, that's the honesty I'm talking about. You would want to sleep with her. You'd be mad not to. Yet, because of me you would choose not to?"

"Correct." Paul gave a definite nod, as if to demonstrate an exaggerated agreement that might not be true. It made me smile. I carried on.

"Choosing not to doesn't mean you wouldn't want to. Still with me?"

"I see what you're saying." He nodded, seeming to indicate that I should carry on.

"There are people that you would like to see undressed, and of course I am the same. From time to time, we will both fantasise about them, about touching them and being touched. It might be someone in a magazine, or on the TV, or in the street. None of that means we want to spend any time with them. None of that means that you and I don't love each other. It is the reality of how people are. The truth."

"Ok. I understand. What does that mean though? Why are we talking about it? I mean, it's interesting, and I can see what you're saying. I don't know if it means anything, for us. Should we start telling each other who we fancy?"

"Why not? You asked me to be honest and tell you about my fantasies. I've been thinking about it a lot and I want to do that, but I need to let you know that I've worked this out first. I've understood that whatever I tell you is just about sex. It doesn't undermine or affect anything else about our relationship. I love you, and I can love you without trying to protect you from the fact that I am sexual, and I have fantasies."

"Ok, I understand." He paused and seemed to relax as his thoughts unfolded. "I completely agree. You can speak openly about anything. We might never fulfil a fantasy, but at least if we communicate about it, we will understand each other better. It's already proved to be fun." I nodded and smiled in agreement. "There might be a fantasy that we would both enjoy, and if we don't have the conversation, we'll never know. How daft would that be? In trying to protect each other we'd actually be depriving each other of something."

I smiled. "Exactly. I looked up common female fantasies online. I found a top ten list from a magazine vote, or something. Do you want to go through them with me and see if there are any you like?"

"That sounds like a great idea, I'll get us some more wine."

We moved from the kitchen to the sofa, and I opened up the list. I'd been careful to bookmark it on my phone. I sat with my leg's half crossed so I could face Paul and began to read.

"Ok, number ten. Drum roll please. Sex with a stranger."

"You've already said you like the thought of that," said Paul. "It's no surprise that it's in the list. It would be an easy one to try."

"At first glance it does, but it's one of the things that got me thinking. In the imagination everything would be perfect. The stranger would be handsome, gentle, an amazing lover. In reality, if you don't know anything about them, and you're not incredibly confident, it's quite unlikely to work out. It made me think about the reason's women cheat with someone at work. Someone they know. Someone who they know they'll be safe with. It might not be the ultimate fantasy, but it's so much less likely to go wrong."

"I suspect you're right," said Paul. "People would play safe and go for a vanilla relationship with someone they know, rather than try and fulfil a real fantasy. Even if success in fulfilling a fantasy might be exciting, a bad experience could be awful. Worse still, dangerous. You're right, it's not as straight forward as it sounds. What's number nine?"

"Group sex. It's a bit vague this one, it just says sex with groups of people. I'm not sure who it would be?" I was puzzled by exactly what the fantasy would entail. Paul looked a bit unsure about what that meant as well, so I decided to press on.

"Number eight is domination." I paused as I read. "I think it's more about getting exactly what you want, rather than any kind of kinky stuff. Being in control and giving the orders. That sounds like fun."

"That depends on what the orders are," joked Paul. "That's something we could do though."

"Number seven is being an exhibitionist. I might be one of those. Putting that picture online turned me on."

"Is that what it means?" Paul asked.

"It seems to cover a few things" I replied. "Being in porn pictures or videos, but it mentions naturism, and having sex in front of people as well."

"What do you think?" Paul tried to gauge my interest.

"I'll think about it. I definitely want to take some more naughty pictures. I'd enjoy that. How would you feel about me being in erotic photos?"

"I'd love it. Who wouldn't want to be married to a nude model?"

"What about harder stuff?" I pushed.

"I think every man wants to have sex with a pornstar, but not necessarily be married to one." Paul replied.

"What if no one knew it was me?"

He paused and looked thoughtful. "In that case I don't see why not. It depends on what it is though? I like what you said earlier. Knowing that there would be no lies, and no affairs, makes the thought of sexual experimentation seem exciting. The openness seems to remove any of the feelings of betrayal that is associated with cheating."

"I'll check everything with you first, we need to talk about it all before any fantasy actually happens."

"Perfect. That's an easy one then, we can tick that one off the list. At least we'll get to do one out of ten." He smiled.

"At least." I smiled back. "Being dominated is at number six. I suppose that's the reverse of number eight." I looked up and Paul nodded. I carried on. "Number five is having sex with a woman."

"Has that ever crossed your mind?" Paul quizzed.

"I don't think so, but perhaps because I haven't thought about it. I don't know if it's something I'd like to do. Let's leave that one for a bit." I moved on. "Number four is being paid for sex". A little shiver went through my spine as I read it. "That has an appeal, because it's a taboo I think!"

"An appeal to you?" questioned Paul.

"Maybe." I answered honestly, without thinking. "Being paid for sex might not work out, but getting paid for pictures or a video or something could be fun?"

"You don't want to have stuff like that on the web Soph, that can always come back and haunt you."

"Of course not, but they won't know it's me, remember. Getting paid for a few photos without my face in would feel good. Being desired enough that someone would pay. A couple of the guys who commented on my picture said they'd pay for more. That's what made me think about it."

"Fair enough, I suppose the rule is that no one ever knows it's you." Paul agreed.

"Number three is having a threesome with two men."

"I don't know about that one," said Paul looking uncomfortable for the first time. "Is that a fantasy of yours?"

"Not specifically. I suppose it's about being desired, having two people want you would be fun. Two people pleasuring you would be good as well. Would you like to sleep with two women?"

"It depends on who they were. That might be a bit like the stranger fantasy. Good in the imagination, but unless it was thought through carefully, it could be rubbish in real life."

"What if one of them was me?" I teased.

"That would be great, but I didn't think you liked girls."

"I said I'd put some thought to it. I'll think about that as well. Anyway, it was a threesome with two men that was on the list. I'll think about them both." I was very turned on by the idea of a threesome with two straight men focussed on me. The thought of having a cock in my mouth and inside me at the same time was something I often fantasised about in the past. I would tell Paul at some point, but not right now. After all, he didn't need to be involved if he didn't like the idea.

"Number two is fucking a man with a strap on!"

"That is out of the question," stated Paul with a comically worried look on his face.

"No problem," I laughed. "I have absolutely no desire to do that. I can't believe it's on the list."

"And the winner is, rape fantasy? That's shocking."

"That is shocking, but it does say fantasy," Paul noted. "It's not actual rape."

Something in my feminist core didn't like it, but Paul was right, a fantasy was different to actual rape. "It should say role play then, not fantasy."

"You're probably right," Paul agreed. "Let's leave that one, should we?"

"Yes, good plan. Well, that was interesting. Which is your favourite?" I asked.

"They're fantasies for women," he replied. "I'm not supposed to pick."

That was a good point. I had forgotten the confident new me for a second. Remembering my promise to myself, I felt brave and decided to take the bull by the horns.

"How about we pick three and talk about them some more. One day we can try one if we both think it would be fun?" I looked up at him.

"That depends on which ones." Paul looked a little bit taken aback by my request.

"Of course. We can decide together. It's only a plan to talk about it some more. To keep communicating!" I paused and smiled, with a look that tried to say, "more communication, like you wanted." He smiled back at me with a nod. "I'd like to think about number seven, by being in pictures or a movie. For fun, not to share with anyone." Paul looked ok with that, but I carried on before he had a chance to speak. "Then number six. I'd like you to order me to do whatever you want." This didn't seem to fit with my new power and confidence, but I wanted to do something cantered around Paul. It felt like if I was making the choice to be dominated then it was in my control, and I still had power. It would be good to see what he would make me do. I'd find out a lot about him and what he liked.

"Ok, we can talk more about that for sure," I could tell Paul was still a bit hesitant.

"Excellent. Finally, erm.... I think I like the idea of being with two men. I'm not sure I'd ever be brave enough to do it in reality, but it's a good fantasy to discuss. Maybe we should talk about having sex with a stranger instead?" I had expected to wait longer than a few minutes to bring this up, but I felt good, so I decided to try. I waited to see Paul's response.

"I suppose we can talk about it," he said, still hesitant. "Talking about fantasies will be fun. We'll learn loads about each other."

"It might not be something I want to do, once I've thought about it more," I suggested. "Let's leave that one until last and see how we go."

"Deal." Paul seemed happy with the option to delay thinking about it until another time. I put the phone down and looked up at him.

"I've missed you these past few days. Why don't we have some time away together somewhere. Even if it's only a long weekend. We could have a sexy weekend, maybe even have sex outdoors. What do you think?"

"That's a great idea. Where are you thinking?" He relaxed a bit, and looked thoughtful, as if thinking about potential destinations.

"It depends how long you can get off work. We don't want to spend too much of our time travelling." I had excited fluttering in my stomach at the thought of a sexy holiday.

"A long weekend is a good idea. I can do that pretty much at any time. Should we go somewhere hot?" Paul suggested.

"That sounds perfect. Sun, sea, and sex. How about Spain? Cheap and cheerful!"

"Ideal. Let's have a look for something." Paul picked up the laptop with purpose.

We sat with the laptop on the couch and spent an hour or so looking at package trips that we liked the look of. There was a reduced weekend package in a few weeks' time, which looked good. It must have been a sale to try and fill the hotel, as it was a lot better value than many of the others. Big rooms, five-star rating, a big pool. It looked lovely. We booked it and my stomach fluttered for about the hundredth time that week. Fluttering in my stomach hadn't happened for so long. I think my body was making up for lost time. I thought I had grown too old for it.

Chapter 7 – My Interview

My shifts at work over the following week seemed to take forever. I kept thinking about our trip. Looking forward to it seemed to make time slow down, to the point where it felt like it was almost standing still. I'd downloaded a dating app on my phone, and I had started to play with it. I'd asked Paul if he minded me trying it, and he was happy with the idea, as long as it was anonymous. It was exciting to be contacted by guys on there. It was nice to be getting attention. I had posted three pictures of me on my profile. Nothing that revealed who I was. There were some cleavage shots and a full-length selfie in the gym changing room mirror. The camera was blocking my face. Most of the blokes who contacted me were from London. London seemed the ideal place to meet people for sex. A big city, awash with anonymity. No chance of bumping into a conquest in a local pub or restaurant, as you might do in a smaller town like ours. It was good to have London on our doorstep, but not be engulfed by it. I started to reply to a couple of people. Whilst I did, I texted Paul.

"I'm thinking about asking someone to take some sexy photos of me, would you mind? I could send you some." I messaged.

"Who?" He texted straight back.

"I'm not sure yet, I'll try and find someone online." I kept my messages brief. There was a slight delay before he came back to me.

"Ok, but make sure you're safe." He didn't seem enthusiastic.

"I won't do it if you don't want me to?" I felt the need to check. I couldn't judge his reaction via text, and I wanted to be sure. There was another slight delay.

"Sorry, in a meeting. Go for it, but you've got to send me loads of sexy pictures." Came the reply I'd hoped for.

"You can see them all." I assured him, and returned to the app.

There was one gym fit guy from West London who interested me. He hadn't shown his face on the app either, but his body was fantastic. Muscular, without looking ridiculous. You could tell from the pictures that he would be good looking. Worth taking to bed, at least. We'd chatted using the messaging service on the app. He'd complemented me, without being crude, and seemed genuine. I had let him know straight away that I wasn't looking for anything serious. I didn't want to mess anybody about. He had replied that he was only dating and not looking for anything serious either. I had downloaded the app on an old phone. I didn't want anyone to know my number, or my name, so I'd set up a completely false identity on a burner sim card. All I needed was a phone number, an email address, which I set up on Google, and a name. I stuck with Sophie. I didn't see any need to change that. No one could find me from my first name. It would make things easier. The second name of my alter ego was Martinez. It was as far away from my married surname as I could realistically get away with, and it sounded exotic to me. Sophie Martinez. I liked it. I sent my number over the app and suggested we that we could message. I got a WhatsApp through on the phone immediately. His name was Nathan. He could have been doing exactly the same as me, I thought. His real name could have been anything. The profile on his phone said Nathan, but mine said Sophie Martinez, so that wasn't proof of anything. There was a picture on the message profile. Although he was wearing sunglasses, I could tell that I would fancy him. He was very attractive. I thought I'd get straight to the point.

"Are you free tomorrow night?" I messaged.

"I could be. Why?"

"I need someone to take some sexy pictures of me. It's a fantasy of mine."

"I'd love to. What sort of pictures, and where?" He asked.

"The plan would be to meet in a café in central London, to see if we get on. If we do, you will take me underwear shopping. Then we'd go to a hotel, and I'd try on the underwear for the camera. What do you think?"

"That sounds amazing. What would I get out of it?" It was the first time he'd sounded a bit pushy, but it was a message, so it wasn't easy to tell how it had been intended. I gave him the benefit of the doubt, but thought I'd push back.

"Taking pictures of a naked woman isn't something you'd like to do without reward?"

"Of course, sorry. I meant I'd be incredibly turned on and would want to touch you." He redeemed himself to some degree.

"If you are respectful and you take good pictures, then we'll see. No promises."

"Ok. Where would you like to meet?"

"Let's meet on Oxford Street. Lots of places to get a coffee, and to go shopping." I replied

"That's good for me. What time?"

"Let's meet at three. I'll ring you when I arrive."

"Looking forward to it. See you tomorrow." He closed the conversation, and I didn't reply. I wanted complete control. I was nervous, but I'd planned it in such a way that I would always be in charge, and I would always be able to back out at any point.

I still had a few hours left on reception, so I replied to a few other guys on the dating app. I didn't commit to anything, I only let them know that I liked their profile or pictures. It was up to them to chase me from that point. I gave my Martinez number out to a couple of them but didn't reply when they sent messages. I'd make them wait a bit. Tension is a big turn on I was learning. Men want nothing more than something they can't have. A lot of what I'd seen on the porn site was about the power of the woman, and the desire that men had to see and touch her body. Holding back, teasing, and delaying that pleasure was almost always part of the plot of a sex scene. The experience I'd had with messaging men on the dating app was exactly the same. The more they had to wait, the more desire they expressed. I loved it. I was going to maintain that power and control at all times. That's one of the big differences between a long-term relationship and casual affairs. You can't manufacture the tension of seeing someone naked or touching them for the first time. Once you've been together for a few months, that experience has gone. This might be a good way of recapturing that feeling.

I had been messaging on the dating app all morning. I enjoyed it partly because the thrill was a novelty, and it was also a real confidence boost. More importantly, it was taking my mind off the afternoon. I had been pushing my CV out a bit more than normal recently, and I'd been invited to an interview. I was sick of doing interviews. I didn't enjoy them, and constantly attending them wasn't getting me anywhere. I seemed to be in a cycle of being asked to interview and then getting nervous. I would take time off work to attend, and then feel relief when it was over. I hardly ever got calls back, and when I did, it was to inform me that I hadn't been successful. This afternoon's interview was for a job with an events company. They were based in town a few miles from where we lived. They weren't a big company, roughly twenty full time staff, from what I could see on the website. They seemed to be doing quite well. The job role was an events manager. The majority of the events that they seemed to manage were corporate functions. I was nervous. I hadn't had an interview for a job that interested me for quite a while. This could be a start of a career shift towards something more exciting. As soon as I finished work, I was going home to change and then make my way over there.

I arrived at the interview venue half an hour before my allocated time. My nervous energy meant that I was always going to be early. The office was on a modern business park, not a dissimilar setting to the gym I thought, as I drove into the complex. I parked up a little way away from the building. I didn't want anyone to see that I'd arrived so early. I took a moment to breathe deeply and calm my nerves. I thought about the morning I'd had, all the attention I'd been getting online. It gave me a little boost. No interview could need the same amount of confidence to do what I was going to do tomorrow. Stripping for a stranger in a hotel room was far braver than facing what I was about to face today. I had also been feeling calmer and happier over the past few weeks. Paul's desire for me had increased since I'd started to be more overtly sexual. My life was feeling more like the life that I wanted to have. Anything that happened in this interview wasn't going to change much. There was nothing in there that could hurt me. This interview was about whether they could enhance my life. This was my choice, my control. I felt good. I got out of the car and went for a short walk to get some air. Although I was still nervous, it felt like a positive thing. My pep talk to myself was having the desired effect.

The front door was closed, I pushed it and realised it was locked. There was a series of four buzzers on the wall to the left. I found Brightstar Events and pressed. A lady with a soft Scottish accent answered.

"Hello, Brightstar Events."

"I'm here for an interview." I stated.

"I'll be right down." Came the reply.

A few moments passed until a small, middle-aged lady pushed the door open to let me in. She looked like she belonged in a library, quite churchy, with glasses and badly brushed hair. It wasn't what I expected. Perhaps my perceptions of the events industry were wide of the mark. We exchanged pleasantries about the weather, and my journey. She was warm and welcoming. She asked the obligatory interview arrival questions about my journey. The questions seemed to be quite genuine coming from her. I liked her immediately. I followed her upstairs as she explained that she would go and see if everyone was ready for me. I took a seat in a small waiting area, whilst the lady bustled off. She had introduced herself, but I had been too busy trying to make a good impression to remember her name. I hope that didn't come back to bite me. It wasn't long before she returned.

"They are ready for you." She smiled. I stood and followed her again. A real shiver of nerves running through me for the first time.

"Thanks Sheila." A man in a suit nodded as the lady opened the door for me. "Sheila", I thought, at exactly the moment I should have been focussing on making a good impression. "Get out of your own head", I chastised myself. I smiled throughout the introductions to three men and one lady. After the handshakes, they took their seats opposite me. I sat down and wondered where the confidence I had felt outside had evaporated to. I couldn't remember any of their names, but Sheila's name was engraved on my brain.

The questions were standard, and my answers were standard as well. It was travelling along like any other run of the mill interview. The kind of interview where I didn't get the job. The comfortable conformity of the process was at least calming my nerves. My lack of any meaningful experience had taken all the hope out of the eyes of the interviewers. I was resigned to my fate. After only ten or fifteen minutes I could feel the interview being wrapped up. I knew that they hadn't been impressed and were looking to close things down. It was unusual for me to see it happening. Usually, I would have been so focussed on getting to the end of the process, that I wouldn't have recognised what was going on. I felt a slight anger burning inside me. It was confusing. What was I angry about? I was angry that they weren't taking me seriously. I was angry that I was being useless. I was angry that I had got dressed up, made my way over here, and wasn't giving myself a fair go at it. I was angry with myself. I was angry that I wasn't being in charge.

"Do you have any questions for us?" said the man in the middle who'd done most of the talking.

"Yes, a couple," I replied. "But first, is it ok if I say something?" The man nodded, with a quizzical expression. He was expecting the usual boring interviewee questions, to round off the usual boring interview. He wasn't expecting an alternative interjection.

"I can tell that you don't think I'm suitable for this role, because of my lack of experience." I began. It wasn't true. They thought that I wasn't suitable for the role because during the interview I had demonstrated the charisma of overcooked broccoli. I wanted to place my lack of my experience in their minds as the reason before I then changed their minds. "I have been a bit surprised by the interview." I continued. "I haven't worked in the events industry, but I imagine it to be vibrant and dynamic. I thought a people-based industry would be personality focussed. Not so concerned with experience. I came to this interview because I want to work for a small company who will see my value. I want to be somewhere that will allow me the chance to prove my ability. I have been good at everything I've turned my hand to, and I know that I will be good at this. Your clients will like me. I will get to know them, build relationships, find out what they want, and then I will deliver it. They will continue to do business with you, because of me. They will like working with me and they will tell their friends about us. I was hoping to show my personal skills during this interview, but I haven't felt the opportunity to do that. I feel like the focus has been on my lack of experience." I paused. I looked at each of the panel. I didn't want to look aggressive. I was trying to look positive and hopeful. Looking to see if anyone would offer me a lifeline. A few seconds passed, only two or three, but it felt like an eternity. "Don't say anything", I was telling myself. "Wait for them to come back. Don't apologise," I pleaded with myself in my head.

"How would you suggest we get you to show us your abilities?" Asked the man in the middle. He looked a bit annoyed that his interview process had been called into question, but not to upset. He was interested in what my answer would be.

"Try me." I stated. "Invite me to one of your events and see how I do. I'm not asking for you to give me responsibilities. Allow me to mingle with your guests and see how I work." I paused again. There was another silence for me to suffer through.

"We'll think about it. Have you got any other questions?" The man in the middle answered for everyone. I'm pretty sure he was the owner of the firm, but I'd missed their job titles when I had focussed on learning Sheila's name.

"I'll ask a few more questions after you've offered me the position." I smiled. The man in the suit smiled back and nodded.

"Ok, we'll be in touch." He stood and shook my hand. I shook everyone else's hand firmly, with a smile, and left the room. I didn't care if I had messed that up. That felt good. Really, really good.

Chapter 8 – Underwear shopping

Another morning at the gym had passed. It was pretty busy, so I didn't have much of a chance for thinking or getting nervous about the afternoon date I had set up. I received a few messages from blokes on the dating app. They were all too old, or too fat. Most of the time there wasn't enough information to decide about whether they were right for me. Blokes seem to think that a picture will do. "Do you fancy me or not?" They seem to be saying. They don't understand that most women need to know a bit more. It's an entirely visual thing for men. A picture of a good-looking girl is all they need, whether she's a Nazi sympathizer or not.

It was soon home time, and I raced back to the house to get changed. I realised I was quite excited, and not as nervous as I'd expected. I put on a pair of my favourite jeans, the ones I would wear on a casual night out, and a tight white, buttoned shirt. I left enough buttons open to look relaxed, but not enough to look slutty. A hotel receptionist amount of cleavage, not a stripper. I wore heels, and underneath my clothes I had matching underwear. It was nice, but not sexy. I wanted to make sure that I was treated to something new. Having sexy underwear on already would only be distracting.

I walked to the station and got the train into the centre of town. I arrived a little bit early and decided to have a glass of wine. I felt confident, but there is always room for the extra confidence created by a good glass of wine. I sent a message to Paul when I had sat down at a table. "Waiting in a bar for my photographer." I wrote. I wanted to let him know that I was being sexual. I wanted to show to him that I was the confident woman that had somehow escaped me these past few years. I sipped my wine and waited until about five past three, then I called Nathan.

"Hello." He answered straight away.

"Hi," I said cheerily. "Are you here?"

"Yes, I'm stood outside the tube station."

"I'm in the wine bar on the opposite side of the road, to your right." I was facing the window but couldn't see the station entrance.

"Ok, I'll come there now, look out for me."

It must have been awkward for him coming into the bar without knowing what I looked like. Sophie Martinez's message profile pic didn't reveal my face. Luckily the bar wasn't busy. As he walked through the door, I was pretty sure it was him. A big clue was that it was a single bloke, who arrived a couple of minutes after I'd spoken to Nathan. His muscular physique was also a giveaway. I stood up so that he would see me. He noticed and smiled, looking relieved. He walked over to the table.

"Nathan?" I asked with a smile as he approached.

"Yes," he said. "Nice to meet you." He leant forward and kissed me on the cheek as he took my hand. He smelled wonderful. He was clean shaven and had made a real effort to dress well. He was wearing a white t-shirt with a blue jacket, jeans, and lovely shoes. I was impressed. I sat back down and waited for him to say something.

"Would you like another drink?" He asked, pointing to my almost empty wine glass.

"Yes please, a dry white wine. A small one!" I watched as he walked towards the bar. A flutter of excitement ran through me. I hadn't felt like this for so many years. The experience with Craig was fun, but I wasn't confident enough to enjoy the sexuality of it. There was also a feeling of guilt associated with it, which I didn't like at all. This was liberating. A man who was here to be used for my pleasure, and Paul was ok with it, I think, up to a point.

He returned with the wine for me, and a bottled beer for himself. He raised his drink to toast.

"It's a bit early, but what the hell." He smiled and took a sip.

"If ever there was a good time for an early drink, this is it." I smiled back.

"How many times have you done this?" He asked.

"A few." I lied. I didn't want to expose my lack of experience, or my potential nervousness. I wanted to keep control. "You?" I asked.

"Never. I don't know any bloke who has. I don't think it's often that a beautiful woman asks a stranger to take photos of them. It's a bit surreal. I'm not sure I can believe it."

"You think I'm beautiful? That's a good start. You haven't seen my face before."

"You're stunning."

"Thank you." The situation, and the prospect of what might happen next might be clouding his judgement. I enjoyed the compliment anyway. I had noticed in porn films that ordinary looking girls can make men desire them. As long as they have enough sexuality and confidence. Keeping in good shape is important. After that, armed with a good understanding of what men find sexy, any woman can seduce many of the men that they meet.

"What about dates? Has the dating app worked for you?" I watched his reactions as I questioned him. He was confident and had an honest demeanour. There were no hesitations in his responses.

"I've been on a few dates. Some have been good fun, but often people are looking for something serious. I'm only dating for fun, and it makes it awkward when someone hopes for more." He looked genuinely concerned about leading someone on or giving the wrong impression.

"I'm not looking for anything serious." I reassured him. "Only fun."

"I assumed so from your messages." He looked like he relaxed after I had confirmed my intentions. "There is a site for swinger couples that I have started using." He continued. "It's much more straightforward. The vast majority of people on there are married and looking to spice up their sex lives. Much less chance of anyone wanting something serious."

"That sounds interesting." I thought, out loud.

"I'll send you the link to it. You'd like it." It was good to hear Nathan discuss the prospect of me meeting other people. It was a good feeling to know that we were both looking for the same thing. I wanted the honesty that I was pursuing in my life to continue with him. The irony of doing it under a false name give me an internal chuckle.

"Why do you want pictures?" He asked. It was a good question. One I hadn't articulated to myself.

"It's not just pictures." I began. "You need to take me shopping first remember? I love underwear. Stockings, negligee, beautiful panties. Anything that shows off a woman's body and makes her look sexy. Then I want pictures of me in it. I want to see how I look and put some on the internet to see what other people think. I could send you some to you as a reward if they're good." I added.

"I love underwear," he was focussing on me as he spoke, without being intimidating or staring. He had a natural way of conversing. "Women look so much sexier partially clothed. Nudity is the end point, not the seduction. Nudity is not as exciting." He seemed to know what he wanted and what he liked. I enjoyed the way he talked, he seemed intelligent, which was exactly what I wanted. If he had been a lad, in a thuggish or brutish way, I had planned to leave the bar straight away. If there was any hint of misogyny, I would leave as well. I had got the feeling that it was going to be fine from our messages. It would be very difficult for a thug to fake decency for even a short time. If they knew how to do that, they wouldn't be a thug. Even though I felt comfortable, I still wanted to be sure. Safe and in control.

"This should be your perfect job then!"

"I hope so. Are you happy? Do I get the job?" He looked nervous for the first time.

"You've made it to stage two. You can take me shopping." I leant back in my chair, smiling, feeling more and more confident.

We finished up our drinks and walked out into the street. Whilst Nathan searched the internet for the nearest suitable shop, I checked my phone. Paul had messaged back, "How are you feeling? Has he turned up?" I replied quickly whilst I had the chance, "Feeling very sexy, we're going underwear shopping." I saw that Paul was typing, so I waited a few seconds. "Send me pictures." Was his response. I replied with a kiss.

We were only a few minutes' walk from a large high street lingerie store. We walked down Oxford Street, dodging the tourists, businesspeople, and shoppers on the busy pavement. How do so many people have the time to be out of work at half three in the afternoon I wondered? We arrived at the store and Nathan held the door open for me as we walked in.

We started to look around, a little sheepishly at first. Browsing through the displays of underwear.

"What size are you?" He questioned, then he checked himself. "Is that a rude question? It would help to know."

I smiled gently, as if to show that there were no issues with such questions. After all, he was going to see me naked soon. "I'm a ten, but sometimes I need a 12 because of my boobs. Thirty-two D for bras" I looked to see his reaction. He looked straight at my tits.

"Makes sense." He grinned. "Do you like this?" He held up a red bustier, which was cheap looking. Quite slutty, but I quite liked it.

"I can try it on. Let's find a few things and we'll see what looks good." We browsed separately for a while. I picked out a couple of lacy underwear sets, one with garters. I also saw a nice white silk slip that I loved the look of. I found Nathan looking at some very strappy bodysuits.

"They look interesting." I commented.

"Very sexy," he nodded. "Are you ready to try some things on?" He looked around for the changing rooms.

"Ok. Are you going to try and sneak some photos of me?"

"If I can. I'll pretend I'm messaging on my phone." He reached into his pocket.

"Not on your phone. One of the rules is all the pictures are taken on my phone or camera. Sorry, but I can't have pictures of me floating about online." I had become quite serious for a second, I wanted to make sure he understood.

"Of course, no problem." He looked worried at my aggressive tone. It made me feel better that I'd put him on the back foot so easily. I wanted to make him feel better though. I liked him. He was perfect for this.

"Here's the deal," I smiled. "You give me your phone to keep safe in my bag for the afternoon and I'll give you mine to take pictures with. I know it might seem over the top, but I don't know you. As much as you seem lovely, it will make me feel better." I softened my tone as I spoke. I hoped it would help put him at ease.

"I completely understand." He handed me his phone. It wasn't a problem for me to hand over my old phone, with Sophie Martinez's profile on it. It didn't contain anything with my real identity. The only thing he'd have if he stole it would be any pictures that he was about to take of me. It had a PIN code protecting the screen lock. I wouldn't give him that. Even if he decided to sacrifice his own phone and run off with mine, he wouldn't be able to see the pictures after the screen had locked. I put his phone in my bag, unlocked mine, and passed it to him. I'd set it to stay unlocked if unused for ten minutes, so he shouldn't need to ask me to enter the PIN very often.

The changing rooms were at the back of the shop, and actually quite out of the way. I passed him the items that I'd selected and asked him to hold them. I took the white slip and went into the changing room. I stripped off and looked at myself in the mirror. The wine might have been helping, but I felt good about myself, and my body. I pulled the slip over my head and looked back at the mirror. I liked it. It was a bit tight around my chest, a size ten, but it pushed my boobs up making my cleavage look impressive. It was how I wanted to look. I reached into my bag for my real phone and took a picture of my reflection in the mirror and sent it to Paul. I replaced the phone and pulled the curtain back enough to look poke my head out. Nathan was waiting. We both glanced around to see if anyone was looking. No one was paying any attention. The shop wasn't very busy. I pulled the curtain back further and revealed my outfit.

"Wow." Nathan gasped. He stepped forward and took a couple of photos. I turned around and lifted my hair so that he could take some of me from the back. I looked back over my shoulder, and then lifted the material on one side of the slip, exposing some of my cheeks. Nathan gulped as he took more pictures. After a few seconds I turned back and took the next piece of underwear from his arm. I went back into the cubicle and closed the curtain. I took the slip off over my head and hung it on one of the hooks. As I picked up the next set of underwear, I realised it was only a pair of panties, attached to garters and stockings. I hadn't paid any attention when I grabbed it. There was no bra with the set. I smiled to myself as I started to pull the panties on. I took another quick picture of me with my real phone when I was finished. I stood topless with the sexy black underwear hugging my legs. I took a couple more shots of my reflection from over my shoulder and sent the best front and back pictures to Paul. I put one arm across my chest, covering my tits as best I could, and opened part of the curtain again. After another quick check to see if the immediate area was clear, I pulled it open and stepped back. Nathan's eye's widened and he began to take more pictures. I posed for him, pushing my hip out to the side, and putting my free hand on my waist. I kept the arm covering my tits in place. After a short time, I turned around. The panties were lacey and framed my arse in a beautiful flow of material. They covered about half of my cheeks in curves over the round of my bum. The garters pushed into my thighs a little and created a shape that I liked. I looked at the mirror as I could see more photos being taken behind me. I took my arm away from my chest and put my hands on my hips. I could see the camera travel upwards. The focus moving from my arse to the reflection of my tits as Nathan took pictures of me over my shoulder. I put my hands on my head and lifted my hair again, swung my hips to one side and tilted my head to the other. I was enjoying myself. I turned around with my mands still on my head and let him take a couple of quick pictures. I stepped forward and said in a lowered voice "touch me." Nathan moved forward and caressed my right boob with his free hand. I shivered as he stared at my chest and grabbed at me slightly harder. "Don't forget the photos." I reminded him. He moved the phone back and took some pictures of his hand on my tits. He had grown in confidence and was enjoying touching me. I didn't let it last for long, I stepped back, smiled, and closed the curtain.

I took off the underwear, and along with the slip, passed it out of the cubicle without opening the curtain. I held my hand out and waited for a new item to be placed into it. I tried on three more outfits, all different, and all very sexy. The strappy one that Nathan had chosen was very erotic. It revealed a lot, but the straps also encased a lot of my body. It made me feel great. I posed for pictures, some with my hands on the wall of the changing rooms, pushing my bum in the air. Some turned around, always trying to achieve a sultry, sexy look. Once I'd tried them all on, I put my clothes back on and came out of the changing rooms.

"Which one did you like?" I asked.

"You looked amazing in all of them." He replied.

"In that case you can buy all of them for me." I smiled. "I want a lot of good pictures."

"Ok," he agreed. I think he would have bought me everything in the shop if I'd asked him to. I hoped he could afford it and wasn't about to bankrupt himself for me. As he queued to pay, I looked through the pictures he'd taken. They weren't the best quality. That was hardly surprising considering the location and the camera that he was using. They were sexy though. I sent a few to Paul. The last one I sent was of Nathans hand fondling my tits, with the caption "I think he likes me."

As we left the shop, I suggested that we needed a sexy dress. I had to strip out of something. I couldn't start in underwear, there wouldn't be enough build up. Nathan agreed, and we went into an impressive looking fashion store a few buildings away. After trying on a couple of things we settled on a very tight, short black dress, with a low-cut neckline. I loved it. I didn't think I'd ever have the courage to wear it in public, but I was looking forward to wearing it in a hotel room.

"Are you sure you don't mind getting this for me?" I checked. "I don't want you to spend all your money on me. You still need to get a hotel room don't forget."

"Don't worry, I can afford it." He said confidently, without it seeming arrogant or showing off. He went over to the till, and I checked my phone again. "That is the sexiest picture I've ever seen," came the reply from Paul. With the follow up, "you look like a porn star." My stomach fluttered. It was what I wanted to look like this afternoon. I wanted to bring those porn stars that men adore back down to earth. Back to reality. I wanted to prove to myself that I could be sexy, that anyone could be sexy. I felt amazing.

Chapter 9 – My First Photo Shoot

I asked for three options of hotels that I could pick from. I trusted Nathan now, but I still didn't want to end up in a room he'd already booked. The fear of hidden cameras was in the back of my mind, and I wanted to stay in complete control. A quick search revealed a few hotels that were close to us, all in Mayfair. I hadn't heard of two of them, but both were five stars. The one I had heard of was Claridge's. I asked if we could go there.

"No problem." Nathan looked up from his phone and flagged down a cab. My stomach was doing somersaults as we climbed into the car and set off.

After a five-minute wait at reception, whilst Nathan sorted the booking, we went upstairs and swiped the door card. The room was beautiful. It wasn't a lot bigger than most good hotel rooms, but it was well furnished. It was impressive. A big white bed in the centre, with huge windows filling the room with light. The bathroom was almost as big as the bedroom, with double sinks, a big shower, and a standalone bath.

"What do you think about some pictures in the bath?" I asked, as we explored the room.

"Sounds like a good idea. What's the plan?"

"You lie on the bed and get relaxed. I'm going to get changed." I picked up the shopping bags and took them back into the bathroom, closing the door behind me. I took out the underwear first. I'd already decided that I wanted to wear the stockings and garters, with the panties that framed my bum. There was a matching black bra, the one that I hadn't picked up in the changing rooms. It wasn't a brilliant bra, but it gave me a huge cleavage and looked sexy enough. After putting the underwear on, I took out the black dress and pulled it down over me. It was tight, but after moving it around a bit, it found a place on me and was a good fit. I looked in the mirror and loved it. I felt desirable and sexual. "Only one person will see me in this today," I thought. Then it occurred to me that I would have the photos. They would give the afternoon a more important, and lasting legacy. I liked that this sexy image of me would be preserved, and that Paul would get to see it. The thought of sharing the photos with Paul sent another shiver of excitement through me. I spent ten minutes putting on some more make up. I added quite a lot to my eyes, in the hope of giving me a very dark, slutty look. I decided against lipstick. It never looks good after about five minutes anyway, and I always felt it looked a bit forced on me. I tied my hair up in a loose bun, so that it was out of the way, and put my heels back on. I was ready.

I walked out into the room. Nathan was on the bed with his hands behind his head on the pillow. He sat up onto his elbows when I entered. His mouth dropped open.

"What do you think?" I wanted to receive a compliment.

"Incredible." He seemed to struggle to find words.

"Let's see if you're any good as a photographer then." I had brought my bag out of the bathroom with me. I took out my camera and threw the bag on the chair by the window. His phone was still safely in there.

"Use this. It's easy, point and press. It does all the work for you." I handed it to him as he moved to sit on the edge of the bed.

"We're not using the phone then?" He looked a bit surprised by the camera.

"If you think I'm going to waste this hotel room, this dress, and some new underwear by using a crappy phone for the photos, you're wrong." I shook my head with a smile. I pulled the curtains back to let as much light in as possible. The net curtains blocked out any opportunity for someone to see us but kept the room as light as possible. I knew that it had to be bright. I'd seen some home-made pictures and video clips on the internet, and they were always terrible. Dark and blurry. I was never going to go to the effort of bringing my own lighting. I would make sure I did the best I could with what was available. I went to the door and turned all the lights on. It didn't seem to make a noticeable difference, but I assumed everything would help.

"Are you ready?" I asked. "You will have to lead this, I won't be able to tell what a good picture is, only you will see from behind the camera. Let me know what you want me to do."

To start with he was quiet. He snapped away as I posed in the doorway, and then in the centre of the room. I leant over the desk. I even pretended to use the hotel phone as I jutted my arse out towards the bed, at right angles to the camera. I moved to the window, and after a few seconds I pulled up the dress, so it was halfway up my arse cheeks. I enjoyed exposing myself to him, and to the camera. I was definitely an exhibitionist. What a thing to realise after all these years.

"I can't see much, because of the light from the window. It's making you into a silhouette."

"You need to be on the window side," I said. I moved to the bed and crawled onto it on all fours. "Then the light will be behind you."

I stayed there in the middle of the bed as he took pictures of me from several angles. Looking up at me with my cleavage underneath me. He took some from behind, my dress still riding up my bum. I rolled back onto the bed and beckoned him over.

"Show me how they look so far." I wanted to make sure we weren't wasting our time. We weren't. They were actually quite good. The camera was advanced enough to make the most of the light from the window. The pictures looked brilliant. It could have been a low-cost porn shoot. These wouldn't look out of place with some of the professional stuff on the web. It gave me more confidence to see my body looking good in the dress. It was fun.

"I've got an idea," I said.

"What's that." He replied, looking at the camera that I'd passed back to him.

"We've got all afternoon here, let's make the most of it. I don't want to rush."

"Ok. I don't have anywhere to be." He looked intrigued.

"Take your pants off." I ordered, with a slight smile.

"Now?" He seemed a bit shocked.

"Yes." He put his jacket on the chair with my bag and started to undo his belt. He kicked his shoes off and then half turned away from me as he dropped his jeans to the floor. He took his socks off as he picked up the trousers and put them with his jacket.

"What now?" He asked as he turned to face me. He was fully erect, his underpants struggled to contain him. This just got more interesting.

"We're going to go through some porn pictures online and find some that we're going to replicate. Then I'll tell you what's next. He lay on the bed next to me and we used Sophie Martinez's phone to search for some good pictures. We searched for hotel strip, shower strip, big boobs in the bath, lingerie, busty stripper. We saved any good ones to the phone, and in the end we had about thirty pictures that we both thought we sexy. By this point I thought he was going to explode. On the bed in his underpants and t-shirt, with his face only a short distance from my cleavage. It must have been like torture.

"Would it be easier to concentrate on taking the photos if you were more relaxed?" I teased.

"If that means what I think it means, then yes." He looked desperate.

"You can cum on my cleavage." I said, directly.

"Will you touch me?" He asked.

"No."

"Will you get your tits out?" He almost pleaded.

"No. I'll take my dress off, but not my bra. I want you to play with yourself and cum onto my cleavage, and I want to video it. After that we can take all the other pictures. You'll see my tits, and at the end of the photoshoot. You'll want to cum again, I guarantee it."

"What happens then?" He enquired.

"I'm not sure yet, we'll see how I feel." I stood up and walked over to the window. I pulled the dress over my head and placed it over the back of the chair. I could feel Nathans eyes on my arse as I bent over more than was necessary to look in my bag. I pulled out a small tripod for the camera and went back to the bed. The tripod had come as a set with the selfie stick. I had thought that it might come in handy. I set the camera up on the bedside table and put a pillow on the floor by the bed. I pressed record on the camera and asked Nathan to stand up. I moved him into position so that the camera was pointing at me. The image was from the side, but also from the front. It allowed the camera to see as much of me as possible without Nathan blocking the view. I knelt down on the pillow and put my hands on his thighs as I looked at the camera. I moved back and stood up to check where I was in the shot. The position was almost perfect. You could see all on me in front of Nathan. All you could see of him was the back of his legs, up to the waistband of his underpants. I raised the angle a little, so that I was centre stage, and went back to my position on my knees. My legs were straight, not sat down on my calves, so that my tits were a fraction below his waist. I looked up at him and said, "go on then".

    He hesitated for a second, as if about to speak, and then he seemed to think better of it. He pulled his cock from his underpants and slid the elastic waist down on to the top of his thighs. He was big. I held back a little gasp as he exposed himself in front of me. The excitement in my stomach felt like it was overflowing. He took hold of his cock and started to play with himself, slowly and deliberately. I placed my hands on his thighs and watched closely, occasionally looking up at him to see him staring at me. His movements became quicker, and his breathing increased. With his free hand he reached down and grabbed my chest. I shivered at being touched and leaned back to let him play with me. He was frantic now and as his hand slipped into my bra to cup me. He began to orgasm. I watched as cum leapt over me, splashing down on my tits in thick showers. There was so much. I was completely covered. I looked down at myself as he slowed and came to a stop. I had never seen so much cum. I stood up and moved over to press stop on the camera. I took it off the tripod and passed it to him. "Take some pictures" I ordered.

    I put my hands on my hips, and then on my head as he snapped away. I pulled the cups of my bra down so that my tits were exposed. The cum started to run down over my chest and onto my nipples. It continued to flow and drip over my stomach and onto my panties and thighs. I looked in the mirror. I was the image of sex and dirtiness. It was thrilling. I took my bra off and he took more pictures of me. Close ups, and shots of me moving around the room. He followed me into the bathroom, and I told him to put the camera back on to video mode. He watched and recorded, as I stood in front of the bathroom mirror and slowly wiped the cum off my tits. One tissue after another. He had lost his erection for a short time when he was taking photos, but it started to return as he watched me cleaning myself.

"Put your clothes back on and we'll take the underwear photos," I smiled at him. He turned the camera off and put it down on the bed as he returned to where his clothes lay and started to dress. I stayed in the bathroom and changed from the cum soaked black underwear into the white slip. The camera was linked via Bluetooth to my real phone. I took it out of my bag and flicked through some of the pictures. They were pretty good. Not bad for a first time. I was happy with how I looked. I loved the sensuality and sexuality of the first underwear pictures. The shots of me covered in cum were thrilling to look at. I sent a couple of them to Paul. I was hesitant, because he wouldn't know the context, but I wanted to see his reaction. I could explain later.

After I'd touched up my makeup and straightened my hair out, I came back out of the bathroom. Nathan was dressed and lying on the bed. We started to work through the first set of pictures that we'd chosen. It was a series in various stages of undress, as a busty girl stripped from her underwear. He took loads of photos, until I was naked in front of him. After some naked shots, I put on the next set of underwear, the strappy outfit that Nathan had chosen. We repeated the process, using a different set of pictures to try and emulate. They were all generally the same series of shots, with some variety in position and location. After I'd ended up naked a couple more times, I put on the last set of underwear. I suggested to Nathan that it was time to mimic a series of photos that ended up with some hardcore images.

Initially, he was clothed, and I was in my underwear. It started with various pictures of me posing in the underwear, similar the previous sets. Then, I put the camera onto a selfie stick, to gain some distance for some pictures of the two of us. The camera was too heavy for me to hold on the end of the stick, so I switched to the phone. It was much more manageable, but I knew the picture quality wasn't going to be as good. I tried to take the pictures as best I could. Some of him groping my tits through my underwear, me undoing his shirt, him taking off my bra. Then grabbing my exposed tits. I tried to get some of him sucking my nipples. I had plenty of time to get it right, as he played with me for several minutes. It was difficult to manage taking the pictures as well as posing. It was frustrating trying to do both. After a while, I took his trousers down and he was exposed again in front of me. I held the selfie stick up to the side and took some pictures with his cock in front of my face. Then I put my tongue out and licked up the shaft, snapping photos all the time. Nathan was erect and breathing heavily. I placed his cock on my chest, across my tits for some pictures. I then put it between my tits, and then rubbed my nipples with the tip, clicking the selfie stick button all the time. I put the head of his cock in my mouth and gently let my lips and tongue surround it. I looked at the camera and took some more shots, moving my mouth down his cock as I did. It was far too big to fit it all into my mouth. I took in as much as I could, about half of it, and looked at the camera again. I took more pictures with him in my mouth, some using my free hand to hold my tits. The material of my underwear was clinging to my mid rift as my boobs hung free. I stood up and he gasped as his cock slipped from my mouth. I took a couple more of us stood together with my free hand holding his cock gently.

"I think it's time you went down on me," I smiled at him. "Would you do that for me?"

"Of course," he nodded.

Chapter 10 – Sharing My Fun

"If you make me cum, I'll touch you and you can cum again." I promised as I put the camera back on the tripod. I moved it into the same position as it was before. It was a relief not to have to bother with taking pictures anymore. I switched it to video mode and started the recording. I sat on the edge of the bed and spread my legs. Nathan kneeled down. He was now naked and started to kiss my thighs. He moved steadily up towards my panties, kissing, and licking the inside of my legs as he went. He kissed across the bottom of my stomach, and then kissing and licking onto the outside of my panties. I was so turned on. I felt shivers flow through me. I grabbed his head and pulled him into me. I was so wet. I was sure he would be able to taste me through my underwear. He slid his hands up my thighs and gently pulled the front of my panties to one side. I moaned out load as he breathed heavily on my exposed vagina. I leant back slightly against one arm, still sat up, exposing my breasts to the camera. My other hand still pulling his head deep between my legs. After what felt like an eternity of gentle kissing and breathing, he engulfed my clitoris with his lips and tongue. Gently sucking and rolling me in his mouth. The feeling was exquisite. I was so turned on from the afternoon, that I was in complete extasy. As he sucked my clitoris immediately an orgasm built up and exploded within me. I moaned with delight as wave after wave of sensational pleasure rolled through my body. It went on for a long time, increasing in magnitude and then slowly fading away. He seemed to recognise exactly when the orgasm was passing. As I became more sensitive, he slowed his licking and sucking to a gentle caress. I slid back and he stood up. I leant forward and took his cock straight into my mouth for a second. "Tell me what you like," I said, as I withdrew to speak. Taking him back into my mouth as soon as the words had departed.

I'd forgotten completely about the camera as I eagerly slid up and down his huge shaft with my lips and tongue. "Be gentle," he said. "That hurts a bit."

"Sorry," I said, taking his cock from my mouth again for a second. If this had been Paul, that comment would have killed my mood, but this was just sex. Even though it made me feel a twist of disappointment, of dented pride, I quickly determined that I didn't care. "Tell me what you want" I repeated.

"Don't suck, just use your mouth to pleasure me." Nathan requested politely.

"Why do men constantly talk about getting their cocks sucked then?" I thought to myself. Men are so stupid. What do they expect to happen? They'll get exactly what they ask for most of the time. I suppose you don't blow, and they're called blowjobs as well, I reasoned. I'd never asked before, so maybe the failure was my communication as much as theirs.

"Ok, let me know if it feels good."

I didn't put my hands on his cock. I grasped his thighs and only used my mouth to stimulate him, sliding my lips and tongue up and down his shaft repeatedly. I felt him pulsing and moving towards my face slightly in time with my movement, up and down. I continued gently encasing his cock with my mouth and tongue. He groaned and stated "that's amazing. Keep doing that." It was less than a minute before I heard him whisper "I'm coming." He was about to explode, I sat back and put my hand on his cock, wanking him towards my face. I held his cock with my hand the same way I had with my mouth, very little pressure, relying on the movement to excite him. I opened my mouth and looked up at him as he started to ejaculate onto my face. I softly wanked him as the hot cum ran over my cheeks and mouth. There wasn't as much as last time, but still a lot. Our photo shoot must have been a turn on for him. I surprised by myself. I hadn't expected to let him cum on my face. I hadn't thought about what I'd do. I suppose it happened quite quickly, and I had done what came instinctively. I'm sure it had something to do with the porn I had been watching. I didn't think it was something I would have chosen to do without the influence of porn. It felt dirty, and fun though. I could tell it was exactly what Nathan wanted to do. It heightened the feeling that I was engaged in a sexual fantasy. I wasn't constrained by some of the extra influences that more intimate relationships harbour.

He stepped back away from me and let out a huge sigh. "That was incredible," he muttered. "Without doubt the best blowjob I've ever had." A little pride rushed through me, along with the still significant afterglow of my orgasm. Perhaps this communication idea was a good thing. I congratulated myself for being a quick learner. I leant forward and picked up the camera, stopped the recording and took it off the tripod. I handed it to Nathan. "Can you take the last pictures, please."

He took the camera and snapped some photos of me sat on the edge of the bed, my underwear messily pulled around my waist. My boobs exposed, and cum dripping from my face onto my chest. I smiled, put my head on one side, and then leaned forward. My boobs hung beneath me, splashed in cum. The camera clicked. I stood up and put my hands on my hips and posed in various positions whilst Nathan took more photo's. We went into the bathroom, and he videoed my cleaning his cum from my face with the tissues. It was erotic, but with a calmness, when compared to the frantic oral sex we had enjoyed.

I took a shower, and he took some more pictures and videos. I was still turned on. It was such a thrill.

After we had dressed, we had a quick look at some of the photos. "Are you happy with them?" he asked.

"Very," I replied. "We look good together."

"Do you want to do more?" He almost pleaded.

"I'll think about it" I smiled. Inside I thought, yes definitely. I wanted to know what that big cock would feel like inside me. "I'll send you some of the pictures later," I promised.

We walked down to reception and out into the street. He kissed me on the cheek before heading off in the opposite direction. There was no awkwardness to our goodbye at all. It felt like we would see each other again, and so there was no need for complication. I turned and made my way down to the tube.

I checked my phone when I got onto the over ground train, and there were a couple of messages from Paul.

"Wow" exclaimed the first one. Followed by "Did you have sex?"

I replied that I hadn't, only a blowjob, and that I'd show him the pictures when I got home. I got a message from Nathan thanking me for an amazing afternoon. I didn't reply, he could wait for a while. I sat back into the train seat, as relaxed as I'd felt in a long time. The afternoon sun shining over the city and through the window of the half empty carriage.

When I got back, Paul looked through the pictures whilst I had another shower. I came out into the bedroom wrapped in a towel and asked, "what do you think?"

"Incredible" he responded, still looking at the screen. You look amazing. Like the world's sexiest porn star. Did you enjoy it?"

I knew most of what he was saying was rose tinted, because I was his wife, but I enjoyed his compliments all the same. I was so glad that he saw me in that way for a change. Gone was the grey, boring middle aged me. He wouldn't look at me like that again. "It was good fun, but now I need sex."

I made my way across the bed and straddled him as he rolled onto his back and looked up at me. He pulled the towel away as I started to ride him. He fondled my tits, still wet from the shower and the water dripping from my hair. We fucked in a frenzy, and both came to orgasm together in only a few minutes. I fell down on top of him breathing heavily. "I love you," I whispered.

"I love you too," he replied between long deep breaths. He held me on top of him in his arms for a few minutes.

I put the towel back around me as I moved to the side and lay next to him on the bed. Paul sat up a bit and uploaded the camera onto his laptop.

"Have you seen the videos yet?" I asked.

"Not yet," he replied, "I looked through some of the photo's".

"There's some more on my phone," I said. "The camera was too heavy for the selfie stick."

We lay together and watched the first video of Nathan wanking over me. It was more erotic than I'd imagined, watching myself being so sexual. It didn't last long, but it was very sexy.

"What do you think?" I asked, a bit nervous about what Paul would say.

"It's awesome, you look so sexy. How did you know where to put the camera? It looks very professional."

"I've been watching more porn," I replied, "I enjoy it, it's interesting to see what men and women want. You can see how many times the clips have been viewed, so I've been looking to see which ones are the most popular. I copied the best ones. Do you want to watch the second video? I got a bit turned on!"

"Sure, let's have a look."

We watched as I orgasmed. "You look incredible," repeated Paul. "Your tits look amazing with you sat up like that."

"I thought you'd like that" I smiled. All the popular videos I'd seen had a good view of boobs. Tits are so curvy and sexual. I was glad mine were big enough. It was a real turn on to see men so captivated by them. We carried on watching me take Nathan in my mouth, and then as he came on my face. I could see Paul was turned on. "Do you think people would watch these clips?" I asked.

"I'm sure they would." Paul exclaimed. "No doubt."

"It's a shame they have my face in them."

"I can crop them down. It's easy," said Paul.

"Go on then, let's see how they look." Paul started working on the laptop whilst I got dressed. Once I was in comfy clothes, I had a quick look at one of the websites I'd been using to watch porn. There was a section for amateurs, where you could upload movies and pictures. I created a Sophie Martinez profile whilst I waited for Paul to finish working on the photos and videos.

He showed me the first clip once it was cropped. It was framed around my cleavage. You couldn't see anything from my neck upwards, only Nathan stroking his big cock in front of my boobs. The anonymity made it sexier for me, although I think most blokes would have rather seen the full view. The amount of cum onto my cleavage was spectacular. The view of my nipple as Nathan slipped his hand inside my bra at the end was very erotic.

"That is a sexy video. You had him very turned on."

"He'd been taking photos of me and watching me try on underwear on all afternoon. I'm surprised he lasted that long."

"Did you enjoy him going down on you?" Paul asked. "Was he good?"

"I did, and he was quite good. I was so turned on from the underwear and the photos, I would have orgasmed even if he wasn't good at it."

"Do you think you'll see him again?" Paul enquired.

"I'm not sure." I replied. "I'm not interested in seeing him again to talk to, no relationships remember. I could use him again for another video if you would like to see it?" Please say yes, I thought to myself. I wanted to get the chance to fuck Nathan. "He's a straightforward bloke, and I know I'm safe with him now," I added to try and help the cause.

"What video would you want to make?"

I thought about how honest I should be. Having just watched me in a porn video, it would seem silly to start lying, or holding things back at this point. "I'd like to have sex with him, if you wouldn't mind?" I waited for Paul's response with a lump in my throat.

"I don't mind. If it means seeing you as sexy as I've seen, you today. I'm happy for you to do what you want. As long as you use a condom."

"Of course," I immediately assured him. "I'll always stick to our rules. How about I make another video for us to watch when we get to Spain? It might be a good way to kick off our sexy holiday."

"That sounds like a very good idea. What do you have in mind?"

I assumed he meant what kind of scene I'd like to do. "I'd like to get taken from behind. Very impersonal. What do you think? What would you like to see?"

"That sounds exciting. Seeing you in charge of your sexuality and enjoying your body is a real turn on. I've never seen you so confident. I've never seen this side of you."

"Should we watch some porn, and decide together what I should film?" I suggested. Paul smiled and nodded. I opened up the new porn account on the laptop and showed it to him.

We watched ten or twelve scenes together. We talked about what each of us liked and didn't like as we watched. It was so good to be so open about it. I felt liberated, and I was getting to know much more about Paul as well. Only little things, but they were little things that brought us closer. The knowledge would definitely improve our sex together. We uploaded a few anonymous video clips and photos of me. We also saved three scenes as our favourites to the porn account. I said I would try and make something similar and bring them to Spain with me.

"Should we put your video on here?" Paul suggested. "See if people like it?"

"Why not, there's no way to tell it's me. It might be a way of meeting people, through the site. We can be sure that people are only there for sex." We uploaded the video of Nathan cuming on my cleavage, and some photo's that Paul cropped to remove my face. I felt a surge of excitement as my exhibitionism kicked in. Paul closed the laptop and pulled me close to him. We made love twice more that evening, and as soon as we woke up the next morning. This was so much fun.

Chapter 11 – A Bad Date

Paul set off to work after we had eaten breakfast together. It was nice to relax and have time for coffee and some eggs with Paul in the morning. I wasn't working until the afternoon, and I had decided to have a restful morning to myself. I made a second coffee and sat down in front of the TV. I had a scan through my Sophie Martinez phone. Some people had posted some complimentary comments about my boobs on the rating site. It gave me a good feeling to read that people had enjoyed looking at me. There were no negative comments, which surprised me a little. I had heard a lot about internet trolls. I had prepared myself for some criticism, even abuse. Up to now it seemed like a much more positive space than I had anticipated. I supposed that the majority of people using the sites were men looking for the opportunity to have sex. Being nasty wasn't' very conducive to creating that opportunity. I suspected that things might turn sour after a rejection. I decided not to let my guard down. I would remain prepared for anything unpleasant should it occur. My dating app had several messages waiting for me. I deleted all the ones which said "hi" unless the guy was really hot. I replied to a couple, asking for details about what date they would take me on. I thought it was a good way to identify who I would like to meet up with and who I wouldn't. A few guys replied in broken, slang English, which immediately put me off. They would actually write things like "I'd take you back to my place and smash u coz u is hot." A very easy opportunity for me to delete the message and unfriend them. It did make me wonder if their approach ever worked. Were there girls on the site who enjoyed with that kind of interaction? I supposed that some people might enjoy the attention. It didn't strike me that those men would be at all respectful. There was a part of me that suspected I would not be safe with them. Maybe I was being judgemental. Judgemental or not, they weren't for me.

I decided to sign up to the swinger's site that Nathan had recommended. I spent an hour reading peoples profiles. I read the profiles of single girls. Then I looked at the kind of guys that they were friends with. I was amazed by how many couples there were on there. I had thought that the conversations Paul and I were having were revolutionary. Apparently not. The internet was full of couples, sharing experiences together. Some were looking for other couples, and many of them were looking for single girls to join them. The search for "unicorns", bisexual girls happy to meet with couples, seemed to get an enormous amount of attention. A lot of couples were looking for a girl to join them, and it seemed like there weren't very many unicorns to choose from. Hence the term unicorn I imagined, very rare indeed. After I had read a good number of profiles for research, I filled mine in. I described myself as married, and a potential unicorn. Looking to meet fun, respectful single men, or couples. I added some pictures, without my face. They were sexy, but non nude. The site seemed classier than the porn site, but more openly sexual than the dating app.

Time had flown past, and my morning was almost over. It concerned me how much time I was spending on my new adventurous lifestyle. I thought it through and justified it to myself in two ways. I was enjoying it, and my sex life with Paul, and my sex life more generally, was more exciting than it had ever been. Why wouldn't I spend time on it? I figured that once I was set up, and I understood the apps and websites more, I wouldn't need to put the same amount of time to it. I was learning a lot about people, and a lot about how to interact with them. Like anything in life, it would become easier with experience. I checked back onto the dating app and read a couple of replies that I'd had. Both were guys in London. I sent them my Martinez phone number and shut down the laptop. I went and got ready for work, planning to get there early and eat in the café.

During lunch I opened the Martinez phone again and looked at my messages. I found it addictive. A little buzz of excitement flowing through me each time there were new messages to read. I had stopped checking the porn site, and the boob rating site. They were fun, but not a way to meet people. The dating app was a bit frustrating. Nathan was right. For everyone who was on there looking for the same thing as me, there were fifty people trying to find a relationship. I didn't want to engage with those people. Two much potential hurt and unwanted attachment. I had messages on my WhatsApp from both of the guys from the dating app that I had sent my number to. One guy called Phil, who was very keen to meet, and a guy called Brian. I looked back at Phil's profile and pictures. He was attractive, balding, so had shaved his head. He was very fit and athletic. There wasn't much information about him, but that's to be expected I suppose. I was very attracted to him, so much so that I definitely wanted to arrange the meet. I told him that I was free after work today, but only if he could get to North London. I let Brian know that I could meet up in the centre of town in a couple of days. Phil came back to me immediately agreeing to travel to somewhere convenient for me. I would get on a train into North London straight after my shift and meet him there.

It started as an uneventful shift at work, but busy enough to make the time pass. I didn't see Craig, which was probably a good thing. I did miss the little ripple of excitement that I felt when he arrived. It wasn't that I fancied him, I didn't. I had decided that nothing further would happen with him, because of the discussion I'd had with Paul. It was the illicit nature of our relationship that stirred the exited thoughts within me. Knowing what we'd done, and knowing he'd be desperate for more was a real turn on. I noticed that I was talking to customers more. James had even taken time to mention to me how much more confident and happier I seemed. It had made me blush, but I did reflect on what he'd said and noticed the change in me. I was smiling more. I felt much more content. It had nothing to do with my adventures, although that was a lot of fun. My contentedness came from my improved relationship with Paul. More important was my improved relationship with myself. I understood what I wanted, and who I wanted to be, and I was achieving it. It seemed like the world was my oyster, for the first time in my life. It was wonderful.

After showing some new clients around the building, I got back to my desk and saw a missed call on my mobile. I checked my voicemail, and it was a man from the events agency asking me to call back. I put up the "back in ten minutes" sign and went into the staff changing rooms to get a bit of privacy. I called the number and the man answered. He had been one of the four who'd interviewed me. He introduced himself as "Dan on the left." He had rung to let me know that Brightstar had an event coming up that he would like me to attend. At least I knew one of their names now.

"Great," I responded, "when is it?" He let me know that it was on Thursday evening. It was black tie, and it would be my chance to introduce myself to some people and see how I got on. He took my email address and promised to send some more information about the evening and the attendees. He would also attach some background information about the company that they were hosting it for. I thanked him for calling and let him know that I was looking forward to Thursday. I was giddy with excitement as I hung up the phone. I'd contained my happiness during the call. Maintaining as calm and professional a demeanour as I could whilst we talked. The truth was the interview and the job had slipped from my mind over the last few days. Sex had distracted me from the world. The phone call had been a real unexpected bonus for me. All my troubles had been forgotten as soon as Paul and I had started communicating. The sex and exhibitionism were so much fun. I didn't feel like things could get much better. Now I had been offered the chance to prove my worth in a job that I wanted. Things were on the up.

As soon as my shift was over, I walked to the train station, and caught the first train South. I had arranged to meet Phil in a pub near the first underground station on the line. It would be easy for Phil to get there, as well as being no hassle for me.

On the train I got the email from Dan at the events company following up from our phone conversation. He provided details of the hotel where I needed to be for the event and confirmed that it would be a black-tie event. My mind turned to potential dresses that I could wear. I had a few to choose from, but nothing inspiring. I looked up the venue. It was a very glamorous looking establishment. He also sent me a link to the company who they would be hosting. I read about them for a while, through various web searches. They were a small company, called Zeno Systems. They sold printing equipment to small and medium sized businesses. They seemed to be doing well and were expanding. The evening was an event where they were bringing current and prospective customers to wine and dine them. I expected this would be as much about showing off as it would be about getting new business, but it looked like fun. I carried on reading until I had a good feel for who they were.

When I'd finished my research, I looked to see if I had any messages on either of my phones. Then had a quick look to see what interest my profile had generated on the swingers site. I had about twenty messages from single guys. A couple of them were attractive, but most of them weren't my type. They had all sent unimaginative, mostly single word messages. I deleted any that weren't of interest to me. I felt a bit bad about ignoring people who had taken time to message me, but I didn't want to get involved in a conversation with someone that I knew wasn't for me. I was here for my pleasure, and I was going to make sure I put myself first. My kindness and compassion were going to be saved for my friends, and most importantly, for Paul. I only had two messages left once I'd done my deleting, and four introductions from couples. Two of the couples didn't interest me. There was a husband and wife, who didn't do anything for me. The guy was out of shape, and the girl wasn't sexy. The other message that I deleted was from a couple who lived miles away. They were a bit older than me, and I wasn't excited enough by their pictures to reply. One message was interesting, from a very attractive couple. They were into spanking and ropes. It had never crossed my mind as something I would be into, but they were very beautiful. I sent them a message asking what they were looking for in a girl who might join them. The other couple were based in London and looked normal. They were very attractive. Their profile stated that they loved each other. They were on the site to experiment and spice up their sex life. I liked that they were open about their loving relationship. He was straight, tall, and very handsome. She was bisexual, a bit shorter than me, with an amazing body. Her curves were a real turn on for me, she looked incredibly sexy. I sent them my Sophie Martinez number in reply to their simple introduction message. I hoped that they would turn out to be a genuine profile and get back to me. I was sure that I'd be checking my phone even more than normal in the coming hours, hoping for a reply from them.

When I arrived at the station, I moved through the concourse and crossed the road. I called Phil's number as I walked. He answered straight away.

"Hello," his voice was brisk, with a higher pitch than I expected.

"Hi, it's Sophie." I hadn't planned my response and got caught up in my head in the seconds before I spoke. Did I need to use a false name? No, Sophie is fine. It had made my reply sound stilted and awkward.

"I'm in the pub, can I get you a drink?" He continued to speak quicky. Nerves must be getting the better of him, I suspected.

"Wait until I get there" I suggested, "I'm thirty seconds away."

"Ok, see you shortly. I'm on the right as you walk in." He added, before I hung up.

I walked in, feeling much less nervous than I would have expected to be, had I thought about it. I was very relaxed, and I felt good. I saw him sitting alone and headed straight over to the table. We greeted each other quite formally, with a light handshake, and I sat down. He looked older than he did in his pictures. I suspected his pictures were from a few years ago. He didn't need to use the tactic, his aging had made him look more rugged, and somehow sexier. He was wearing a tight white t-shirt, showing off his gym physique. He was tanned, and obviously spent a lot of time on himself. His appearance gave the impression of someone quite vain. I suppose that could be a bonus in a situation where fun sex was the goal.

"What are you drinking?" I asked to break the small awkward silence that developed after we had completed our introductions.

"Vodka and soda." He motioned towards his glass as he said it. "Would you like one?"

That was the drink of a gym rat if ever there was one. Chosen solely for its calorific content, rather than its taste. I knew so many people like that at our gym. I had fallen into the trap from time to time. Missing out on life in pursuit of the perfect body. I would now settle for a healthy and attractive body, alongside the joys of some of life's small pleasures.

"I'll have a dry white wine please." I smiled.

"A large one?" He stood up as he asked, revealing his tight jeans, boat shoes without socks, and a small bag to keep his phone and wallet in. Carrying a bag was a small price to pay to avoid his phone or wallet breaking the lines of his skin-tight outfit, I mused. He did look good though.

"Why not?" One of the benefits of living and working so close to London, was that driving was seldom necessary. My first thought when offered a drink was always "what am I doing later? Do I need to drive?" But since moving close to London, I had always been free of such concerns. He moved off towards the bar, and I instinctively turned to watch him leave. His efforts to look good were definitely paying off. He looked great. I glanced at my phone whilst he was gone and saw a WhatsApp message from the couple on the swinger's site. They were Jess and Robert. Their message was brief. They introduced themselves and thanked me for sending my number. My heart skipped a little as I read it, remembering their pictures. They were very attractive. I replied, asking them to let me know what they were looking for. There was also a message from the guy from the dating app, Brian, but I didn't' get chance to read it. I quickly put my phone away as Phil arrived back at the table.

"Was that another potential date?" Phil half smiled but looked a little uneasy as he spoke.

"Potentially." I smiled back. My instinct had been to say no, but I had no reason to lie to him. He was a stranger, and I'd met him on a dating site, so there was no need to hide that I used one.

"Hopefully this date will go well enough that you can tell him you won't be going!" I looked up, expecting to see him indicate that he was joking, but his face gave no such sign. I paused for a second, allowing myself to process what he'd said.

"It isn't a guy!" I kept my eyes on him, judging his reaction, "and if it was a guy, I would definitely still go on the date if he was hot!" I continued.

"Does that mean you're not interested in me?" He was still serious. I could tell he wanted an answer to the question.

"It doesn't mean that. I'm dating for a bit of fun. I'm not looking to meet anyone serious. I'm not looking for an exclusive relationship." I told him. I didn't want there to be any confusion. I wasn't sure whether I'd mentioned this in my messages, but I had definitely spelled it out on my profile on the dating app.

He looked very perturbed. "I'm not used to that." He admitted, looking more and more serious each time he spoke. "I'm normally enough for a girl, she doesn't need more after she's had me."

I struggled not to laugh. I smiled to mask my giggle. In case it came. "Are you looking for a relationship?"

"No, but I don't like to share." His seriousness continued. In my line of work, I need to be in control, and I suppose it's the same in my personal life.

"What do you do for a living?" I hoped that this question would help to change the subject.

It worked. For the next half hour Phil told me about his job in recruitment. He explained the cut and thrust of the Alpha male environment. He often referred to how much money he made, and how much conflict there was in his line of work. He also kept referring back to why he expected women not to date other people when they were with him. I listened, paying attention, and sipping my wine. It was fascinating watching his ego and insecurities unfold in front of me. I finished my drink, and he was still talking about himself. After a short time, I stopped paying attention, and began to think about Jess and Robert. I found myself wishing that I had the opportunity to message them back, instead of listening to Phil. He wasn't offensive, or an unpleasant person. He was insecure, and very boring. I started to wonder how I could escape. I decided to be direct.

"I am going to have to leave soon!" I interjected, at a pause in his conversation that was only just big enough for me to barge into. There hadn't been many such breaks in his flow.

"Oh, I had hoped we could get some food together." He looked very disappointed. He had no idea how boring he was.

Perhaps he was used to boring, or shallow girls. He was good looking enough. His conversations about career and money might have been enough for some people. I was completely turned off. I didn't want to hurt his feelings though.

"Maybe another time." I tried to look sincere. "Tonight, I have to get home. I only had time for a quick drink. Sorry, I should have been clearer in my messages."

"Are you not interested in me?" He asked, "or are you going on to meet someone else?" He followed up before I could respond. This guy was a fruit cake.

"I have to get home. Don't worry. You're very attractive." I assured him. I omitted that he was a boring, vain, insecure prat. Far too serious, and no fun at all.

"Another time?" I questioned as I stood up to leave, not giving him any chance to continue talking.

"Definitely." He stood as he spoke, not able to stand straight due to the table in front of him hitting his thighs. I used the moment as he was trapped by his chair to skip out to the side of the table. I gave him a quick kiss on the cheek.

"Thanks for the drink." I immediately turned to leave, hoping that he wouldn't follow me. He didn't. I walked with purpose straight back across the road to the train station. I found a train that was leaving in only a few minutes. They were leaving London every few minutes during rush hour. I walked along the platform until it arrived, still half expecting Phil to be following me. I checked over my shoulder, but he wasn't on the platform. I boarded the train and slumped into a seat, relieved and relaxed. I hadn't been frightened at all. He wasn't a threat to me. He seemed to have no idea of how to conduct normal social interactions. He was way too serious. Hard work to be around. I took out my phone and replied to Jess and Robert. I had decided, whilst Phil had been blabbering about himself, to be much more careful about who I met up with. I wanted to avoid any experiences like today if I could help it. I asked them if they wanted to meet in town for a coffee after work one day. A coffee is easier than a drink, and there would be less assumption that it would be a few drinks, or a meal as well. I also messaged Brian from the dating app. I asked him to tell me a bit more about himself, and what he wanted from the dating app. I hoped he would be a bit more laid back than Phil.

Jess replied almost immediately, saying that her and Robert would love to meet me. She confirmed the day and time, and suggested a coffee shop, which I knew, and agreed to.

I had received a string of WhatsApp messages from Phil during this time. He thanked me for the date and suggested some potential future dates to meet up. Each message was telling me why he couldn't meet up sooner because of some important meeting. He also explained why he hadn't been himself tonight because of trouble with an important client. I messaged him back saying that I thought we were looking for different things in a relationship. I blocked his number. Cruel to be kind, I thought. I relaxed the minute I knew I wouldn't be in contact with him again.

Chapter 12 – The Beautiful Couple

When I got home, Paul was already there. He had made some dinner, and we sat down and ate together whilst I relayed the story of my date. I realised as we talked that I was now able to be completely open with Paul. I was getting to know him so much more than I had before. I had assumed that because we were married that we knew everything about each other. The truth was a long way short of that. I knew that he would be learning so much about me as well. I was telling him things about how I felt that I hadn't known myself until a few weeks ago.

"If he was so good looking, why didn't you want to fulfil a fantasy with him? Paul had been listening intently to my story, and laughed when I described Phil. His question was a good one. I hadn't articulated it to myself until now.

"Even though I'm not looking for a relationship, to fulfil any fantasies that I, or we, might have, I want to meet someone fun. I don't want to spend a minute of my life with someone boring or serious. The biggest reason is that boring and serious is a complete turn off for me." Paul nodded understanding as I continued. "Imagine we chose to have a threesome with another girl. Neither of us would have to like her particularly or want to spend any time with her. It would be important that she was relaxed and fun. Otherwise, our experience wouldn't be relaxed and fun."

"I see," Paul nodded again as he spoke. "Should we look at the dating app, and you can show me how you're getting on with setting up your three fantasies?"

"Definitely," I grinned. We went through to the lounge and sat on the sofa. I showed Paul my profile. He suggested a couple of small changes, which made sense, and I altered my profile there and then. I opened up the messages, and there were about six from Phil. We both laughed at the site of his name repeated in my inbox. I was glad I was with Paul. It removed any guilt I had about blanking Phil. It put it all in perspective for me, why I was doing it, and why there was no need for guilt. I deleted his messages without reading them, and blocked him on the app.

Brian had replied, saying that he was only looking for fun, with fun people. I was pleased by his replies, and asked Paul what he thought.

"He seems a lot more straightforward. What fantasy would you like to fulfil with him?"

I mused a little before I spoke. "Sex with a stranger. I could ask Nathan to be there to film it, so I'd be safe. Unless you wanted to film it?" The thought occurred to me that he might.

"Maybe in the future. That would be sexy. For now, it might better for you to experience things without me for a bit. It's all new, and a massive change to how you've been in the past. We should run before we walk. Once you're comfortable with things, who knows what we'll want to do together." He paused, as if waiting for me to let me know what I thought.

"That seems sensible. I am learning so much about myself, and about other people. It would be better for us to do things together once I'm more experienced and confident." I opened up the swinger's app whilst I talked and put it in front of Paul when I'd finished.

"What's this?" He asked as he looked over my profile page.

"It's an app that will be much better than the dating app. I wanted to chat to you first, but I'll delete the dating app, and only use this one. Everyone on there is either married or looking to meet up with married women or couples. It seems much more straightforward, and there should be a lot less people like Phil." I chuckled again at the thought of him and his pomposity.

Paul was clicking through the site whilst I talked. "You have a lot of messages from single guys! Are you sure Phil won't be on here?" He smiled. "You might get some more messages in your inbox from him here."

I laughed. "Phil wouldn't want to share, so he would never use a site like this. Women don't need anyone else after they've had him," I mimicked him, in a mocking tone. We both laughed again. "I'll meet up with Brian and see if he's sane. I also might meet up with a couple from the swinger's site, for coffee. I would like to talk to a couple who have had experiences. It would be great to understand what has worked for them and what hasn't."

Paul looked over Jess and Robert's profile and commented on how attractive they were. We put the phone away and watched a film together. I felt content and comfortable. It was a lovely way to feel, and it was a lovely evening. Paul was away for the week from tomorrow, so I was glad we'd had a chance to talk.

Before I went to bed, I messaged Brian to arrange a meet up a couple of hours after I had seen Jess and Robert. I also deleted the dating app from the phone. Glad to have had the experience but pleased to be moving on to something which seemed a bit more straightforward.

Paul set off in the morning before I got up. He kissed me on the cheek as I dozed, and I drifted back to sleep when I heard the front door close behind him. My day wasn't productive, but I managed to get through some chores and housework. I was drinking coffee and dipping in and out of the daytime TV that was playing in the background. As the clock rolled round to mid-afternoon, I put on a light dress, and went outside for the first time. It was a warm day, sunshine with a gentle breeze. The weather enhanced my already calm and happy mood. It was one of the most pleasant walks to work could remember. I was looking forward to meeting the Jess and Robert later. I had so many questions to ask them. Whilst on reception I sent a message to Nathan asking him how his day was going. I attached a few of the photos that he had taken of me, with my face cropped off. Then I went back to the mundane tasks of work. Doing the rounds of the gym to pick up any used towels and see if there was anything out of place. I stopped and chatted with a couple of the regular girls. They were leaning against the running machines. It was nice to catch up with people here. It felt very comfortable after five years. I still hadn't seen Craig again. I knew I would need to talk to him. I'd broken the rules with him, before I'd agreed any rules with Paul. I needed to straighten that out. It was one thing that was hanging over me. Not bumping into him was ok though, I was happy to put it off for a while. I noticed I'd got a message back from Nathan.

"Fucking hot." The first one read, in response to my pictures. "Have you got any more you can share?" Came the follow up. I sent him a couple more, one of me leaning forward with my tits hanging underneath me. I sent him one face down on the bed, my arse framed by the nice panties. Then I sent him a clip of the video. All altered to remove my face. It was only a couple of minutes before he responded with more adulation. He requested more photos and videos.

"I don't have many more. Do you fancy helping me get some?" I responded.

"Of course. What do you have in mind this time?"

"What about you are filming me giving a blowjob to someone?" I asked, already knowing what his response would be.

"That would be fun. You do give an amazing blowjob." Was all he replied.

"I want to try my skills out on someone else. What do you think?"

"What would we do afterwards?" He pushed, to see what was in it for him, as usual.

"I might let you fuck me." I finished the message with a devil emoji.

"Sounds amazing. When?"

"I'll let you know xx"

"Let me know where and when, and I will be there. I'm flexible at work." He closed out the conversation.

I went straight from work into town. I looked around a couple of shops when I arrived, killing half an hour before I had arranged to meet the couple. I still ended up at the coffee shop early. I ordered myself a drink and enjoyed some people watching whilst waiting for them to arrive. When they walked through the door, I recognised them immediately. They had their faces visible on their profile, so it wasn't difficult. The tanned curves of Jess's body were unmistakable. She was remarkable. Robert was handsome, slim, and tall. They both gave the impression of being well-groomed and smart. On his own he would have looked great, but being next to Jess, he somehow looked more ordinary than he was. She had a supernatural beauty which eclipsed his classic good looks. I gave a small, shy wave in their direction. They noticed and came over to my table. They both had beaming smiles as they sat down and said hello. They seemed so calm and confident, they immediately made me feel at ease.

"You look pretty," Jess continued to smile as she complimented me. "I love your dress."

"Thank you," I felt myself blush a little. I could never control my blushes. "You look great too. You both do." I added, in what felt like a clumsy addition to my response. I realised I wasn't very sure of how this conversation would play out. I wasn't certain of what I should say next. It made me feel a bit less confident than I had a few seconds before. I needn't have worried. Jess seemed to know exactly what to say.

"So how are you finding the swinger app?" She was leaning forward, looking intently at me as she asked. It wasn't overbearing or intimidating. It felt like she was very focussed on me and interested in what I was going to say.

"I am enjoying it. I am new to it though." I decided in that moment to be honest during this conversation. I wasn't going to be in control and didn't want or need to be. There was a lot that I could learn from them.

"What made you decide to sign up?" Robert interjected. He'd taken his sunglasses off and was listening as keenly as Jess. I shifted in my seat to address him more directly.

"I had the first open and honest conversation about our sex life with my husband. We'd got into a bit of a rut, and after we'd talked, we decided that trying new things might be fun. I tried a dating app, but I wasn't finding it easy to meet people with the same expectations as me. A guy I met suggested the swinger app, and here I am. It does seem to be a lot more straightforward, but you are the first meeting I've arranged with the app."

"I hope we don't put you off." Robert laughed as he joked. His straight, white teeth glinting and lighting up his face.

"I very much doubt that," I gave a coy smile. "What made you guys decide to use the app?"

Jess sat back, her eyes drifting off to the right. She paused, in thoughtful consideration before she spoke. "We've always been honest with each other. We're very much in love, and that gives us both a lot of confidence. We have never suffered from jealousy. We know we'd never let each other down, so we decided that we could be strong enough to experiment with other people. For us it's about seeing what we enjoy and making the most of those experiences. We're new to it as well. At the moment we are trying new things and seeing if it suits us."

"What new things have you tried?" This was exactly the kind of thing I had hoped to find out about from them.

"I stripped for a bachelor party" Jess grinned. "It was something that had always intrigued me. I always resented girls who were the centre of attention. I found myself being a bit catty, and nasty towards them, without realising why. As I got older, I realised anyone could be the centre of attention, but they were brave enough to do it. I stopped resenting them and began admiring their courage. When I had built up enough confidence, I was able to do it myself."

"Did you enjoy it?" She was glowing with happiness, I expected I knew what the answer would be.

"I was glad I'd done it, afterwards. I don't think I enjoyed the experience enough at the time. I was nervous, and it was completely new to me. I don't remember being turned on when I stripped. I was more worried about doing a good job. Afterwards, I was elated. Rob and I had the most amazing sex, I loved it."

"Were you there, Robert?" He was listening to Jess, his concentration on her broken by my question.

"Rob is fine, Robert makes me feel like I've done something wrong." His boyish grin came back to his face. "I was. Jess wanted and needed to be safe. A bunch of drunk guys all together could be a problem. We made sure it was early in the afternoon, so that they wouldn't be too drunk, and I went along in the role of her manager. They paid me the money, and I told them the rules. It was pretty straightforward."

"Did you enjoy it?" I was fascinated to know what he had felt.

"It was incredible." He responded, speaking with sincerity. "Seeing Jess being so confident and sexual, was so much fun. Seeing how much the guys wanted to see her body was amazing as well. It made me realise how lucky I am to be married to Jess. It made the line between the fantasy women of the movies, and the woman of my every day, seem non-existent."

I'd never thought about it like that, but it made sense. The contrast between women in porn and the wives and girlfriends of normal life is very distinct. The two might never meet in the minds of most men. It has a lot less to do with looks, than it does circumstance and actions, I mused. Jess was beautiful, but anyone stripping, and being the centre of attention, would seem more sexual than a housewife, mother, or career woman.

"Is it something you would want to do?" Jess interrupted my thoughts.

"I don't think I'd have the confidence yet." I replied. "I haven't had a very exciting sex life up to now. I will need to build up to something like that."

"How come you're here on your own?" Rob questioned, with a slight hesitation as he said it. He seemed worried that he was asking something inappropriate. I smiled to reassure him.

"For the same reason. I am inexperienced, and I want to find my feet before me, and my husband do more things together. I want to get through any awkward situations, and learn about myself, what I enjoy, what I don't enjoy. It wouldn't feel right doing that with my husband. I want it to be fun for him, and that will be when I'm confident and comfortable. Being with someone insecure and unsure isn't fun. He would feel like he was looking after me." I looked to Rob to see if he understood my response. He nodded, with a thoughtful expression on his face. Before he could respond, Jess interjected, full of enthusiasm.

"I completely get it," she announced. "Me and Rob are lucky, we had a lot of fun before we met, travelling and meeting people. Our sex lives were fun, and we had learned a lot about ourselves. That's why we're able to be here, talking to you. Without that, I know I wouldn't feel confident in trying things like we are." It was lovely to hear her understand my thought process. I couldn't imagine someone as beautiful and confident as her ever being in my position. It was empowering to know that she understood me, and that one day I could come across like she did.

"What do you want from me?" My question was passive, and I was ok with that. I felt very comfortable with them, and I wanted to see them again, in whatever capacity they chose. Being around them made me feel good.

"We loved your pictures, and both find you sexy." It was the first time that Jess had seemed shy. Not embarrassed, but hesitant about being so open with me. It was endearing, and a huge confidence boost for me. "We have talked about inviting a girl to be with us, but we've never done it. When we saw your profile, we both agreed that we'd like to meet you. We hoped that we'd know whether we wanted to go ahead, after we'd met someone."

"Do you?" I pushed. I was watching them learning and growing, as I was. I realised we were all in a similar position.

"Well, we haven't had a chance to talk." Jess looked across at Rob. He smiled at her but didn't give the impression that he was going to say anything. Jess turned back to me, "I'd love to see you again, have a few drinks, some fun, and see what happens. Only if Rob wants to." She added and turned back to Rob.

"Sounds wonderful to me." He seemed so relaxed and confident. Jess was definitely the driving force behind their adventurous side. Rob seemed to be happy as long as she was happy. He had such a calm and positive demeanour.

We chatted a little longer, about some other experiences that they'd had. I told them about Nathan, and about Phil. As we finished our coffees, I let them know that I was away for a while. We agreed to message when I got back to arrange something.

We left the coffee shop at the same time, after we said our goodbyes. I walked towards Covent Garden where I'd agreed to meet Brian. I dropped him a message letting him know that I was early, and ready to meet whenever he was free. I stopped and had a glass of wine and some pasta. I enjoyed people watching whilst sitting in the restaurant, and the time to myself. I reflected on my conversation with Jess and Rob. I hadn't had any expectations, but I could never have predicted or hoped that it would go that well. I liked them. I had learned so much from talking to them and had enjoyed their company. I would look forward to seeing them again, regardless of sex. I was thinking about ordering a second glass of wine, when my phone buzzed. It was Brian letting me know that he was ten minutes away. I settled the bill and left the restaurant. There was a bar on the opposite side of the road. I went in and found a table by the window. I messaged him back to let him know where I was and waited for him to join me. I was starting to feel more comfortable playing the sexy new role in my life. It felt good to throw myself into it. Now that'd I'd had some experience, I could settle back and decide what I wanted to do with my sexual freedom. I got a message from Paul asking if I was on my date yet. I replied that I was in a bar waiting for him. Paul asked me again to be safe and asked me to update him.

My thoughts were broken by the arrival of Brian. He saw me and headed over towards the table. He was good looking, his body filling his clothes beautifully. He was tall with a handsome face.

"Sophie?" His voice raising at the end, indicating he wasn't sure it was me.

"I am." I stood up and he kissed my cheek.

"What would you like to drink?" He asked, motioning towards the bar with his hand.

"I'll have a dry white wine, please. A small one."

"Coming right up." He Left, and I stared at his bottom as he walked across the room. I texted Paul. "He's arrived, and he is very attractive."

Brian returned with my wine and what looked like a gin and tonic for himself.

"What are you drinking?" I checked.

"Soda water." He looked embarrassed. "I've got a big day tomorrow."

"What do you do?"

"I work in the city for an insurance company. It's not interesting, unless you're involved the industry, I suppose. I quite like it. It pays the bills." I could tell from the way he was dressed that it more than paid the bills.

"So, what's a successful, good-looking guy like you doing with a profile on a dating site?" I asked, naively I realised as soon as I'd said it.

"Sex is fun, right?" He smiled. "Isn't that why you're on there?"

I looked down at my drink, feeling a bit daft. "Of course. I wondered why use the internet? Aren't there other ways to meet girls?"

"Well, I work a lot. I don't drink very often, and I'm not looking for a relationship. Going to bars and clubs isn't my thing. When your friends introduce to you someone who they think is perfect for you, it's hard to mention to the date that you're looking for no strings sex. That's the kind of thing that gets reported back during the post blind date debrief."

"I suppose it would be." I smiled.

"The web is great," he continued, "you can meet people who want the same things as you, without all the hassle of meeting a thousand other people who don't. I have come straight from work to meet a beautiful woman who wants what I want. What could be better than that?"

"I suppose so," I agreed. "I'd never thought of it like that."

"Are you new to this then?" He asked.

"No, I've met a few people." I didn't want to admit that I was still a beginner, I felt it would give him the upper hand somehow.

"How did it go?" He enquired.

"It's been a bit mixed. Some fun experiences, but some that weren't quite right. Sexual chemistry is a tricky one. It's hard to make it work the first time you're with someone isn't it? Especially for a woman, it's easier to be satisfied if someone knows you well. How have you found it?"

"I enjoy it. There are a lot of women who want to experiment with me because I'm a black guy, but I don't mind that. It would probably be frustrating if I was looking for a relationship, but at the moment, it suits me fine. There are some good-looking girls on the site. I wasn't expecting so many when I joined. You're a great example. If I saw you in the street, I'd never think you were so forward and open about sex. It's great."

Until a couple of weeks ago he would have been right, I thought to myself. I hadn't been that kind of person at all. I was enjoying talking with him. It was making me more and more comfortable that this was a lifestyle that I could, and would, enjoy for a bit. I could feel myself growing into the role of Sophie Martinez.

"What do you want from tonight then?" I asked.

He gave a little laugh. "The same things all men want when they meet a beautiful woman, to see her naked, and then to have sex with her."

"Are men really all that simple?" I couldn't believe it was true of everyone.

"That is exactly how simple men are. There is very little else going on, trust me. There will be people with different fetishes. Some dudes will want to suck your feet or whatever, but it'll all come down to the same thing in the end. Nudity and sex."

"I see. Do you have any fetishes?" I thought I should check, seeing as he'd brought it up.

"No, nothing weird, don't worry. I like boobs. That's what drew me to your profile."

"Good. I can satisfy that fetish easily enough." I sipped my wine, watching as he involuntarily glanced down at my chest.

"What do you want then?" He returned the question. "I'm pretty relaxed, and you seem lovely, the evening will probably go the way you choose it to. How does this play out for you in an ideal world?"

It seemed like the perfect opportunity to try and get exactly what I wanted. Why wait? He seemed genuine. I liked him. "We leave here, and you take me shopping, for a beautiful dress, and some unbelievably sexy underwear. Then we go back to the hotel room where I will get changed into my new clothes, and I'll see if my friend is available to take loads of sexy pictures of us together. You taking off my dress, touching me, me taking you in my mouth. All kinds of sexy poses. It might feel a bit staged, but I like the nudity and touching, without the sex to start with. It's a long slow build up. Then, my friend will video whilst we fuck. Whatever position we want, for as long as we want. Hopefully for a long time. How does that sound."

"Fantastic," he gestured with open hands, as if to express his agreement with my plan. "What are we waiting for?"

"I'll have to make sure my friend is free." It won't stop us having fun if he isn't, don't worry, but I would like to have him there. Brian nodded his agreement. I messaged Nathan to see if he could meet me at such short notice. I explained that I needed a cameraman, and that there would be rewards. It was less than a couple of minutes before I received a message back. "Sounds fantastic, even if I was busy, I'm sure I'd cancel most things to see you naked again. Let me know a time and place."

Chapter 13 – Dress Shopping

We left the bar and walked for a few minutes. There was a slight chill in the air as the cool of the evening started to set in. I pulled the collar of my coat up around my neck in an attempt to keep warmer.

"I've got an idea where might be good to find a dress." Brian motioned to the right as we turned down a side street. "I get shirts here sometimes."

We entered a lovely boutique, fashioned with wooden panelling and ornate ceilings. The kind of shop you imagined looked the same in the nineteen twenties as it did now. There were men's suits and shirts on the right, and on the left was the women's section, full of dresses and gowns of all types. We started to browse through the dresses, picking out one to hold up and look at in more detail. From a couple of rails away Brian held up a pink ball gown for me to pass judgement on. It looked more like a prom dress than a ball gown and would have made me look a bit like I should be sat on the top of a Christmas tree. I smiled and shook my head. I hoped he was joking. I saw a charcoal-coloured dress, which I liked. It had a halter plunging neckline and was elegant and beautiful. It might have looked a bit slutty on me though. My boobs would have been very on show. That would have been good for this evening. I had decided that I wanted to wear this dress for my job trial tomorrow evening. I found a red sequin evening gown, which was perfect. I pulled it out and asked the shop assistant if they had it in a twelve. It was tight fitting, sleeveless with a mermaid hem. A ten would have been a little small. She disappeared into the back to see if they had it in stock.

"Have you found one you liked?" Asked Brain.

"It's worth trying on, to see what you think." I carried on looking through the hanging rails.

"Will it feel like you're being paid for sex if I buy you this?" He asked, with a smile on his face to indicate a light-hearted tone.

"Not if I'm paying for the hotel room." I replied, "You'll still need to get me some lovely underwear before we're even, otherwise it means I'll be paying you. The dress is only a hundred and ten pounds, it's on sale." I was pleased with my response. Even though he seemed nice, and genuine, I didn't want him to take the upper hand. I know what powerful businessmen can be like. I wasn't going to be dominated in any way. I remembered the fantasy about being paid for sex when Paul and I had chatted through the list. If I ever did that, it wouldn't be subtle. I wanted someone handing me a fat fold of twenty-pound notes as I stood in front of them. In a cheap hotel room, wearing stockings and a negligee.

"Fair enough." Brian interrupted my thoughts. He took his phone from his pocket. "I'll have a look at where we can find some."

"No need." I replied. "There is plenty over there." I nodded my head towards an alcove at the back of the store, with a decent display of elegant items. "Go and see if there is anything you would like to see me in."

He moved off towards the underwear section, as the lady came back with the dress. I went over to the changing rooms and tried it on. It felt lovely on me. A ten would indeed have been too tight, but this hugged my figure without clinging to me. It was comfortable, but I liked the way it looked. I don't think I had ever tried a dress on first time that fitted so well. It was probably the benefit of spending a bit more money. It was a dress that would cost over two hundred pounds at full price. For that amount you'd expect the cut to be good. The neckline came low but wasn't as revealing as the first one I'd seen. I loved it. I was going to buy it even if Brian wasn't.

I changed out of the dress and went back out into the shop. "It's perfect," I said, handing it to the lady who had looked after me. "I'll take it. We'll only be a minute if that's ok?"

"Take your time. I'll put it behind the counter for you." She moved off, and I turned towards the underwear. "Which ones do you like?" I asked as I walked up behind Brian.

"Either this one, or this one." He pointed to two bodice type garments, that were both nice.

"This one won't work with the dress. That strap would be on show." I pointed out. "Should I try the other one on?" He nodded, so I picked up a size twelve and headed back to the changing rooms. This time the twelve was too big. It didn't look good at all. I wasn't sure the ten would look any better, but I threw my clothes back on and went to find the smaller size. Once back in the changing rooms I undressed again and tried the ten. It wasn't perfect, but it was pretty good. It hugged my waist well, and there was enough room in the chest for my boobs. I turned to the side and looked again. I got a shiver of excitement as I thought of what was coming next. My focus on dresses had allowed my upcoming sexual adventure to slip my mind for a moment. Time to get ready, I thought with a smile, as I turned back to see myself front on in the mirror. I looked good. I felt good. I got changed and went back out to the counter.

Brian saw me and came over. "Any good?" He checked.

"Ideal." I replied. The lady put the underwear and the dress in a bag, and Brian handed over his card. He picked up the bag and we walked out of the store and back towards the hotel. I took my phone from my bag as we walked and called Nathan.

"Hello," he answered, almost immediately.

"Hi, we'll be at the hotel in ten minutes, if I send you the address, do you want to meet us there?"

"I'll be there in fifteen or twenty. I'll be as quick as I can." He sounded rushed.

"No problem. We'll see you there."

"Was that the friend who's going to film us?" Asked Brian.

"Yes." I kept my response brief.

"Who is he?" pushed Brian.

"He's a friend. He's a good photographer."

"Just a friend? Does he ever get to be in the photos with you?"

"That's none of your business," I teased him. "You don't need to worry," I assured him. "You'll forget he's there, trust me."

I chose a hotel that I had known from a work event that Paul and I had been to a few years before. It was impressive, without being too expensive. At the hotel there was a guy behind reception who nodded and smiled as we came in. I asked what rooms he had available, and he went through several options.

"I'll have to take a basic room." I gave a look of sorrow at the reality. "Work budgets don't allow me any luxury," I explained my choice to him.

"That's a shame." He agreed, rolling his eyes at the penny-pinching meanness of my imaginary employer.

"They wouldn't know if I was upgraded." I put the final piece of my plan into action. It couldn't hurt to ask.

The receptionist gave a knowing nod and turned to his computer. He printed out my receipt and passed it over. He had upgraded us to a luxury room. I beamed my gratitude, before thanking him. I messaged Nathan the hotel name and room number, before joining Brian on the other side of the lobby.

Once in the room I told Brian to make himself comfortable. I started to feel horny as I went into the bathroom to change. I put the underwear and dress on straight away, and then put a few curls in my hair before putting on my makeup. I went even darker than last time around my eyes. I loved the way it made me look, dark and dirty. I'd never wear it out in the street like that, but in here, for the camera, I could do whatever I wanted. I stood back and liked what I saw. This was definitely a hair down dress. I walked back into the room, and Brian looked impressed.

"Fuck me," he said, almost involuntarily. "Sorry," he checked himself. "You look amazing." He corrected.

"Thank you," I smiled, as a knock came at the door. I opened it and Nathan entered. I kissed him on the cheek and introduced him to Brian. It was much more relaxed than I expected. Nathan got the camera ready whilst I did my routine of turning on all the lights. Nathan asked how I wanted to start.

"Let's do photo's first. You tell us how and where you want us, I'd like a full set, right through from strip to sex. We can do the cumshot pictures later. Would that be fun?"

"That sounds good." Nathan agreed. Brian nodded. "Let's start with you both entering the room."

I took Brian by the hand, and we posed at the door. Nathan spoke his instructions every now and again as we moved into the middle of the room and kissed. It was a passionate kiss. I could feel Nathan circling us with the camera, taking photos from several angles. The next stage was taking my dress off. Brian pulled it off my shoulders and caressed my cleavage as it became exposed. He kissed my neck and chest for a few minutes as I pulled his head into me. Nathan asked for the dress to come off fully, and it dropped to the floor as I slid it over my waist. I stood there in my underwear. Brian became more excited, as he licked and groped at my body. We kissed again, before Nathan asked me to bend over the table. I put my arms out in front of me and kept my legs straight as I leant forward. Brian caressed my back before bending down and kissing my arse cheeks. I arched my back and pushed myself higher, exposing myself more. He kissed down and onto the material covering my vagina. After a couple of minutes of tantalising pleasure, he stood up at Nathan's request. He reached around and held my tits firmly from behind. Nathan moved in front of us to take photos as Brian groped at my chest through the underwear as he kissed my neck. I lay my head back onto his shoulder and groaned as his hands slipped inside the material and stroked across my nipples. He released the straps off my shoulders, exposing my chest as he continued to play with me. He held my tits for pictures, as if on display, and grabbed at them as the camera clicked away. It crossed my mind how amazing these photos would look. After a while I turned around so that Brian could look at my boobs directly for the first time. He couldn't take his hands or eyes off me. He began to lick and kiss and suck me. It was so pleasurable. I was in heaven for what seemed like an age. I think he would have carried on fondling me and kissing my tits for hours if Nathan hadn't interrupted.

"Keep doing that whilst she gives you a handjob." Came the photographer's request. Brian happily carried on playing with me, as I undid his belt and zip. I rubbed the material of his trousers. Fondling his cock, before reaching into his underpants and grabbing hold of him. He was hard, and big. Not as big as Nathan, but very impressive. I used my free hand to slide his underwear down onto his thighs, as his trousers fell to the floor.

His cock in my hand, as he continued to suck and kiss my boobs as they were pushed up by his hands. I didn't play with him. I wrapped my hand around his cock and admired it. The movement would spoil the pictures, and I didn't want to turn him on too much. I wanted this sex to last as long as possible.

"Let's take some blowjob shots." Suggested Nathan, after he had got several pictures of me with Brian in my hand. I bent my knees and dropped down. Brian let go of my tits for the first time since I'd revealed them. Once I was level with his cock, I looked at the camera as I held it in front of my face. I tried to remember some of the poses from the pictures Nathan and I had picked out the other day. I opened my mouth and put my tongue out, his cock only a few centimetres from my face. I was still looking at the camera. I could feel him pulsating in my hand, desperate for me to take him into my mouth. I licked the tip of his cock, posing, making sure my tits were facing the camera. I held the position for a few seconds, flicking my tongue again over the end. I could taste the pre-cum that was waiting for me. I stood up for a second and moved to one of the chairs by the table. My legs were getting tired of squatting, and I wanted to get my tits up to the same height as his waist. Once sat down I placed his cock across my boobs and looked at the camera again. I used it to rub my nipples, and then put it between my tits and squeezed them around it. He instinctively thrust upwards, his cock coming out from between my tits towards my face. It was big enough that I could lick the tip of it again, whilst the base of it was still between my boobs. I waited for Nathan to take pictures, as I moved my tits up and down his shaft. Not quickly enough to excite him too much, but enough to give the camera lots of different view. After several moments passed, I took hold of him again, and put the head of his cock in my mouth. I looked at the camera, as Brian let out a long sigh. I massaged him with my tongue whilst the camera snapped. Almost as if pleasuring him secretly whilst the camera saw only my still lips. After a few moments I began to move my mouth slowly down his shaft. Pausing for pictures at regular intervals, before moving further and further down. After a while, I couldn't fit any more in my mouth. I put my hands on the back of his thighs and pulled his cock into me. Even with the use of my arms to pull, I didn't even reach halfway down his shaft. There was enough of hm left exposed put one of my hands around him as well, which I did. I took him out of my mouth and put his shaft between my teeth and posed for the camera some more. I moved to hold his cock above me as I flicked my tongue around his balls and the base of his cock. After a few minutes Nathan decided that he had taken enough blowjob pictures. He asked me to take off Brian's shirt. I stood up and Brian took my tits in his hands again as I undid his buttons. His throbbing cock was brushing against my stomach as I placed my hands on his chest and pushed his white shirt open. His body was exactly as I'd hoped. He was like an Olympic athlete, muscled and toned. He had a big frame. I seemed quite small in front of him. He looked good in his clothes, slim and fit, but naked he seemed much bigger. His white shirt framing his dark torso. I kissed his chest and ran my hands down over his body to his waist. Then I brought my hands back up, touching each sculpted part of his body as my fingers passed over him. I pushed the shirt off his shoulders. As it fell down his back, it revealed his arms, muscular and even bigger than his chest. The curves of his muscles akin to the sensual curves of breasts, or hips. He had a beautiful body. I put my hands on his arms and kissed him passionately. He undid his cufflinks as we kissed and dropped his shirt to the floor. He then wrapped his arms around me. Our passionate embrace became more thrilling as my tits pushed against his hard body. He slid his hands down my back and onto my bum cheeks. He grabbed me firmly and pulled me towards him as we kissed. His cock pushing against my belly as we squeezed together.

"Ok, let's take some sex shots," Nathan suggested. I'd forgotten he was in the room for a few moments. I'd become intoxicated with our passionate embrace. Brian and I stepped back away from each other, and I went to the table to get a condom from my bag. I passed it to him, and he unwrapped it and put it on. I noticed he had to stretch it out it to get it on. I had a fleeting thought back to sex education at school. Our school nurse had rolled a condom over a carrot, as easy as could be. I bet she'd never had sex like this. It wouldn't have been appropriate for a class of thirteen-year-old girls to watch her try and wrestle a condom over a cucumber.

Nathan could see that we were unsure of what to do next, so he started to give us more direction than before.

"Start by fucking her on the bed."

I moved over to the bed and lay down on my back. Brian moved carefully over the top of me, and between my legs. I pulled my underwear to one side, and then took his cock in my hand. He was so hard. I became breathless as I moved him into position. Brian started to push himself into me. I felt like he was filling me, even before he had penetrated me completely.

"Hold it there." Nathan took more pictures. "Ok, carry on."

Brian then pushed the rest of his cock inside me, and I gasped with pleasure. We held the position and kissed. He started to withdraw from me, and then pushed into me again. I grabbed his buttocks and pulled him towards me. The hardness of his body surprising me still further.

"Now from behind?" Nathan suggested.

I could have got carried away. I wanted to have sex now, but I remembered Paul, and how I'd promised him some pictures. Brain pulled out of me and kneeled up, and I turned around onto all fours in front of him. I could feel him lay his cock across my arse cheeks for a moment as he moved into position.

"Hold it there, that's a good picture," said Nathan. Brian put his cock in different positions on my arse, as the camera clicked. Then I felt it slide down and he put the head of it inside me. I gasped again, even though he'd only been out for a few moments. He waited whilst the pictures were taken and then pushed further into me. I guess he was only halfway, but as he paused for more photos, I wondered how much more I was going to be able to take. The angle from behind was allowing him to get much deeper into me than he was before.

"Slowly." I requested, as he started pushing into me again. I put one of my hands back onto his hip to slow his entry, as I gasped with pleasure. I felt his hips push against my arse when he had inserted himself. I took deep breaths as a few seconds passed. Nathan moved around the bed to take shots from different angles. Brian pulled back and I braced to be penetrated again, but it didn't come. Nathan interrupted, suggesting some pictures by the table. We got out of bed. I bent over the desk between the two chairs, briefly thinking about how the pictures would look. My thoughts were interrupted by Brian's cock starting to enter me again from behind. It happened slowly again, pausing for pictures. Getting deeper and deeper inside me. I wouldn't be able to stand much more. I was so turned on I could hardly breathe. I was about to tell Brian to fuck me, when Nathan suggested that we had enough photos.

"Is there anything else you want?" Nathan asked me, as Brian pulled out of me, and I stood up.

"No, thank you." I felt heady with the constant sensations running through my body. "Let's get dressed and make a video." I wanted to have sex without restraint. I felt like I'd had enough teasing to last for a lifetime.

Chapter 14 – Sex

I went into the bathroom to put my dress back on. I looked a little bit dishevelled already. Although nothing particularly energetic had happened yet. With my underwear on, I touched up my makeup. I took my real phone out of my bag and took a selfie in the mirror and sent it to Paul. "The date went well, I'm about to make a porn movie for you," was the message underneath the picture. I checked my photo's gallery. The phone had picked up the pictures from the camera via the Bluetooth connection. I flicked through them and was happy. I sent a few over to Paul. A few of us kissing, and Brian playing with my tits. He could wait until later for some of the other shots. I put the phone back and pulled my dress back on. After running the brush through my hair, I went back into the bedroom.

"Now for some fun." I looked suggestively at Brian as I walked to the far side of the room and put my bag down in the corner. "We'll start as if we've just arrived back at the room, and we'll see what happens. Video everything, with different angles. You know what you're doing." Nathan nodded. "After we've fucked can you help me in the shower?" I requested of Brian. "Keep filming right through." I smiled at Nathan, who nodded again. Brian was dressed again, so we moved back to the door, and I looked at Nathan. I saw him press record on the camera, and I pulled Brian towards the centre of the room again and kissed him. I could forget about the camera now and enjoy my first extra marital sex. The first sex with anyone except Paul for almost ten years.

With all the build-up, we were both very turned on. It felt quite frantic, desire swept over us and took control. We kissed and he immediately dropped the shoulders off my dress and exposed my tits again. Things slowed a little as he played with them for a while. I held the back of his head as he lifted my boobs against his lips and tongue. I took his shirt off again, desperate to see and touch his body once more. Before long we were naked. I was about to bend down and take him in my mouth when he picked me up. With one hand under me, and one arm around my back, he lifted me towards him, and I wrapped my legs around his waist. His cock pressed into me as we kissed, and I felt the full power of his body as I clung to him.

"Put a condom on." I whispered to him. I wanted him inside me. He put me down and I ran across to my bag. I should have thought to get one ready, but it hadn't occurred to me. I took my time, slowly walking back towards him. I took in the sight of his mighty body, with his big erect cock looking magnificent above his strong legs. I swayed my hips a little more than usual, and felt my tits bounce under me as I walked back to him. He was staring at me with a fierce intensity. I felt amazing. I passed the condom to him. He put it on without looking as I threw my arms around his neck and kissed him. Our tongues sliding together as our lips met, erotic and passionate. I heard the snap of the base of the condom fit into place, and Brian moved his hands to my arse cheeks. With his hands on my bottom, with one move he jumped me back up into position, my legs around his waist. Locked around him once again. I carried on kissing him for a moment, and then reached down and positioned his cock underneath me. He lowered me down and pushed into me. I put my arm around his neck to hold myself up as he dropped my body down onto his shaft. As I slid down on to him, I yelped with pleasure as he penetrated deep into me. His hands lifted me and then dropped me down onto him again, with more force than before. We started to find a rhythm as I moved up and down his body, his cock pushing into me harder and harder as I bounced. I wasn't sure how he could hold me up for so long. We fucked like that, frantically, for what seemed like minutes. The pleasure was extraordinary. I could feel myself contracting as an orgasm started to swell. He took a couple of seconds to walk back to a flat part of the wall next to the door, still with me sat penetrated on him. I was clinging to his neck and waist with my arms and legs. He pushed me back against the wall and began to thrust into me again. With the wall for support, he could push harder into me, and I felt the orgasm immediately start to swell again. I came with a violent pleasure as I started to bang against the wall. His body driving his cock into me as hard as he could. I shuddered and groaned with pleasure as the penetration continued, hard and fast. I could feel the moisture of perspiration on his smooth back. He worked himself continuously back and forth into me. Thrills cascaded through my body. As my moaning subsided, he slowed down. Our fucking came to a stop as I sat, mounted on his cock. I tried to gather my breath. He lifted me off his shaft and let me down to the floor. My knees were weak as I landed, buckling slightly as I took responsibility for my own weight. He took my hand and led me over to the bed, where I sat down. He went down onto his knees and pushed my legs apart. I held his head in my hands as he put his face between my legs and began to lick me softly. It was nice. It wasn't as intense as normal, probably because I'd recently orgasmed, but it was good to rest. I'm sure he was glad of a break. He licked and sucked me for a few minutes, before climbing up off his knees and onto the bed.

"Take me from behind." I demanded and lay on my stomach. I had seen a video like this, and it had looked sensational. I moved my legs apart, so that he could penetrate me, but didn't raise myself onto my knees. Brian moved in behind me and started to kiss my neck and shoulders as he began to slowly fuck me. I raised myself up on my elbows and turned to kiss him over my shoulder. The rhythmic strokes of his cock pushed into me. My bum cheeks pushed forwards with each penetration, rocking me back and forth on the bed. My tits hung beneath me, and I could see Nathan moving in front of me as the camera watched us. I stopped kissing Brian and turned to face the camera. I grabbed hold of the sheets as the extasy of the sex started to take hold of me again. My eyes rolled involuntarily as I tried to look at the camera. Brian's cock getting further into me. My cheeks were now being squashed by the impact of each penetration. He fucked me into the bed, hard. He kept going and going. He was lasting much longer than I expected, it was wonderful. I guessed he was used to having sex. Perhaps it took more to turn him on than less experienced men. After several more minutes, he rolled me onto my side, without his cock leaving me. He continued to fuck me from behind. I lifted my top leg and moved it forward, exposing myself to him more, and enabling him to thrust more deeply into me. His rhythm didn't slow at all if anything it got quicker. I looked at Nathan and the camera in front of me. The lens watching my tits jumping up and down as Brian's cock repeatedly pushed into my body. Brian reached a hand over and started to play with my clit, whilst the fucking continued. It was enough to send me over the edge almost immediately. The extra stimulation, which was only gentle, coincided with the pulsating penetration. I orgasmed again. It felt different to the first one, less intense but it affected my whole body. My legs were shaking as Brian banged into me with his hips. I had to use my hands to stop me banging into the headboard as his thrusts surged me up the bed. I was able to push back against him using the headboard. My orgasm overtook me as the sound of our bodies slapping together intensified. He continued to rub my clitoris, adding more pressure as he sensed my orgasm rolling though me. My body spasming and contorting with ecstasy. As the pleasure started to ease, I started to become sensitive. I moved his hand to stop him touching me and placed it onto my boobs. I could feel he was becoming more frantic, as he grabbed me and continued to slam into me from behind. I watched as his toned stomach and muscled legs worked together to drive his lovely cock into me. His hand moved from my boobs back onto my hip to steady me as he fucked me harder still. The contrast of the colours of our skin, highlighted by the white sheets of the bed. It looked beautiful.

"I want to finish you in my mouth," I said to him over my shoulder.

"Not yet," he said. "Soon." He slowed down and almost stopped. I was surprised by his restraint. I was sure he was ready to cum, but he managed to control it. He was definitely experienced. He kissed my neck and shoulder, only gently moving his cock inside me as he did so. Then he pulled out and lay on his back. "I want to see you on top of me," he requested.

"What a good idea." I replied. It was my favourite position. I had been enjoying the sex so much that I hadn't put much thought to what I wanted. I hadn't expected it to last so long. I moved into position on top of him, as he put a couple of the pillows underneath his head. The pillows lifted him up, so that when I guided his cock back inside me, and sat down onto him,

my tits fell into his face. He immediately started to play with
them. I looked down at him. His hands and mouth exploring my
breasts, as I worked myself up and down the full length of his
shaft. He was so focussed on my tits that he kept his hips still. I
had complete control of how fast, how deep, and how much of
him I wanted to ride. I rode him for a long time. He was
captivated by my boobs. The sensations of his tongue and hands
working over my nipples was wonderful. He sucked at one then
the other, the wetness of his mouth making my nipples glisten
with saliva as I watched him. I looked up at the camera as it
captured my boobs being worshipped in his mouth. I followed the
lens with my gaze as the camera moved down the side of the bed.
It focussed on me from behind, moving up and down as I gripped
the mighty cock that was inside me. I looked back over my
shoulder and arched my back. The pleasure from being watched
heightened the intensity of the moment. I focussed on putting on a
show for the camera, speeding up the movements up and down
his shaft. I lifted myself right to the top. Almost to the point
where he would come out of me, before immediately sliding
down the full length and pressing into his hips. I turned away
from the camera and looked at Brian, who had stopped sucking
me for a moment, and was looking up at me. I leaned forward and
kissed him, plunging my tongue into his mouth, whilst driving
down onto his cock. I was fucking him harder now. He started to
push back with the rhythm of my downward pushes meeting the
upward thrust of his hips. I was shocked to feel the beginnings of
another orgasm stirring within me. I'd never cum three times
during sex before. I didn't know I could. Perhaps it wasn't going
to happen, maybe I was just enjoying it. We carried on kissing,
and our fucking increased in intensity. I sat up, taking my tongue
out of his mouth, as my breathing increased. My tits jumped
beneath me, and we slammed together, over, and over. He
couldn't resist the sight of my bouncing boobs. He arched
forward, taking one in his mouth again and holding the other with
his hand. I drove down onto him and moaned, as the pleasure
increased all over my body. The orgasm was coming, it was real.
I worked up and down his cock harder and harder as my body
was sent into explosions of sensation again. It seemed to rip

through me at speed, and was over quite soon, but it was as intense as the first one. The exquisite sensation of my nipples being sucked added to the experience. As the excitement subsided, I slowed my movement to a stop. Sitting with him deep inside me. I pulled my tits from his hands, leant forward, and kissed him again. I was sensitive now, all over. My nipples reacting to the slightest touch. I was completely fulfilled. I climbed of the bed and took his hand so that he stood up next to me. I sat down on the edge of the bed and pulled the condom from his incredible cock. I looked up at him and smiled as I took it into my mouth. He moved around so that he was in front of me, and I put my hands onto the back of his legs and pulled him into my mouth as far as it would go. I set myself the challenge of making him cum without using my hands. Giving Nathan a blowjob had opened my eyes to the art of it, and I wanted to consider myself an expert. I softly encased his cock with my mouth and moved gently up and down the top of the shaft. I felt his thighs and grabbed at his bottom as I used my tongue to completely envelop his cock in the warmth of my mouth. I didn't stop. I stroked his balls with my fingers a couple of times but continued to move up and down his cock in a perfect rhythm. I could feel it was beginning to work. His cock grew harder in my mouth, and his bum cheeks clenched as he pushed towards me. I didn't alter the firmness of my caress, or the speed of my movement. In the past I'd reacted to the excitement by sucking harder or moving faster. What had worked him up to the point of orgasm, was the same thing that would make him cum. Why change? I felt turned on by feeling him becoming more excited. He was twitching in my mouth as I continued to move up and down. He became more frantic still, and his hands moved onto my head, digging into my hair as he began to explode into my mouth. I kept moving up and down his shaft as I felt the cum fill my mouth, bursting against my tongue. I kept going until the pulsing ejaculation had stopped. Only then did I slow my movement, caressing his cock with my tongue as the last of his orgasm drained out of him. It was hard to keep the cum in my mouth, there was so much of it. I let him slip from my mouth onto my chest as I sat back on the bed. I looked up for the camera, and saw it focussed on me. I looked directly at it and let the rest of Brian's cum drip from my mouth onto my tits. I let it fall of its own accord at first. It slid onto my left boob, running over the curve of my breast and across my nipple. It continued to run over me, down onto my stomach. I moved my head and dropped the rest onto my right boob, forcing the remaining cum out of my mouth and onto my chest. I stood up and posed in front of the camera, holding my tits, presenting me cum soaked image to the audience. I took hold of Brian's cock, and gave it a gentle squeeze, smiling at him.

"That was fun. Time for a shower?"

I took Brian's hand and led him to the bathroom. Nathan followed us in and filmed as Brian washed my breasts. He ran his soapy hands all over my body. He was almost erect again by the time we'd finished. "Fancy going again?" he asked.

"Not today," I refused. "We'll definitely do that again though, you lasted a long time, it was great."

"The condom makes it last longer," admitted Brian. "I wanted to do a good job, so I'd get a second chance."

He dried himself off and got dressed. Nathan sat on the bed and looked through some of the pictures on the camera. I wrapped myself in a towel and started to dry off my hair with a hand towel. Once dressed, Brian said his goodbyes. It was strange to see him say goodbye to Nathan, as if they were acquaintances from work or something. What a strange circumstance I had created. It's amazing how people take things in their stride. I kissed him, on the mouth, but not with passion, and promised to send him some photos. The door closed behind him and I turned to Nathan.

"What do you think? I asked, as he was focussed on the screen of the camera.

"They are amazing, even if I do say so myself," he stated. I hope you like them. I've taken loads. You deserve to have a professional shooting you. I'm worried I won't have done it justice."

"Don't worry, they will be fine. I don't want to be a porn star. I only want some pictures to look back at. They don't have to be perfect." He put the camera down and moved to the edge of the bed. I stepped over to him, and he pulled the towel away from me as he put his arms around my waist.

"Can I ask a favour?" I asked

"What is it?"

"I don't think I can take your huge cock yet. Do you think we could wait a while? We've got all night." He looked disappointed. "I'll give you a handjob now, we can go out for dinner, and then we can come back and fuck." I promised.

"That sounds like a good plan," he responded. I was glad he agreed. I was too sensitive and too tired to have sex again. I did still feel horny, but my body couldn't take anymore.

"Take your clothes off then." I ordered.

He stripped off. He lay back and I moved round and sat with him. The towel was around my waist as I leant over him and started to massage his enormous cock with my hand. It felt wonderful. I started slowly and got quicker as he became more excited. I wanted to be the handjob queen as well as the blowjob queen. "How is that?" I asked.

"Incredible," he muttered through gasped breaths. I continued to stroke him, holding him with what I hoped was the same pressure as my mouth would have offered. Very gentle, with regular rhythmic strokes. I once or twice bent forward and put the head of his cock in my mouth for a couple of seconds. I still stroked up and down his huge shaft when he was in my mouth. He didn't last long. His body twitched and tightened as he started to cum. I dropped my tits down and aimed his cock at my chest. He exploded onto me, even more than the first time when he'd cum on my cleavage. It was everywhere. I slowed the stroking of his cock until I came to a stop. He relaxed into the bed and with a deep sigh. I put one of my forearms under my tits and pushed them up, using my free had to play with some of the cum that was running over them. I smiled, and licked the finger that I'd dipped in the cum.

We didn't go for dinner. As soon as he'd cum he was satisfied. The male post orgasm change happened, and he wasn't thinking with his cock anymore. I didn't want to sit and eat with anyone except Paul, and I didn't want to get to know Nathan. I had suggested dinner to put off having sex for a bit, but I was glad I didn't have to go through with it. It was nice to say goodbye and make my way through London to catch the train home. Flicking through the pictures on my phone during my journey. Glowing with excitement at the memory of the day's events.

Chapter 15 – My First, Second Interview

It was late the following afternoon, and I was getting ready for my trial at the events company. I'd finished a morning shift at the gym and eaten a salad in the gym café before I'd come home. I had the afternoon to myself to relax and get ready. I was glad the second interview was happening whilst Paul was away. I could get ready in my own time, and it filled an evening that might have otherwise been spent on my own in front of a movie. It had been a busy week, and I was tired. I rested for a few hours, half watching some awful reality TV, and half playing with my phone. I had got into the habit of checking my swingers account a couple of times a day. There was always a slight thrill when looking through new friend requests. I enjoyed seeing what new messages I'd received. I had a routine of deleting anything that wasn't interesting to me. At the same time, I sent my Martinez phone number to anyone who was attractive or had sent a fun message. Usually only once or twice every couple of days. I was being picky. Why shouldn't I be? It meant I had built up a list of sexy contacts in my illicit phone, most of which I'd met on the swinger's app. There were a few contacts from the porn site, but I'd not used it as a way of meeting people. It was very international, and there was no way of telling if a profile was genuine. You had to pay to be on the Swingers site. The need for a credit card seemed to weed out a lot of the fakes. There were a couple of exceptions to my online double life. A guy working in a coffee shop had flirted with me on my way back from London one evening. I'd given him my Martinez number. He was good looking, very pretty, but that wasn't why I gave him my number. It was a real thrill to be able to do it. I couldn't remember ever doing it before. I'm sure I must have done when I was younger, but I was shy back then, and it wouldn't be a surprise to me if I never had. There was also a sales rep who'd called into the gym. He'd been very flirty and left me his card. He wasn't selling anything that the gym would ever use, some sort of software I half remembered. I didn't think I'd ever see him again at work. I messaged him from my Martinez number but didn't tell him where he'd met me. I wouldn't be breaking any of the rules if I met up with him. I'd sent him a picture of me in underwear, revealing, but no nudity. I'd wait and see how it progressed.

When people messaged me, I had perfected a way of deciding whether they were worth speaking to. I would tell them what I wanted. A sexual adventure, which would give me photos and videos for my husband. This was the perfect place to begin. It made it clear that I was married, that I didn't want a relationship, and everyone knew that it was only about sex. Their job was to tell me what they would want to do with me. I asked about location, what they would want me to wear, if they had any fantasies to fulfil. One way of finding out about them was to get them to send me links to porn that they liked. It was pretty easy to understand the kind of person they were from these messages. I would learn whether they would be a gentleman. Whether I would be safe, whether they would pay for things, whether they would mind being filmed. It all added up, and I got a good picture of who they were. More than half of the people who messaged me got deleted at this stage. Lads who wouldn't be suitable for me would never be bothered with answering my questions. Quick and easy sex is very straightforward to find. Searching for a more fulfilling and interesting encounter takes a bit more effort. Idiots needed to be removed. It was working well for me.

In the next phase, I asked them to send me some pictures. It was quid pro quo, which was easy for me as I now had many pictures on my phone that I could use. If someone wasn't prepared to share anonymous pictures with me using their phone, there was no chance they'd be the kind of person that I was looking for. The pictures were also important to see if I was attracted to them. Another half of the people who had passed the first stage, didn't make it past the attraction test. This left very few of the original people I'd given my number to.

Finally, I asked them if they'd do an audition with me, to see if we got on. This would mean a hotel room, taking their clothes off, and me giving them a handjob on video. I was looking forward to doing this. I liked the idea of the control I would have. I also liked the idea of making a lot more pictures and videos. The best bit would be getting fucked by the camera man after the audition. If people could last long enough, and they were respectful, then they would get to do a sex scene with me at some point. I hadn't been doing this for long. I hadn't put the whole plan into practice from start to finish, but it seemed to be working well so far. I wanted to have a phone full of contacts that I knew I could call on when I wanted an adventure. I wanted to do everything on the list that Paul and I had talked through. I also wanted to do a few more things that had come to mind over the past few days.

I had a different plan for people who I'd met in real life. It would have to be different from the people I met online, who already knew from my profile what I was like, and I wanted. It was exciting that I would be introducing myself as sexually liberated woman in real life. It seemed somehow naughtier, more illicit, to be so forward with people who I had met in normal situations. I was looking forward to that.

I paid particular attention to girls, and couples who messaged me. I had invited several to be friends over the past few days, and almost all had accepted. I liked the idea of having another girl with me, taking the photos, or perhaps getting involved. I liked the idea of filming a girl in an erotic situation. Watching her fulfil a fantasy of hers. Then reversing the roles, so that I could play out a fantasy and be filmed by her. It would be safer, and it seemed sexier with two of us. I would try and do that as soon as possible. My dream would be to do this with Jess and Robert. It also occurred to me that the getting paid for sex fantasy would be very easy to fulfil if there were two girls. The ability to grant a man his dream threesome. If we put sexy pictures together up on our online profiles, I didn't expect it would take long for two of us to be offered financial rewards for a threesome. The thought of it turned me on a great deal.

I had spent about an hour lounging on the sofa, sorting through all the messages on my phone. There was a message from Nathan asking when he could take advantage of the sex that I had postponed with him. I let him know that I was away for a few days, and that I would be in touch when I got back. I asked him to send through some links to porn scenes that he'd like to make with me. He seemed happy to wait.

With only a couple of hours left before I had to set off, I showered and washed and dried my hair. It always seemed like such an effort, but I liked the way it felt and looked after I'd done it. I enjoyed putting my new dress back on. I wore the same, new underwear that Brain had bought me along with the dress. I hadn't washed it, but I'd only worn it for a few minutes before it was taken off me. It made me feel sexual, and confident. I didn't think there would be any situation during the evening that would need me to be as confident as I was yesterday. I drove to the venue for the event, almost without any nerves. I was feeling good about who I was, and my confidence was as high as I could ever remember it. Sex is such a powerful part of the human psychology, I mused. It must impact so much of our exitance. Indeed, the fact that we exist at all. I chuckled to myself at the thought.

When I arrived, I found Dan at the entrance to the venue. It was still half an hour before guests were due to turn up, so he took the time to introduce me to his team. There were seven of them, five guys, all in tuxedos, and two girls wearing long gowns. No one struck me as particularly glamorous, which surprised me. I had been expecting the world of events management to be a bit more like Hollywood than it was in reality. The girls were lovely. Kind and welcoming to me, even if only for a few minutes, before things started to get busy. After my introduction, the guys acknowledged me, and then continued to talk amongst themselves. Dan came over after the girls had moved off and gave me a run through of how the evening was going to go. We were to have introduction drinks, followed by dinner, with speeches after dinner. There would then be dancing and partying, which I could stay for if I wanted, but it wasn't expected of me. He showed me an area in the entrance to the kitchen where there were several drinks, ready poured on a tray.

"These are non-alcoholic drinks for the team. We don't have a strict no alcohol policy, but we advise not drinking too much at these events. We're here to work." He smiled, to reassure me it wasn't too strict and boring. There were various drinks, they all looked like they could be alcoholic. He saw me looking at them and ran through them.

"Non-alcoholic beers. Tonic waters with a slice of lemon. Lemonade in the tall glasses. Apple juice in the tumblers, and sparkling apple juice in the champagne glasses. There's ice in the fridge for you to add whenever you take one."

"That's a very good idea," I observed as he moved a few empty boxes off the work surface. "I'm driving, so having these here is clever."

"Many people will offer to buy you drinks. You can either take them and pour them away, or decline. It's up to you. It depends on the situation. You'll be sat with a table, all from the same company. I can't remember who you're with off the top of my head. The seating plan is in the lobby. Any questions?"

"I don't think so. Thank you."

"I'll be around if you need anything. Don't forget, we're the conduit. It's the relationships between the customer and their guests that are important. You can introduce yourself as working for us. After that, any time talking about us is a minute where we could have been talking about the customer. This whole evening is about Zeno Systems selling more printers to the companies that have been invited."

"I understand. What is my job role for the evening in case anyone asks?"

"Well reminded, I'd completely forgotten." He asked me to follow him, and we went back out into the reception area. He went behind the desks and looked in a bag for something, which turned out to be my name badge. "Brightstar Events," it read at the top, with "Sophie Valentine – Events Coordinator" underneath.

"Perfect, thank you." They were very organised. It seemed like everything was prepared and every eventuality covered. It was very positive for me to see, although a little bit intimidating. Working for an organised, efficient company would be brilliant. I suppose there was a little bit of doubt in me whether I would be able to match their standards. I banished the thought from my mind, looked down at my dress, and remembered the new confident me.

"Guests will be arriving any minute. Grab a drink and have a mingle. I'll see you later."

People started to arrive and introduce themselves to the receptionists. Sat behind their computer screens, with their permanent smiles in place. I checked where I was sitting on the table layout plan and went back to the kitchen to pick up a sparking apple juice. Armed with my fake champagne, I wandered into the dining hall to search out my seat. I wanted to know where everything was before things got busy. I was sat at a table named SportsTech International. I took out my phone and googled them. I found that they were a company who dealt in a variety of sports equipment. Despite their name, the product portfolio seemed to be fairly low tech. Most of their range was made up of clothing. They had some footballing accessories like shin pads and goalkeeping gloves. They had a wide range of what looked like low-quality bat and ball products. Table tennis, badminton, baseball, and rounders. They were geared up for the wholesale market. From what I could gather, they sourced most of their products in the far East. They were based in the Netherlands and were expanding into the UK. I looked around the table at the name cards. I was pretty sure they were all blokes, although a couple of the Dutch names could have been women. This might be quite a tough induction. Alone, on a table with five guys who work in sport. I could only imagine the topics of conversation. This was going to be difficult ground for me.

I moved around the hall and looked at some of the other table names. As far as I could tell, they were all names of companies. After my exploration, I went back through to the reception area. I was a little nervous. I knew that I needed to look engaged and busy. This was a job interview, I kept reminding myself. I decided my initial strategy would be to single people out who were on their own. I would then introduce myself to them. I found that the initial conversation flowed after I'd asked them who they were here with.

After half an hour, my strategy had engaged me with three current customers of Zeno systems. They had introduced me to several other guests as we'd talked. It didn't feel very productive, but at this point I was keen to establish myself and build some confidence. Another fifteen minutes passed having various conversations, before there was a tapping on a glass. It was announced that dinner was about to be served. I said goodbye to the lady that I was talking to and headed to my table. I stopped on the way to pick up another sparkling apple juice. As I arrived, the last of the guests at my table were taking their seats.

"Hi everyone, I'm Sophie." I introduced myself with a small wave and a smile to the group. Everyone acknowledged me with a nod or a smile. I added, "I'm from Brightstar, we're running the event this evening, so if there's anything you need, just let me know. I'll be joining you for dinner if that's ok?" Everyone was warm and reassuring in their welcome. They seemed friendly. The guy to my left stood and drew back my chair for me as I sat down. I relaxed a little bit after my introduction was made. I felt that the hard part was done. There would be more small talk at the table. A few drinks consumed over dinner, which would make the rest of the night a lot more comfortable for me.

It was actually interesting chatting to the team about their business. They were paying a lot of attention to me. As the only woman on the table, I had expected it. They were very keen to brag about the growth of their business. They were telling me how aggressively they planned to move into the UK market. I learned that they were looking for a premises. North of London was the perfect location for them. They had been invited to the evening without having any connection with Zeno systems. They assumed they had ended up on a database. Probably because of their interests in commercial properties in the area. I filled the time during dinner, trying to find out as much as I could about them and their company. I needed to find a way to make myself useful tonight, my job opportunity probably depended on it. As desert was served the conversation moved away from work. All the guys were drinking. The three chaps on the opposite side of the table seemed to be involved in a conversation about football. I wanted to avoid that at all costs. The guy to my right spent his time checking his phone. The chap to my left continued to make conversation. He'd had a few glasses of wine and seemed like he was even getting board of himself. He was middle aged, but I suspected he looked a bit older than he was. He hadn't looked after himself. Business seemed to be his first priority.

"So how do we go about seeing you again?" He asked.

"How do you mean?" I answered, not sure where he was going with his question.

"Well, we've enjoyed meeting you. We're in the UK for a few more days, would you like to meet up with us again? You could bring some friends?"

Now I understood where he was going. He wanted the company of girls whilst he was in a different country, away from the wife at home. "I'm crazy busy over the next few days," I let him know I wouldn't be meeting them.

"That's a shame. Here's my card in case you get a free evening." He handed it to me. "Will we see more of you if we buy printers from these guys?" He gestured over to the top table, where Zeno systems were sat. This was the sort of flirting I expected from a guy who knew he wasn't good looking. It was all about power, money, control. I could use that to my advantage. It was an opportunity to prove myself useful.

"I don't work for them, but we manage their events. I'm sure if you become a customer of theirs, we'll bump into each other again." I smiled. "Do you want me to introduce you?"

"Sure, why not." He lent back in his seat.

"Wait here, I'll set something up. Back in a moment." I assured him with a touch on his shoulder as I left.

Chapter 16 – Not Sleeping My Way to The Top

I went to find Dan, who was standing to one side of the room, using his phone. I don't think he'd sat with anyone during dinner. He had left the leg work to us. He put the phone in his pocket as I approached and asked how everything was going.

"Good thanks. The guys from my table would like to be introduced to the customer, who should I take them to?"

Dan nodded approval and motioned to follow him. I assumed he was going to take me to the Zeno table and introduce me. Then he seemed to have a change of heart. He turned back to me. "You see the older guy on the left of the table as we look?" He pointed and I nodded. "He's the owner of Zeno systems. He'll point you in the right direction." Dan was about to go back to his phone.

"What's his name?" I could tell I was being tested, and I realised that I wasn't fazed by it. A wave of confidence moved through me as I admired my new confidence.

"Bill Turner. He prefers Bill, he's quite informal." Dan smiled.

"Thank you," I gave a confident nod, before heading over to the table at the far end of the room. As I approached, I could see that Bill was using his phone, which was out of sight, below the level of the table. Tapping away at the screen, oblivious to anything going on around him. The table was bigger than ours, eight or ten sitting at it. Bill was on his own. Others had pulled their chairs into groups and were having side conversations. Alcohol and the end of dinner started to turn people's attentions to partying and having a good time. I approached him and placed my hand on his arm.

"Bill?" I asked, checking to see if it was the right person. He immediately looked up at me, and then put his phone into his pocket.

"Yes. What can I do for you?" He responded, in a polite, but friendly manner.

"I'm with Brightstar. I'm sitting with a group from SportsTech International. They'd like to speak to someone about their requirements. Is there anyone from your team I can introduce to them?" I waited for his response.

"Indeed. I'd like to meet them." He stood up from his chair. I could tell he hadn't been drinking. He seemed keen for the opportunity to do something other than sit with his phone.

"Follow me." I smiled. I led him back to the SportsTech table, and to the guy I had been talking to. "This is Bill Turner, the owner of Zeno Systems." I made the introduction, not remembering even the name of the person I'd been speaking to. I kicked myself. I was quite pleased to have remembered Bill's second name. That was more important.

"Ian Longstaff," my dinner partner announced as he stood up and shook Bill's hand. "a pleasure to meet you." My name slip hadn't mattered at all.

"Ian and his team are based in the Netherlands and are currently looking for offices in the UK." I informed Bill. "I'm sure Zeno Systems could be a big help to them as they progress. I'll leave you gentlemen to it." I smiled and backed away from the table, as both Ian and Bill thanked me for my help. I walked out of the hall to get another drink. I was feeling quite proud of my work. Maybe I'd have something stronger to celebrate, a double shot of apple juice on the rocks perhaps. I smiled to myself as I entered the kitchen. Dan was there filling up his glass with lemonade.

"How did it go?" He enquired.

"No problem. I made the introduction and left them talking. Is there anything particular you'd like me to do now?" I checked.

"No. There's only half an hour left before we become surplus to requirements. Carry on as you are." He picked up his drink and faced me. "How have you found it tonight?"

"Interesting. I've enjoyed meeting people. It seems like the event has gone well." I was in full interview mode now. I could tell that Dan was pushing to see how I had done. I'm sure he'd be getting feedback from various sources in the coming days. I kept my cards close to my chest. I hoped that other people would sell me, and that I wouldn't have to push myself too much.

"It seems like you've been very well received." Dan admitted. He had done some digging already. "I love the dress, is it new?"

"Thank you. No, I've had it for a little while. I like it, it's comfortable, which is good for long evenings like this." I had an internal smile at the thought of the real story behind the dress. "I'm going to get back in the room and mingle. See you in a bit." I thought I'd make it clear I was there to work, and not stand around and chat, even it was chatting to the boss. I felt I'd made a good impression so far. A bit more work and I'd have got through it. It was fun, but I was looking forward to it being over. It's hard, concentrating for so long. Knowing that you are being always examined. It was quite stressful.

I did my best to mingle as I re-joined the room, and even did a little flirting as several guys offered to buy me drinks. I managed to take a couple more potential customers to the Zeno table and introduce them. Bill had disappeared, but several of his team were still on hand. Most of the people I talked to were already customers, so I didn't see much of an opportunity to impress.

After another half an hour of mingling, the volume of the music had gone up. It was becoming quite hard to talk to anyone. I had noticed that a few of the other Brightstar team had disappeared. I went to find Dan in the hope that I could head home. I found him in reception, chatting to some of the people from the hotel. I waited until he had finished talking.

"How is it in there?" He asked, as he saw me waiting and made his way over.

"It's starting to turn into a party. Not much chance for me to engage with anyone now. Has it been a success?" I was asking about the evening in general, but I was looking for clues about how I had done.

"They're happy," I assumed he meant the customer. "We've done our bit now. It'll turn into a bit of a mess, as people get drunk and do stupid things, but that's not our concern."

"Do we stay to the end?" I checked.

"I'll stay here, with the Brightstar manager responsible for this project, but everyone else can go. We stay to make sure the hotel staff are supported. In case anything goes wrong. They look after everything practical from here, but it wouldn't be right if we all left. Someone from Brightstar needs to say goodbye at the end of the night. Someone might be sober enough to notice if we didn't." He looked at his watch. "Probably three or four hours to kill whilst they party." He gave an expression of boredom for effect. He paused, before adding, "would you like a drink before you go?"

"Another apple juice?" I smiled. "I've had one too many already. I'm driving don't forget."

He laughed. "I'm sure the law allows you one drink. I'm sure we could find some proper champagne." He seemed to be flirting now. I had noticed him looking at me from time to time. The comment about my dress was definitely more than a professional compliment. It made me think that the evening had gone well for me. I doubt he would be offering me a drink if he was going to ring on Monday and tell me I hadn't got the job. I felt I shouldn't refuse the offer. It was a good chance to sell myself further.

"Ok, sure. Real champagne would be nice after all those soft drinks." There were a few tables on the side of the lobby, opposite the reception desk. I went and sat down whilst he went to find a waiter. He was gone for quite a while, before coming back with a bottle in an ice bucket.

"They only sell this by the bottle," he placed the bucket on the table next to me. "It's good though, worth the three hundred pounds, as long as it's company money." He was showing off, not even in a subtle way. There were a couple of glasses upside down in the crushed ice, he lifted them and placed them on the table. I watched as he stood and opened the bottle. He as a very handsome man. I hadn't considered it before. I never do when someone is in a position that isn't conducive to attraction. It's a strange thing, but I would never be attracted to a friend's husband. It didn't matter how good looking or sexy they were. My brain would put it off limits, without my conscious brain needing to be involved. I knew this didn't apply to everyone. You didn't have to watch daytime TV talk shows for long to realise that people are often attracted to those that they shouldn't be. Proximity infatuations always seemed like a sign of weakness to me. There were so many ways to meet people. Falling for the married guy at work, or worse still, a sister's boyfriend, was such a lazy way to find someone. I smiled to myself as I recalled my methods of meeting people over the last couple of weeks. Dan had opened himself up to my scrutiny with his flirting. It now needed to be considered. He was very, very handsome, to the point where I was surprised that I hadn't noticed it before, even objectively. He finished uncorking the bottle and poured both glasses. He sat down and raised his glass towards me. I leant forward and clinked my glass against his.

"What are we toasting?" I questioned. "Have I got the job?" I may as well try and close the deal. Any good salesperson would try in this situation. He should think less of me if I didn't.

"You've done well. I've got a few more people to speak to, and I'll need to catch up with the other directors on Monday, but I can tell you that you've been very impressive." He was leant back in his chair. He was still showing off. Powerful men were always a bit of a turn on for me, but as I'd got older, I'd realised where true power existed. Pushing around people who worked for you wasn't power. Nor was sleeping with your secretary. Real power was having the opportunity to utilise your position or wealth for personal gain and choosing not to. The power of control was something much more impressive.

"How do you feel it went?" Dan asked. "Is this something you'd like to be involved with?"

"Definitely." I responded. I didn't want to give too much away. I'd had a successful evening, and I didn't want to give Dan the option to think less of me for any reason. I tried to steer the conversation on to more general topics. I imagined he liked the sound of his own voice enough to make that easy. "How long have you been with the company?"

Dan went through an elongated description of his career. He placed himself as the desired party in each situation. Never once admitting that he had wanted a job or aspired to anything. It was always companies that "saw him as a good fit," or "wanted to bring his experience to the table." If I had met him through the porn site, I would take him to a room and shag the life out of him. He was incredibly fuckable. In this situation, I was never going to do that, and so I had to listen to him go on about himself. This would be the problem with affairs. To have sex with a guy who looked like this, you'd have to put up with the tedious conversation. It had been nice for Sophie Martinez to be able to ignore the drinks and dinners and get straight to what she wanted.

"What brings you to our firm?" Dan broke my thoughts with his question. I still wanted to avoid the subject of me if I could.

"I'm keen to learn new things and expand my horizons." I sounded like I was having an interview now. I don't think Dan noticed. He wasn't listening to my response. He had picked up the bottle from the ice bucket and topped us both up. I'd barely had a sip of what he'd poured the first time.

"I'm staying over tonight." He said as he finished pouring and sat back in his chair. "We use this hotel quite a lot, they always give us a couple of rooms to use, if they have any spare."

"That's handy. It saves driving after a long night, I suppose." I'd rather be in the room ripping your clothes off than sat here listening to you talk, I thought to myself.

"You're welcome to use one if you fancy staying on for a bit? We have three put aside for us."

"Thank you," I smiled. "I'm tired, it's been a long evening, another time?" I wanted to refuse, without upsetting him or disappointing him. He had put me in a very strong position. It would be almost impossible for him not to offer me the job now. Nothing he said had directly implied that he wanted to sleep with me. He wouldn't be in trouble for inappropriate behaviour if he didn't offer the job to me. He would struggle to explain why I didn't get it. He'd already told me how well I'd done tonight. You don't ask someone who hasn't been good enough during their trial to stay on and work late. I had him where I wanted him. I was never going to sleep with Dan. It was against the rules I'd agreed with Paul. I'd be upset if he had been sleeping with someone he worked with. It changed it from sex to a relationship of sorts. That was never going to happen. I wouldn't have slept with him even if I was single. The fact that he can't have me would mean I'd have the upper hand. As long as I showed restraint, he'd always want me. As soon as he'd slept with me a few times, he'd get bored and move on. Men like that always do. Not fucking Dan, or anyone else at work, was great for my career.

"Will I hear from you on Monday?" I asked, setting up the conversation to instigate my departure.

"It'll be someone from the office that calls." Dan used the opportunity to show that he was above making such calls himself. "The directors will meet in the morning. I expect you'll find out in the next few days."

"Great," I smiled. "I hope it's good news. It would be fun working together, I've enjoyed tonight." I leant forward to pick up my glass. I exaggerated my lean in order for my cleavage to be on show. I noticed him looking, before he saw me and turned his eyes away. I stayed leant forward, my arms pushing at the side of my tits as I took a sip of my drink. He couldn't help himself. He took another glance.

"Thank you for the drink," I stood up. "That was a lot nicer than the apple juice."

"Indeed," he laughed. "Are you sure you won't stay and finish your glass?"

"I'd like to," I lied, "but I've got to go. Hopefully I'll see you soon." I put my hand out to shake his, as he stood up.

"Thank you for your hard work tonight. Enjoy your weekend."

"You too." I made my way past him and walked through the lobby, towards the entrance. I could feel his eyes watching me as I walked away. I gave a glance over my shoulder and caught his gaze. He smiled, and so did I. He wanted me.

Chapter 17 – Setting Up a Fantasy Situation

Before I set off to work in the morning, I called Paul. It had been too late to call him when I'd got back the night before. I'd sent a goodnight message when I got home, letting him know I was back safe. We chatted through how the previous evening had gone. It was nice to be able to be positive about an interview for once. It had been so often that Paul had the job of cheering me up after a failure. He asked me if I had anymore dates planned. I had confided in him that I was becoming more confident. My sexual awakening was happening far faster than I had expected. I wanted to continue with it, whilst I felt good. With Paul away, it was an exciting distraction. Much better than being at home on my own. I mentioned I felt brave enough to try meeting two guys at once and tried to gauge Paul's reaction. Although I had been learning so much, and finding out so much about myself, I was aware that Paul had been away for the past few days. I wanted to make sure he was ok with everything. We talked for a while about what it might involve and how it might work. He said he was fine with any adventures that I would arrange, as long as I was safe. He would look forward to hearing about it and seeing some pictures when we he got back.

A plan had started to form in my mind during my morning workout. I decided to play about and see if it would work in practice. Once I'd showered and changed and settled myself behind reception. I went back on the swinger app and had a look through some of the guys who had messaged me. There was a younger guy, twenty-six or twenty-seven, who'd sent me a very complimentary message. I sent him my Martinez phone number and told him to message if he was interested in meeting up.

A message came through to my phone almost immediately. He had either been on the app as I'd messaged, or he'd set alerts to notify him of any activity. That told me that he must be a single bloke who doesn't have to worry about anyone looking at his phone. I was cautious to start with, I needed to see what he was looking for. "Hi, it's James, you messaged me," his first message read.

"Hi, I'm Sophie." I replied. My confidence was high.

"Nice to meet you. What are you looking for?" He asked.

That was a surprise to me. I suppose it was a fairly benign introductory question, but it did get straight to the point. "I'm here for fun, no strings attached sex." I replied. He had been direct, so I decided not to waste any time.

There was a brief pause. It probably takes a few minutes to process a message like that, and then to figure out how to respond.

"I'm your man," came the brief, but functional response. I waited for another message. He hadn't asked a question, and it wasn't going to be down to me to progress the conversation. He could do the work. After a couple of minutes, he must have realised I wasn't going to respond, and he followed up.

"What do you have in mind? I've never done this before." Was his honest, if somewhat passive reply. Passive was ok, I was looking for someone to do exactly as I wanted.

"I've always wanted to make a porn video. Would you be ok with that? Your face wouldn't need to be in it. I want to make a blowjob video." I got straight to the point.

"That is very sexy. I'd love to." It was the response I expected. It would be a lot harder to find a man who didn't like porn, and didn't want a blowjob, than one thousand who did.

I sent him a link to a porn clip. It was a video of a woman going down on two attractive men as a thank you for moving some furniture for her. It was sexy. I added a follow up message, "How about something like this?"

"Who would the other guy be?" He asked.

"He would be another random, the same as you. A friend of mine would be there to video it, and make sure I'm safe. Are you up for it still?"

"It's not what I expected, but OK." He definitely wasn't as confident now. I sent him a couple of pictures of me in the underwear, and one with my boobs on show. Then I sent him the video clip of Nathans cumshot on my tits.

"These are all me," I assured him.

"Wow, are you a pornstar?" Came the reply. Through his messages I got the impression he was quite young, younger than the 27 I'd originally guessed. That wasn't a bad thing. All I needed was an attractive guy for an hour.

"No, I'm normal. A pornstar would definitely have their face on show. I'm going to need to see what you look like before we meet up!" I thought I'd push it a bit and see if he would do as I asked.

"I thought you'd seen my pictures online?" He was missing the point.

"Take your clothes off for me." I spelt it out.

"You could be anyone though!" He was worried now. This was a good test to see if someone was all talk.

"I could be, but who cares. You don't need to put your face in them. I'll know if it's not you." A few minutes passed, and I assumed he'd chickened out. I thought I would put him out of his misery.

"Don't worry, you'll find something that's right for you. Good luck."

A few moments later my phone buzzed, and I opened up a message to a reveal a naked picture. It was a selfie in a bathroom mirror, with the phone covering the face in the reflection. The guy was topless, and in good shape. Not a physique I would choose, a bit too thin, but fit. He had pulled his trousers and boxers, down on one side to reveal most, but not the entire length of his cock. It was enough to see he wasn't small, not big, normal.

"Thanks James. I like what I see. I definitely want you in my movie." I put a smiley emoji at the end of my message. I felt like he had worried a lot about taking that photo, and I wanted to put him at ease.

"Thank you. When?"

"Can you do tomorrow afternoon in London?" I asked.

"I'm working, could we meet in the evening?"

"Sorry, tomorrow afternoon is the only time I have. Don't worry if it doesn't work. Another time maybe?" He would make it work, I thought to myself. A couple of minutes passed before he messaged back.

"I can take the afternoon off work. Where should we meet?"

"Head into town for two o'clock, it'll be somewhere in the West end. I'll message you when I've checked in. I'll need to get a hotel room. Are you ok to go halves with me on the cost of the room?"

"Of course, let me know how much."

I closed the conversation. Now onto the next part of my plan, to find the second co-star for my movie. I checked through the app some more but didn't see anyone who would fit the bill. There was a lot of what seemed to be nice guys on there, but not anyone that I wanted to jump into bed with. Why settle for second best? I may as well choose someone I fancied. I realised there's a big difference between someone you'd like to jump on, and someone you could fall for. I wasn't interested in anyone I could fall in love with. I didn't want to, and I couldn't anyway. I was completely in love with Paul. For my adventures I wanted someone who made me want to rip their clothes off. For this video I didn't care how stupid they were, or what they were like to talk to. I wanted the ultimate sex toy for an hour. Phil would do, but I wasn't going to risk contacting him again. I could imagine the constant spam of messages I'd receive.

I went back onto the porn site, for the first time in a few days, to see if my videos and pictures had got any more attention. They had been viewed a few times. They all had one hundred percent approval rating, from a thumbs up or thumbs down system. Some had received comments. I clicked on the comments section straight away. Some said things like "great tits, let us see more." Some were a bit more personal, "I love your boobs Sophie, I wish I was that guy." One message was from a girl, and it said "Nice." I looked back at my profile, and I'd had twenty-four friend requests. I clicked through them one by one. Most of the profile photos were pictures of dicks. Men from all parts of the world. I declined anyone who didn't have more pictures or was from too far away to meet up. There were two couples, one from London, and one from Bristol who had requested friendship. They both had picture galleries and seemed genuine. I accepted both. I accepted a couple of very fit looking guys based in

London. I sent a message to one of the guys asking, "how would you like to be in a video with me?" Once I'd cleared the friend requests, I closed my phone and went for lunch. At some point I would have to do some work, or people would start to notice that my mind was elsewhere.

Later that afternoon, I took my ten-minute break, and went to the café. I went online and booked a hotel room close to a bar for the following day. It had big rooms, and looked well lit. Many hotel rooms are dark, lit only with wall lights or lamps. One of the benefits of being there in the afternoon was the natural light. The room had an early check in available, which was essential. I checked the porn website again and I'd had a reply from the good-looking guy. The response to my offer of a video shoot was met with delight. I messaged him my Martinez phone number. I told him that if he could make tomorrow afternoon, he might get the chance to be in the movie. I went back to my desk and left my phone in my bag for a bit. Things started to get a bit busier on reception. The after-work rush was beginning, and other members of staff were stopping by to use the phone or computer. I didn't want to lose my job or be embarrassed in front of anyone at the gym. I had pride in being good at what I did, even though I would hopefully be moving on soon.

Once at home I read several new messages. There was a message on the porn site from the guy who wanted to be in my blowjob video. His name was Andy, and he could get himself free tomorrow afternoon. I replied with a link to the video of the woman with the two men helping her with the furniture.

"That's a lot for a first date." He returned.

"It's not a date." I stated. "We're making some porn together. Would you be ok with that?"

"It looks like fun, but I'm not gay. I'm completely straight."

"Don't worry," I tried to put him at ease. "I'll be the only one touching anyone, like in the video. I want to be the centre of attention."

"Ok, that sounds fine. Where should I meet you?" I sent him the nearest tube station to the hotel and told him to ring me when he got there.

I sent a link to the scene I'd chosen to Paul, with a message that read "I think I'm going to make this one tomorrow."

The attention was so stimulating. Not to mention the messages about sex and engaging with sexy websites and apps. I wished Paul was around. I wanted to share this feeling with him and take him to bed. My sex drive had increased so much over the past few weeks. I was loving it. I got a reply from Paul saying, "That video is very sexy, you'll look amazing doing that. Who are you doing it with?"

"A guy I who messaged me after he'd seen my pics online, and one from a dating app." I replied.

"Make sure you're safe." Paul worried, as usual.

"Nathan is going to film it again. I'll be safe." I assured him.

"That's good. You'll have to send it to me. I can't wait to see it."

"I thought I was going to show it to you in Spain," I teased him.

"Can you send it straight away? It's boring up here on my own." Paul had never liked working away.

"Ok. I'll send you some pictures, and a clip from the video." Paul ended the conversation as he had to go out to dinner with some colleagues.

Chapter 18 – My First Group Experience

When I got home, I went straight to the sofa and started playing the porn clip on my laptop. It was the one that I was basing tomorrow's adventure around. I slipped my hand into my panties and touched myself. I fantasised about it being me in that same situation tomorrow afternoon. The build-up of my arousal during the day was released through a powerful and wonderful orgasm. It wasn't a great substitute for Paul, but it was still very pleasurable.

I didn't have a morning shift at the gym the next day, so the whole day was my own. I woke up and felt a surge of excitement at the thought of the day ahead of me. It was mingled with the thrill of the thought that we were off to Spain tomorrow. My morning was lazy. A coffee and toast in front of daytime TV. I took my time showering, drying my hair and getting dressed. I put the camera, tripod, selfie stick, underwear makeup and a few other bits in my bag, and set off to the train station. I would have time to get some lunch before my arranged meeting with Nathan at a bar.

I couldn't eat much of my salad. Nerves, or excitement, was taking hold of me. It was a relief to meet up with Nathan and have someone to talk to. We had a drink, and then went up to the hotel room. He suggested getting a bottle of wine to take with us. Although my first thought was "what a good idea," I decided against it. I wanted to be completely in control, and I also wanted to enjoy this experience as much as possible. I didn't want it to be dulled by the effects of wine. The hotel room was exactly as described in the pictures. The Bathroom wasn't very big, but that didn't matter today. Nathan sat on the bed.

"What should we do whilst we wait?" He asked, with a smile. My phone started buzzing in my hand.

"Too late" I grinned as I answered the phone. It was Andy. I answered and told him the name of the bar next to the hotel. I arranged to meet him there in ten minutes.

"If anyone asks, you're an amateur photographer again." I smiled at Nathan. "We're friends and you're helping me out. Same as last time."

"Whatever you say boss." He laughed.

"Good, because if you take some more good pictures and videos, I'll give you the fuck of your life later." I picked up my bag, which still had everything in it. "Do you mind looking after the bag when they are here?" I checked. "I'll put their phones in there."

"No problem. Do you want my phone?" He asked.

"I trust you." I had to at this point, and I was pretty certain he was a good guy. It was in his interests not to run off with my camera. If he waited around, he was going to have sex. I still held the cards, even though I was sure I didn't need to.

"I'll meet the first guy in the bar, I want to make sure he's ok. Then I'll bring him here before I meet the second guy in the lobby. Are you ok waiting here with him?"

"No problem. See you shortly." He lay back on the bed as I headed out of the door.

I saw Andy and knew it was him immediately, even though I hadn't seen his face online. He was on his own, the right age, and obviously waiting for someone. He looked very nervous. I tried to put him at ease, but he didn't relax much. He asked me how much the room was and handed me eighty pounds for his half. I asked him what porn he liked on the site, and why he had signed up. I think he liked the idea of promiscuous sex, but I don't think he was ready for the reality of it. Our conversation was interrupted when James called. He was five minutes' walk away. I gave him the name of the hotel and told him I'd meet him in reception. I walked with Andy from the bar, across the street and up to the room. I wondered if the receptionist noticed that I was coming in with a different bloke? Probably not. Paranoia was kicking in because of my nerves. Once upstairs, I introduced Andy to Nathan and went back down to the lobby. It occurred to me on my way to reception what a convoluted set of circumstances I'd created. Three blokes I didn't know, who didn't know each other, all in a hotel room with me. "Oh well," I thought. "Let's see what happens." I smiled to myself, it felt good to be doing something out of the ordinary and unusual. Brave and exciting. Not to mention incredibly sexy.

I kissed James on the cheek as we met in reception. He was the only bloke in the lobby. It wasn't hard to pick him out. Two girls were checking in at reception. This distracted the receptionist from seeing me going to the room with a third man. As we climbed the stairs to the first floor, I took his hand.

"Are you looking forward to this?" I asked

"Yeah." He replied. He looked even more nervous than Andy.

"It'll be fun. Don't worry, do what I say, and you'll enjoy it." I wanted to at least pretend I knew what I was doing. In that moment I did look forward to being a bit more experienced. Having more confidence in these situations would be good. The only way to get there was to gain the experience, and that's exactly what I was doing.

"The room was one hundred and sixty pounds. I hate to ask, but I can't afford to pay for it all."

"No problem," he replied as he counted four twenties out of his wallet and handed them to me."

"Thank you." I smiled at him, and we continued along the corridor to the room. It felt odd, taking the money, but the alternative was for Paul and I to pay for it, and that seemed even worse.

We entered the room, Nathan was sat up on the bed talking to Andy, who was sat on one of the chairs at the back of the room. There were two chairs, one either side of a table, and I indicated to James to sit in the other chair.

"Ok, let's get straight to it." I said to them both. "I'm going to strip down to my underwear for you, then I'll give you both a blowjob. You've seen the video I sent, so you know what to expect. I'll want you standing on either side of me so that I can do my thing. Does that sound ok?"

They both nodded in agreement. "My panties will stay on the whole time, there won't be any sex. If you impress me, and last for long enough, you might get to do more with me in the future. There is one other thing. I want you both to pleasure me before we start. I want to be satisfied before you two are. Does that sound fair?" They both nodded again. "OK, you can go first." I pointed to Andy and started to take off my jeans. My socks came off with the legs of the jeans. I folded them and put them on the desk where the TV sat on the other side of the room. I threw my shoes over towards the door so that they would be out of the way. I stood in my panties, and my tight, white top in front of the three men. They were all staring at me.

"Where do you want us?" I turned to Nathan.

"I'll film from the window side. If you move the chairs out a bit into the room so that they're away from the window, that will be perfect."

As they moved the chairs I went and turned the lights on. I put the bedside lamps on as well, and the lamp on the table. The two lads were loitering near the chairs, and I moved over in front of them. Nathan had got the camera, and nodded as he pressed the record button, and began to film.

I sat down on one of the chairs and beckoned Andy to kneel between my legs. He put his hands on my thighs after he had knelt, looking to me for instruction. I used one hand to move my panties to one side, exposing myself to Andy, James, and the camera. I felt a shiver of excitement as I did so. With my other hand, I gently pulled his shoulder and moved him towards me. He brought his head down between my legs, and immediately started to lick me. I gasped with the suddenness of his approach, but I felt myself writhe as the pleasure started to flow through my body. I looked up at James, who was watching us, wide eyed. I kept my eyes focussed on him as I put my hands on the back of Andy's head, pulling him towards me. I loved the feeling of being watched. It was different to having the camera there, or Nathan behind the camera. James was doing nothing except watching me. He looked captivated. During the build up to my experiences, the thought of what was going to happen was like sub conscious foreplay for me. Without knowing it I had built up anticipation and tension all day. Perhaps for a couple of days. Once Andy began to touch me, I knew that I would orgasm before long. I kept staring at James, placing one of my hands on my chest. I was enjoying showing off. Focussing on looking sexy for James, and the camera, as Andy brought me to climax as he knelt in between my legs. My eyes closed and I moaned. Forgetting about my audience and enjoying the extasy that overtook my whole body. I moved both my hands to the back of Andy's head again and manipulated the pressure he applied by holding his head. I made sure I enjoyed every last drop of my orgasm before I released him.

"Thank you." I breathlessly muttered, as he stood up. "Your turn." I beckoned James's forward. "Be gentle, I'll be sensitive now." He looked worried as he knelt in front of me. I shifted back in the chair, so I was more upright, and he moved between my legs. I shivered as his mouth engulfed me. I was sensitive, but I had cum so quickly the first time, that I would definitely have no trouble in orgasming again. I closed my eyes for a moment and enjoyed the sensation. He was gentler than Andy and seemed to be more intent on giving me what I wanted. I had made a good choice in the order that I had asked them to perform for me. I opened my eyes and looked up at Andy. I took the opportunity to enjoy my exhibitionist side. I pulled my top up and lifted it over my head. I then removed my bra and watched as Andy starred at my tits. I let him enjoy the view for a moment as I closed my eyes again. I pulled James into me, encouraging him to be firmer with the pressure of his tongue. After a few moments I looked back up at Andy.

"Touch me." I ordered, nodding towards my boobs. He moved in at the side of the chair on his knees and caressed my tits with both hands. He was staring at me as he fondled me, like a kid in a sweet shop. I looked straight at him as he played with my nipples and caressed the curves of my boobs. Having the pleasure between my legs, and the excitement of being touched by a second man, started to heighten my feelings again. My whole body stirred towards fulfilment for the second time. As the thrill built up, I grabbed urgently at Andy's arm, and pulled him towards me. I put an arm on the back of his neck and brought his face onto my tits. I moaned in pleasure as his tongue found my nipple and started to flick and play across and around it. His licking and sucking became more intense as I writhed in pleasure. I pulled James harder into me with my other hand, urging him to intensify the stimulation between my legs. As my whole body felt like it was being pleasured to ecstasy, I looked up at the camera. The thrill of being watched, and the erotic moment being captured on film, tipped me over the edge. I yelped out loud as a more powerful orgasm than the first one started to rage in my body. My senses were on overdrive as my tits felt the constant attention of Andy's tongue and lips. James licked and sucked as electric pleasure poured through me. I opened my eyes, and looked at the camera again, groaning with the intense pleasure of the moment. I moved James' head back as my orgasm subsided. Andy seemed to sense that it was time to move back as my writhing stopped. I stayed still for a moment, eyes closed, relaxing into the chair, and enjoying the moment.

After a few seconds, I got up, my legs feeling weak underneath me. I took Andy by the hand and sat him in the opposite chair. James turned around as he stood up, and I motioned for him to sit in the chair I'd stood up from. They had earned their reward. I turned around in front of the guys and bent over a little, pushing my arse towards them. Then I turned to face them and leaned forward again, exposing my boobs. I moved my shoulders from side to side, both of them were transfixed on me. Showing off still wasn't natural for me, but I relaxed a bit as I saw how much they were focussed on me. I stood up tall. I had their full attention now. I leaned forward again and cupped my tits with my hands. I turned around a second time and looked at the camera. I leaned forward for the camera this time, showing off my boobs as I had to the guys.

"You can touch me." I said over my shoulder. I felt hands caress the skin of my bum cheeks, and then grab and grope at me. The hands on me becoming more urgent as their confidence and arousal grew. I bent over again, stretching out in front of them. I grabbed a pillow from the bed as I turned to face them. Standing only in my panties, I put the pillow on the floor in front of the chairs and ordered them to stand up. I turned to face the camera and stood between them, first putting my arm around Andy's shoulders. I leant over and kissed him. The kiss didn't last for long. I pulled his head down onto my chest and he started to kiss and lick at my breasts as I turned to James. I pulled his head to mine and kissed him passionately. This lasted much longer. My inhibitions had completely gone now. The sensations from Andy kissing my boobs tingled through me. I snogged James for a few more moments and then stopped. I sank down and fell to my knees on the pillow. I looked up at Andy.

"Take your cock out for me." I commanded. As he started to undo his trousers, I turned to James and undid his myself. I pulled his boxers and jeans down over his thighs and his cock appeared in front of me. He wasn't erect, which surprised me. I felt a tinge of disappointment, but ignored it, and took his cock in my hand and began to stroke it. I turned to find Andy, already with his trousers around his ankles playing with himself. His cock was bigger, but only because he had been playing with it. He moved his hand away as I put my hand on his thigh and took him in my mouth. He wasn't fully erect either, but he was getting there. I moved my mouth up and down his cock, and he got harder as I worked. After a few minutes he was almost fully erect in my mouth. I put my hand back on to his cock as I stopped sucking him and turned back to James. He still wasn't hard at all. I looked up at him, and he looked almost apologetic. I smiled, hoping to relax him, and took him in my mouth. It was strange, sucking a flaccid cock. I'd never done it before. I expected him to get harder in my mouth, as Andy had done, but it didn't happen. After a couple of minutes, I stood up, wanking both slowly, one in each hand. They both grabbed at my tits with their free hands. Andy leaned forward and started to suck my nipple. I shivered with pleasure, and I felt James getting harder in my hand. He had one hand on my boob, and one grabbing my bum cheek. I closed my eyes and enjoyed being touched for a few more minutes. I was wanking them very gently, careful not to get Andy too excited. James still wasn't erect, so I turned to him and pushed him down onto the chair. I bent over, pushing my arse towards Andy. "Do you want to play with that for a moment?" I asked him. I turned back to James and brought my tits forward into his face. He held them with both hands and started to suck at each of my nipples in turn. It felt amazing. I stroked his cock as he continued to play with my tits, hoping that he would get hard. I could feel Andy kissing at my cheeks, then he stopped, and I felt him start to rub his cock up and down the tops of my legs. Nathan had moved closer, and Andy gently slapped me with his cock. I leaned over more and took James's back into my mouth. As I sucked, Andy's cock stroked at me, getting further and further between my cheeks as he played with himself. It felt great, but I didn't want him to cum, and I definitely didn't want him to penetrate me. He wasn't wearing a condom. I stood up and beckoned James to his feet. I went back down to my knees and started sucking each of them in turn. Nathan had moved in front of us. I could sense the camera focussed on me as I took each cock in my mouth for a few seconds at a time. Andy started to push himself into my face each time I turned to him. I could see it wouldn't be long before he orgasmed. I slowed my sucking and concentrated more on James for a couple of minutes. I continued stroking Andy with my hand at the same time.

After a short while I sat up on the chair and let go of James for a moment. He started to play with himself as I took hold of Andy's cock and placed it between my tits. I grabbed my tits on each side and let him tit fuck me as he held my shoulders. His pace increased and he thrust between my tits harder and harder. I moved back and took him in my hand, and held my free arm under my tits, as if presenting them for him. I wanked him more quickly as he groaned and ejaculated all over me. Cum leapt onto my tits, some of it going across one of my cheeks and hitting my ear. I slowed my hand as he shuddered to the end of his orgasm. I took the head of his cock in my mouth and licked the remaining cum from the tip. I kept my hand on his cock as I turned to James. He was clearly excited by what he'd seen, and the sight of me covered in cum knelt in front of him. I put my hand back on his cock and took it into my mouth. He still wasn't fully erect, which must have been so frustrating for him. I moved my mouth up and down his cock at full speed, resisting the temptation to suck. He quickly pulled back and began to wank himself. He obviously needed things to be a certain way, and I didn't know what that was. I didn't care. I let go of Andy's cock, who moved away behind me, and used my hands to present me cum covered boobs in front of James. He wanked furiously. After a minute or two began to edge closer to me as his orgasm started.

His knees trembled as he almost pressed up against me. I looked up at him as his cum gushed onto my tits. It didn't go as far as Andy's but there was more of it. He had time to move his cock across my tits and completely cover me in cum. As he slowed, I leant forward and sucked the head of his cock as I had done to Andy. I then turned to the camera and presented my tits to Nathan. During the experience I had forgotten that he was there for a moment. I moved my hands away and moved my tits from side to side. Some cum ran down onto my thighs. I gave the camera a little wave goodbye, and then stood up.

Chapter 19 – Thanking the Cameraman

It was nice not to have much cum on my face. Only the bit on my cheek. I didn't mind cum on my face. I expected I would do it more as my adventures continued, but I didn't like leaving it there for long. The experience of being so close to a man ejaculating was exciting but having semen on my face wasn't pleasant. I didn't like the smell, or the feeling of it. I didn't like it as it cooled. It was good having it on my tits. I felt dishevelled and dirty. That was much more fun.

"Get dressed and see yourselves out guys. I'm going to have some pictures taken. I've got both your numbers, so I can send you some of the photos later." They sheepishly pulled up their jeans. I passed them their phones from my bag, and they hurried out of the room. James saying a notional "bye" over his shoulder as he left. Nathan had started to take pictures of me as I moved around the room, close ups of my face and boobs. I posed more, now that we were alone, lifting my arms up to show off my chest.

"Do you think I need some more cum on here?" I asked.

"Yes, I do." He replied with gusto.

"Cum on my tits now, and then take some more pictures. Afterwards I want a good long fuck. You won't last two minutes if you fuck me now." I assured him. He nodded agreement and came towards me. I went back down onto my knees on the pillow. I reached into his underpants after pulling down his jeans. His big cock required a little bit of strength to pull from the cloth, as his erection made it hard to extract. It sprung out in front of me, completely hard. I enjoyed the feeling of having turned someone on so much. I was sure that the other two had been as excited, but his erection was such an obvious sign of his desire. I took as much of it as I could into my mouth, softly wrapping my lips around it and quickly getting up to full blowjob speed. It can't have been thirty seconds before Nathan pulled out and exploded over me. He almost covered my face and chest, completing me cum drenched image. His knees buckled a bit as he came to a stop and moved back. He looked at me and sighed, relief flowing out of him.

"I told you." I smiled through his cum. "That wouldn't have been much of a fuck, would it?"

"Sorry. After what I've watched, I couldn't help it."

"Don't worry. Take some pictures, we can take our time." Nathan pulled his jeans up and took more photos, like the ones he'd taken before. After a few more shots with my extra covering, I went to the bathroom to wipe the cum off my face. Nathan followed with the camera.

"Are you filming?" I asked.

"Yes." He replied. "Is that ok? It's always one of the best bits of a porn film. I don't know why."

"It's fine." I had that noticed videos with footage after the scene were always very popular. Maybe it was seeing the girl in a real setting, rather than a staged porn shoot? Paul had liked that bit when I'd made the film with Brian, so I wanted to check that Nathan was capturing the experience.

After I'd cleaned up, I took a quick shower. Nathan tried to take a couple of photos, but the room was a bit small, and not well lit. I didn't stay in for long. I didn't want to turn him on too much. I wrapped a towel around myself and went back through to the bedroom. Strip for me then. I lay on the bed as Nathan took his clothes off. His cock starting to stiffen again as he removed his underpants and stood before me. He was in great shape. I admired his body.

"Come here," I beckoned.

He joined me on the bed, and I kissed him as I began to stroke his cock. He moved the towel away from my chest and pulled away from the kiss to suck and lick at my tits. We stayed there for only a few moments. His cock was hard again now, and I reached over and pulled a condom from my bag. I leaned down and wrapped my mouth around the top of his cock, enough to make it wet. I then unwrapped the condom and began to roll it down onto him.

"I'm not sure it'll fit!" I exclaimed.

"It will," he assured me.

I pulled the sides of the condom apart and stretched it down. It covered most of him but didn't get down to the bottom.

"Will that be safe?" I asked.

"It should be fine. We will be careful." He pulled me towards him. I climbed on top of him and kissed him again. I took hold of his cock and held it still whilst I moved into position and sank down onto him. I was so wet. I'd been so turned on by giving three blowjobs that afternoon, that I couldn't have been more aroused. Even so, it still took a while before I could work my way down fully onto him. He was so big, it felt amazing. I stayed there for a moment, kissing him between gasps. Then I started to gently rock back and forth, trying to get used to having something so big inside me.

"Be gentle." I said, as he started to push into me. He slowed and I sat up a bit. Once my position had altered, I began fucking him a bit harder. He took my tits in his hands and then into his mouth. He sucked and played with my nipples. I gathered speed and started to orgasm almost immediately. It was no surprise to me that it happened so soon, even though it was my third of the afternoon. I moaned and fell back down on top of him as my body pulsated with each thrust. He was fucking me as hard as I was riding him, and wave after orgasmic wave ran through me. I continued to groan with pleasure, as the orgasm seemed to linger for such a long time. He continued to fuck me, getting more excited. I moved forward and slid off him. He looked up, disappointed.

"Get behind me." I smiled. I climbed off him and placed myself on all fours next to him on the bed. He got up onto his knees and moved behind me. I felt him push himself back inside me. It was easier than before, but his cock still went in slowly, as I gave way to it a little at a time. He put his hands on my hips and started to fuck me.

"As hard as you can," I told him. His speed increased, and he started slamming into me as he pushed deeper and deeper. I rocked violently as he moved one hand up onto my shoulder. He started pulling me towards him, as well as thrusting as hard as he could with his hips. I lifted one hand to touch myself and struggled to steady myself with my one remaining hand due to being fucked so hard. I put my chest down onto the bed so that I could lift my hand and rubbed my clitoris as another orgasm started to grow. My knees gave way and I slid down onto my front as he pushed my hips down into the bed with each thrust. He was laying on top of me now and fucking me as deep as I'd ever felt. Spasms of pleasure shook me, completely taking hold of me. The driving of his cock into me seemed to get somehow faster and the orgasm increased in intensity. It was as much pleasure as I could stand. The release of all the arousal from the day. As my body relaxed into the bed Nathan was grinding into me with everything he had. After a few seconds he pulled out. I heard the snap of the condom being pulled off, and cum gushed onto my arse and up my back. I could feel him wanking himself onto my cheeks, the top of his cock rubbing against me. I stayed, face down, breathless, and exhausted. Nathan reached over and picked up the camera. I heard him take some pictures, his cock lying on my bum in front of him.

"That was fun." He said, as he climbed off me, and then off the bed. He went to the bathroom and came back with a hand towel, which he used to wipe my bum and back.

"Thank you." I said, as I rolled over. "That was fun. You have a brilliant cock."

"Thanks," he lay back down on the bed next to me. "That's a compliment that all men want to hear."

"Well, it's true," I said.

"My wife doesn't seem too interested in my cock." He stared at the ceiling as he spoke, as if drifting into deep thought.

"Wife?" The revelation shocked me. "I didn't know you were married."

"You never asked." He responded, which was true. It took me back a bit, I wasn't sure why.

"What about the dating site? Aren't you worried you'll get caught?" I asked.

"I was a bit worried about that, but the site doesn't have much information about me. If she found it, I could say it's an old account from before I met her. I don't use it much anyway. I should delete it."

"Don't you feel bad?" I quizzed him further. I realised why it had taken me aback. I had thought Nathan was a good bloke, and this might be proof that he wasn't what I had thought. I also felt bad for his wife. I had enjoyed the afternoon sex, knowing that it was for fun, and that Paul was ok with it. Had Nathan had felt differently about the whole thing? Maybe it was tinged with guilt for him.

"You don't need to worry," he said calmly. "I'm not worried if she finds out. She cheated on me last year, and we haven't been the same since. I'm not sure whether we'll get through it. I'm not sure I even want to, anymore. I'm going to have some fun anyway. Me and her don't have a sexual relationship at the moment."

He was putting his clothes on as he talked. He was almost dressed by the time he'd finished. I tried to process what he'd said. I concluded that it didn't matter to me. I was here for sex. The fact that he was married made it easier for me to get what I wanted. No extra hassle.

"Are you with anyone?" Nathan asked.

The question caught me off guard a bit. I took a couple of seconds to think.

"Yes, I'm married." I answered. Why not be honest? We were both in the same boat. Well, similar boats.

"Aren't you happy?" He continued.

"Very happy." I answered. "I want to explore sex whilst I'm young. Have some fun."

"What would happen if he found out?"

"He'll never find out. What you don't know doesn't hurt you." Nathan didn't need to know anything about me or my life. Knowing I was married would stop him doing something ridiculous, like leaving his wife for me. I didn't need to tell him anything about my life. He didn't even know my real name after all. I probably didn't know his.

After Nathan had left, I tidied up the room a bit. I put my stuff back in my handbag and set off home.

Chapter 20 – Sharing My Porn

Paul got home on Friday, the night before we were due to travel to Spain. It was so good to see him. I'd missed him more on this trip than any I could remember. My new sex life was off the charts exciting, and I'd wanted to share more of it with him. Messaging and calling were nice, but it was different to being able to sit down and talk. Our relationship had improved so much recently, and I wanted that to continue. Only by being together and communicating would we keep on building on what we'd started. It was going to be great to be together for a few days, with no work to interrupt us. I couldn't wait to show him my videos. I was like a kid at Christmas. I'd sent him some of the posed sex pictures of me with Brian, and he'd loved them. He kept asking for more, to the point where I had sent him most of the good ones. We sat together on the couch as soon as he got back, and I presented him with the laptop.

"They're all on there." I grinned as I kneeled close to him on the sofa.

"Have you posted any online?" He asked.

"Only a few. I wanted to experiment to find out which ones were the most popular." We started to go through the pictures. They followed the order that they were taken, so the build-up was quite thrilling. We deleted any that were out of focus, or no good. Each time we both agreed that one was sexy, we put it into a folder for editing. The pictures progressed to ones with me having my tits exposed. Brian playing with them as the top of my dress hung around my waist. I liked looking back at them. They looked so glamorous. As the pictures moved through the series, I could feel my heart rate increasing at the sight of me with Brian's cock. First in my mouth, and then pushing into me. There was a shot of me on all fours looking up at the camera. Behind me you could see five or six inches of Brian's cock ready to be pushed into me. It was a truly erotic photo.

"That's the best one so far!" Paul exclaimed.

"Why do you like that one?" I asked, interested in his thoughts.

"It's sexy, and it shows your whole body off. Your tits look good underneath you, and your bum is on display. You look gorgeous. Your face is showing your pleasure, and the guy you're with looks like he's come straight from the set of a professional porn shoot. What's bad about it?"

"Nothing. I love it. I wanted to know what you liked specifically. The more I understand, the better." He carried on looking through the various poses of us fucking. They stopped after the doggy style sex on the bed.

"Didn't he cum?" Paul asked.

"He did, but those photos were taken before the video. We set up again after that and then filmed us."

"That's a great idea. What made you think of that?" Paul asked.

"It was when I met the first guy, and it was difficult to take pictures as well as having sex. Even though it was only oral. I thought the same would be true of videoing and taking pictures. You can't do both. I liked the idea of making sure I got some good pictures, and then doing a video. It's like intense foreplay, it takes quite a bit of control. I enjoyed it though. I liked the restraint and the suspense."

"It shows in the pictures. You're incredible." Paul complimented again.

"Should we watch the video?" I asked.

"Sure." He clicked it open, and we saw us come into the room. We watched as Brian played with me, and then picked me up. It was amazing to watch. I'd watched it few times in the past few days, each time I enjoyed it more. Watching Brian's physique manhandle me was such a turn on. As Paul watched I took his cock from his trousers and slowly wanked him. He was as hard as I'd ever known him, almost bursting. I didn't want him to cum, I wanted to tease him into a state of ecstasy. As the video finished, I took my hand away and asked him what he thought.

"Did you cum?" Paul asked.

"Three times." I informed him.

"Wow. Why so many do you think?"

"Do you mind?" I was worried that it would bother him.

"Not at all. Quite the opposite, I'm happy that you enjoyed yourself. I love seeing you achieve pleasure, until now I hadn't realised quite how much I like it. I was interested to know what it was that turned you on that much."

"It was the build-up. The extended foreplay, posing for the pictures that led to it. The elicit nature of what I was doing heightened the pleasure. I don't think that kind of experience can be fabricated between people in a relationship. I've been thinking about it a lot. If I wasn't married, it wouldn't have felt the same. The fact that it was only sex, nothing else in the background, no worries or hang ups made it entirely sensual. Normally people would consider whether they fancied someone. Whether they wanted to see them again. My body reacted to the freedom from those concerns and enabled me to focus on the sex. Our sex is more like that now. Free somehow of the constraints that relationships put on everything. We seem to be able to enjoy sex without any hang ups, now we're communicating more." I stopped talking for a second, to give him a chance to respond.

"I think you're right," he said, after a couple seconds. "Having seen you like this," pointing to the video, "I see you more like a pornstar. Someone utterly sexual, not a wife, or friend, or partner. It makes things very sex focussed when we desire them to be that way."

"That's why men like the idea of pornstars," I added. "A woman who likes sex and wants to have sex. Someone who won't moan at them for not putting the bins out, or for snoring. You never see those interactions in a porn film, do you? It must be quite hard on women generally. Men struggling to find a balance between sexual fulfilment, and a life partner. I guess it takes a lot of communication to address that. I can't imagine how much more difficult that would be with kids involved."

"You're right," Paul agreed again. "We seem to be getting there though."

"We do," I nodded. I pulled off my jeans and straddled him on the sofa and we made love. The first of three times that evening.

We lay in bed together the next morning, having sex and dozing. Paul cropped a few of the photos and I added them to the album on the porn site. He took a clip from the video that didn't show my face and I uploaded that as well. I loved that people would be looking at me.

"It's a shame I forgot to get pictures of the cum on my tits after we made the video." I mentioned, quite disappointed not to be able to complete the set pf photos.

"You can take them from the video! Watch." Paul showed me how to take a picture from the movie, in a couple of clicks. He sent some cropped ones to me, and I added them to the end of the picture series. It was a perfect end to the set of photos.

We had breakfast and made our way to the airport. I was tired and very relaxed. I slept on Paul's shoulder on the train, and then again on the plane.

We landed in Spain in the late afternoon. It was hot and humid. A heat that made you feel sticky, encouraging clothes to grab at you as it became impossible to stay cool. We only felt the heat as we left the airport. The air conditioning was hiding the true nature of the afternoon heat inside. The cab wasn't air conditioned, so we had a very hot forty-minute drive into town. The windows were down so that the airflow provided some relief from the heat. It made the ride noisy and uncomfortable. We arrived at our hotel, and the air conditioning hit us again as we walked through the doors into reception. We checked in and went up to the room. We unpacked and had a look around. It was an impressive room, with a balcony that looked out over the sea. There were big windows that went right across from one side of the room to the other, making the most of the view. The middle two panes of glass opened onto the balcony. We walked out into the early evening warmth. There was a table with two chairs, perfect for breakfast, or an evening glass of champagne.

"I've got a surprise for you," I said as we leaned on the balcony rail. "A start to our sexy trip." I smiled as I went back into the room and picked up the laptop. Paul had followed me and sat on the bed.

"What is it?" He asked, a little nervous.

"You'll see." I opened the laptop and clicked into a folder where I'd put the video from my afternoon in London. I opened it up and sat next to him on the bed. "I made this for you as a surprise."

We sat and watched as the guys took their turns to go down on me, and then me rewarding them as they stood either side of me. The video was only ten minutes long and didn't look as professional as the video with Brian, but it was a very sexy scene. I loved seeing all the attention of the two men, focussed on me. It finished up with me posing with cum all over my tits and I asked Paul what he thought.

"It's amazing. I'm speechless. Did you enjoy it?"

"I loved it. I was a bit unsure, and the guys weren't who I would have chosen now that I have a bit more experience. I'm sure I can make a better one."

"They weren't as good as your first co-star. I can't believe the guy on the left wasn't hard."

"He was nervous, he was quite young. I didn't get any photo's either. I'm glad we can get screen shots from the movie."

"Was it the same camera man again?"

"It was. The guy who I met the first time, who bought me the underwear. He did a pretty good job didn't he. Those lads paid for the hotel room as well." I was quite proud of myself.

"Did you have sex with the cameraman?" Paul was sat forward in his chair, still watching the end of the video.

"Yes. He deserved it after he'd made the two videos for us.

"You had a busy day!" Paul seemed impressed. He sat back as the scene came to an end.

"I did. A sexual experience with two guys. A first for me."

"Can I see the video with the camera man?"

"I didn't film it." I explained, immediately wondering why I hadn't.

"Why not?" Paul looked a little bit put out.

"I didn't think about it. Is that a problem?" I waited during a slight pause in the conversation. Paul hesitated for a minute before responding, as if in thought.

"I suppose not." He seemed deflated somehow, a worried expression had crept into his face.

"You seem a bit upset?" I pushed. What's wrong? Tell me?" I leant across and put my hand on his leg.

"I wondered why that one was different? It's a turn on to watch you making porn. Knowing you did something with someone without capturing it doesn't feel the same. It's not a problem."

"I'm glad you've told me. I didn't think I had to film it." I defended myself a little bit, although I did worry that he felt bad.

"You don't have to. We never talked about it. Sorry, I'm not upset." Paul's face lifted. "I like the idea of you enjoying sex, and I love seeing you as a pornstar. I guess I don't like the idea of knowing you're spending time with someone else." As he spoke it made complete sense to me. If I hadn't filmed any of them, it wouldn't have been an issue, but the fact that one was different was a worry.

"I understand, sorry. It's not like that at all." I started.

"You don't need to explain Soph, I trust you."

"I want to explain. The more we communicate the better, remember?" He nodded. "It wasn't any different with him than with the guy in the film. I enjoyed them both, it was great fun." I wanted to be honest, it was the different approach that had upset Paul, not whether I had enjoyed the sex. "I wanted someone to film me, so the movie would be better for us to watch. Sex was always going to be the best incentive for someone to do that for me. I'm not going to pay anyone to film for us. After the lads left, I was focussed on rewarding him for helping me. I wasn't thinking about making more videos, but it was the same. Impersonal, just sex, great fun. It's not easy getting a good video from a tripod, but I could have put it on anyway. I always will in the future. He's married." I added at the end, to make Paul aware that there was nothing more to it. I waited a few seconds to gauge his response.

"I understand. What was it like?" He still seemed a little unsure.

"He didn't last very long when he wanked over me the first time we met, and I wanted good sex. I'd got so horny making the first video. He came on my tits as soon as the lads left. I put him into my mouth, and he didn't last thirty seconds. I got some pictures of that." My face lit up as I remembered. I clicked into the folder and brought up the images of me with the three loads of cum dripping over my chest.

"That's an incredible picture," Paul said. We had clicked onto one of me leaning forward, pushing my cum soaked boobs together. "That's my favourite one so far."

"I'm glad you like it." I smiled. He was relaxing. The concern that I'd seen a few minutes before was leaving him. "He took these shots of me in the shower whilst he recovered himself, and then he we had sex."

"Did you cum?" Paul wanted to know.

"Yes. Twice I think, I can't remember. I was very horny after the experience I'd had that afternoon. There's a picture of afterwards here somewhere." I clicked through a few shots that Nathan had taken of me in the shower. Then there were the photo's he took of me from above after he'd cum. I stopped on the picture. "That was the end. It didn't last long." The picture showed a lot of cum on my bum cheeks and back. Nathan's huge cock lying semi erect on my bottom. I hadn't seen it before. It sent a shiver of excitement through me. It was deeply erotic.

"He's big." Stated Paul.

"Very," I replied. "I like that picture. I've got a video of him cuming on my cleavage from the first time we met!" I found the clip and we watched it together. It was only a couple of minutes long, but it still turned me on.

"It's brilliant. You'll have to do another scene with him on camera. If you want to?" It seemed that the filming misunderstanding was forgotten.

"He doesn't last long, but I'll give it a go. What would you like to see?"

"I'm not sure, should we pick something out together later?"

"That sounds like a brilliant idea." I apologised again for making him feel bad. I promised to make it up to him. "We're learning all the time. It'll get better and better," I assured him. "Do you fancy some champagne?" I asked.

"Sounds great," he smiled. "We are on holiday after all".

I rang reception from the phone by the bed. After I'd ordered, I got the travel speaker from my case and put on some music using my phone. A mix that seemed like the right kind of relaxed vibe for the evening.

There was a knock on the door, and I went over to answer it. Paul had gone back out on to the balcony, leaning over, and looking at his phone. Someone from the hotel had brought up the champagne in an ice bucket. She was dressed smartly, but not in a uniform.

"Thank you". I smiled as the door opened. "Come in".

I opened the door wider, and she came through into the room. "Where would you like it?" She asked, speaking English in a soft Spanish accent.

"On the side there." I pointed to the desk where the television was situated.

"Is it a special occasion?" Her English seemed a bit broken, but very good. She was pretty, with a full, yet athletic figure. She looked like she might have a good body under her shirt. I decided to try and flirt a little. I was feeling a bit heady after watching myself in the videos. The fact that we were on our sexy trip made me feel even more horny.

"It's Paul's birthday" I replied, nodding towards Paul on the balcony. "We're here for a romantic weekend."

"Welcome," she said with a smile, "I hope you have a lovely stay."

I signed for the drink. I caught myself looking at her chest as I scrawled my name. I paused and added a twenty-euro tip to the bill. She tipped her head to one side as she saw the extra.

"Thank you," she had a look of shock in her smile. "Is there anything else I can do for you?" She asked.

"Would you like to have a drink with us?" I went for it. "You seem fun." She looked even more surprised, but the shock soon disappeared from her face, and I could see her thinking.

"I can't drink at work, it's against the rules." She apologised.

"No problem", I said. I hoped I hadn't been too obvious. She may have felt uncomfortable. I started to worry. She may tell her friends about this, but she didn't have any grounds for any sort of sexual harassment complaint. I was taken aback by what I'd done, and the reality of the situation hit me. She thanked me again and went to leave. She stopped and turned as she was about to open the door.

"I finish in an hour. Would you like me to join you then?" she smiled.

"That would be good", I responded, desperately trying to seem calm and confident. Inside my stomach leapt and swirled at the thrill of what she had said. "Birthday drinks." I followed up. I watched her leave, her hips swayed as she walked through the door. She seemed so exotic, and liberal. She had an air about her that was seductive. I think that's why I'd felt ok to ask her. I wasn't sure I'd ever been attracted to a woman before. Jess was beautiful. I'd been attracted to her when I'd met her and Rob, but I hadn't thought about actually having sex with her. I was feeling horny, which could be the reason I'd felt the impulse. Was she just coming for a drink I checked myself, or is this going to go somewhere? She reacted very comfortably and confidently to the situation. If this did lead somewhere, there was no way this would be her first threesome, or her first time with a woman.

When she left, I poured two glasses of Champagne. I needed a drink. I walked out onto the balcony and passed a glass to Paul. "Cheers", I said. "Happy Birthday", as I clinked his glass.

"What do you mean?" He looked bemused. "It's not my birthday for months."

"Well, I've got you a present, so let's pretend it is," I smiled. "It's been a long day, I'm going to have a shower, do you want to join me?"

"Good idea." Paul seemed to forget about the birthday thing as I took his hand and we walked back into the room.

We stripped and walked into the shower together. It was a lovely big area, with a waterfall head that gave enough water for us both to be under it. It was lovely and warm, we spent ages washing each other and kissing. We didn't speak much. After we'd showered, we dried off and I asked Paul to lie face down on the bed. He had a towel around his waist. I started to give him a massage on his back and shoulders. I worked down his back kissing and caressing him all over. I peeled the towel away and continue to massage the backs of his legs and all around his backside. Then I turned him over and kissed him. We spent nearly half an hour, kissing, and touching. After a while I put him into my mouth, gently, for a long time. As he was getting to the point where he's starting to breathe heavily, there was a knock at the door.

Chapter 21 – My First Girl Experience

Paul stayed on the bed. I pulled the towel over him as I got up. I wrapped one of the bath towels around myself and answered the door. The girl had changed out of her work clothes and was wearing jeans and a vest. She had long brown hair and looked very pretty. Her shapely figure accentuated more by her casual clothes than her uniform. She didn't seem phased at all that I was in a towel. It was clear that she knew what she was here for. I was feeling so aroused, as soon as the door closed behind her, I turned towards her and kissed her. If she wasn't interested, then I may as well find out straight away. She accepted my kiss, and immediately used her tongue. The touch of her lips sent an intimate, and passionate feeling flowing through me. She tasted amazing, like she'd had a breath mint before meeting us, to make sure her mouth was fresh and sweet. Paul watched in amazement from the bed. I took her by the hand and brought her over to where he was lying. He sat up and we both sat to join him, on the edge of the bed. I leaned across and kissed him.

"Happy birthday." I reminded him.

As we kissed the towel fell away from me, revealing my breasts. I could feel the Spanish girl looking at me. I glanced round at her. She had her eyes fixed on my body. I took her hand and pulled her towards me. I kissed her again. We kissed delicately and deliberately. Our tongues touching gently and my lips brushing against hers. She kissed my neck and put her hands on my breasts. She kissed lower down my neck, moving further down my chest until her tongue flicked at my nipple. Paul had moved behind her and he started to pull her top up over her head. She didn't mind at all. She helped him remove her vest, whilst she still focused on playing with my tits.

She wasn't wearing a bra. Her tits fell from the material of her top as it rode up over them and bounced a little as they fell back into place. They weren't as big as mine, which I secretly quite liked. I didn't want to feel second best in a fantasy of my own making. Paul was still behind her, and he put his hands on her tits for a moment as I lay back onto the bed and opened my legs. Without hesitation the girl leant forward and kissed my stomach. She quickly moved down between my thighs. She licked and sucked as expertly as you'd imagine from someone who knew exactly how it felt. Within seconds I was in complete ecstasy. As she played with me using her mouth, she started to use her fingers as well. Paul was taking her jeans off. She helped again, by altering the angle of her legs so that he could slide them over her hips. I looked across at her almost naked body, covered only by the scant material of a black G-string. Her bum cheeks exposed to Paul. The atmosphere was electric, and the scene in front of me was so intensely erotic. In no time at all I had the most powerful orgasm of my life, shuddering through me for what seemed like minutes. I was taken aback by how it felt. It was like it was the first time I'd ever had one.

As I stopped shaking, she rolled onto her back to finish removing her jeans over her feet. I climbed on top of her into a sixty-nine position. I wasn't ready for Paul to be involved yet. He was sat on the edge of the bed, watching us intently. She started to lick me again, and I pulled her panties to one side and began to go down on her. I hadn't had a girl in my mouth before. It was a strange sensation, but one that I enjoyed. It was odd trying to mimic what I liked having done to myself. It felt almost abstract, especially as it was happening upside down. Her expert oral sex brought be back to reality. I shuddered at the pleasure of her touch. I moaned as she heightened the intensity of her play. She began rolling my clitoris around on her tongue, sucking and using her lips to pleasure me. I already started to feel the stirrings of pleasure building in me. I would definitely cum again, given time. Paul moved around to the other end of the bed and kneeled behind me. He pushed himself into me whilst I writhed on top of the girl, and I let out a stifled scream of pleasure. She continued to lick me whilst Paul started to fuck me, above her face, faster and faster, harder, and harder. I forget about pleasuring her, as the intensity of my feelings became too much. I lay with my head on her thighs as Paul fucked me. She sucked at my clit, and I came again, somehow even bigger than the previous record. It lasted longer, with huge intensity. I almost wept as I shivered and relaxed onto her body.

Exhausted, I climbed off her, sliding off Paul's cock as I did. I turned around and took Paul in my mouth. I sensed that he was about to cum. I sat up and leant back with my tongue out and wanked him so that he came over me. The girl had sat up next to me and started to play with the cum covering my tits. She leant forward and licked the last of the cum from the end of Paul's cock and turned to kiss me. I couldn't taste any cum, only the sweetness of her mouth, mixed with the taste of myself. I lay back down on the bed, and she licked my stomach and breasts. I realised she hadn't been satisfied.

"Sit back and watch for a moment." I told Paul. I wanted to return the favour for the girl. I hadn't been able to concentrate on her before, when I was in her mouth as well. I wanted to focus on her. I wanted to see if I could make her cum. I started to lick her again. Never taking my tongue off her, circling round her clitoris, then softly sucking at it. Rolling it between my lips. I concentrated on her sounds and movements. Listening to her groans and gasps, trying to work out what she liked. I felt some movement on the bed and glanced up from between her legs. I carried on pleasuring her as I watched her pull Paul closer to her. She moved her head to the side and put his cock in her mouth. With her arm around his waist, she started to move up and down him, becoming excited as she did so. It wasn't strange to see him being sucked by another girl. It seemed completely natural, like we were all enjoying the moment together. I could feel her grind herself into me, as her body started to contort and tense up. She pulled my head into her, I forgot about Paul for a moment and focused on bringing her to climax.

I felt her cum. She writhed from side to side as her clitoris was pushed into my mouth. She spasmed as she orgasmed, her legs moving around as her body danced on my face. As I felt her relax, and I started to slow my movements. I looked up to see her, still taking Paul into her mouth. He had begun to thrust as his urgency increased. She was concentrated on his cock, but she reached out and pulled my head towards her to get me to continue. I was surprised, but I started to increase the speed of my stimulation again. Sucking as I had been before, engulfing her clit in my lips. It only took a few moments, and her movements began to increase again. I heard Paul moan and looked up from between her legs. He was thrusting quite hard into her face now, as she managed to take almost the full length of his cock in her mouth. It was impressive to watch. She became more frantic as she could sense Paul was going to cum. I watched him tense and orgasm, and she started to cum again at the same time. As if his orgasm had turned her on. The writhing was the same as before, but not for as long. I was able to watch as Paul emptied himself into her mouth, gasping in pleasure as he did so.

As she relaxed this time, she didn't complain when my sucking stopped. I gently licked her, until the last remnants of her second orgasm had left her body. I didn't know how she'd been able to do it. I didn't know it was possible to cum so quickly twice in a row. I carried on watching as she swallowed what was in her mouth. She still had Paul's cock between her lips, engulfing him. He looked down at her and fondled one of her breasts as she drained every last drop of cum from him. I sat up as she let Paul's cock slip from her mouth. She lay back on the bed and put her hands over her face, panting and smiling. I felt a glow of pride that I'd made her feel like that. It was my first time with a woman, and she'd cum twice. Not a bad start I thought.

I had expected the moments after sex like this to be awkward, but they weren't. She sat up and smiled at me, her boobs looked lovely as they fell into place beneath her. I instinctively reached out and touched them. She put her hand on my arm, as if to urge me to continue, which I did for a moment. Paul stood up and went into the bathroom, and as he did so the girl got up and started to get dressed. I realised I didn't know her name.

"What's your name?" I asked, as I lay on the bed.

"It doesn't matter." She grinned at me.

"I suppose not." I agreed. "It would be nice to know it though, in case we see you around the hotel."

"It's Pillar." She nodded. "Perhaps I will visit you again?" She was confident and sexual. She had such an ease about her. That's why it wasn't awkward at all.

"We're here until Monday, you're always welcome." I smiled at her again. She pulled her top back over her, and I watched as her boobs pressed into place by the fabric as it slipped onto her. She blew me a kiss as she went to the door, looking both ways before leaving and pulling it closed behind her.

"Has she gone?" Paul asked as he came back into the room.

"A minute ago. How did you enjoy your birthday present?"

"Fucking amazing," he exclaimed as he dropped onto the bed beside me. "You looked like you enjoyed my birthday present more." He looked across at me.

"I did. I've never been with a woman before. It was fun. Did you want to fuck her?" I wanted to know.

"I thought about it," admitted Paul, "but we don't have any condoms here." I liked his answer, and his honesty.

"We can get some, in case she comes back." I suggested.

"What, today?" Paul asked. "I don't think I've got another fuck in me!"

"No, not today," I laughed, "but maybe before we go home."

"Did you get her number then?" Paul was laid out on the bed, looking relaxed.

"No, but she knows where we live. She's very sexual, I'd be surprised if she doesn't come back. She's definitely into men more than women. She loved taking you in her mouth."

"She was good at it," agreed Paul.

"Better than me?" I asked, with a mock defensive tone.

"Absolutely not my love," he rolled closer to me and smiled, "you have become the queen of blowjobs."

"I've been practicing quite a lot," I bragged. "I'll get good at a lot of things if I keep this up." I paused for a second. "We could do this more you know. It wouldn't have to cost us anything. Paul looked confused.

"There are people from all over the world with profiles on dating apps and porn web sites. I'm sure that people would chip in for travel costs, if I wanted to go abroad and make some sexy films." I looked over at him.

"I suppose so. It's no different from paying for a hotel room," he mused.

"Exactly. I've been thinking about it quite a bit. We could even rent a villa somewhere hot and ask people we know to come and visit for a day. To be in a sex scene. I'm sure blokes from the UK would do it and pay towards the costs. Imagine if me and Pillar were both on offer!"

"Who's Pillar?" Paul looked puzzled.

"That's the name of the girl we had sex with a few minutes ago," I laughed again at Paul's bewilderment. "People would pay for a threesome like that. That could be a way to get paid for sex, like on the fantasy list."

"Would you like that?" Paul asked.

"I would. Not necessarily with her, but with a beautiful girl, driving a man, or men wild would-be great fun. Being paid to fulfil a fantasy would be a turn on. I'd prefer it if it was only me. Knowing that my body was so desirable that someone would pay me to let them touch it."

"You'd get lots of offers for that. You're gorgeous." Paul stated. "I'm not sure you'd want to be with the guys who would be willing to pay you though."

"You may be right, although I could take offense."

"I didn't mean that, and you know it."

I smiled at him. "An older guy might be an option. Someone in good shape, board of being married for twenty years, happy to pay a younger woman for a change of scenery."

"Would that be a turn on?"

"It would. He'd have to be attractive," I stipulated.

"What else on the list are you thinking of experimenting with?" Paul let the conversation evolve.

"I loved having two guys in front of me," I said, thinking back to a couple of days ago. "I'd like to have sex with two men. Not those two, but two who I know would do a good job. I like the idea of having a cock in my mouth whilst having sex. Would you like to be either of those?" I turned to Paul.

"No. Not at all." His reply was blunt.

"How come? Wouldn't you be ok with that?"

"It would be fine, as long as I wasn't one of them." He must have noticed the confusion on my face. "I don't want to be the same as any guy who is used for sex. I want our relationship to be different. I don't mind seeing it on video, it's a real turn on, and I would even be ok with watching it happen or filming it myself. I just don't want to be the same as the other guys. Me and you can have more intimate sex. The kind of sex that only we can have."

"Did you think of me the same as Pillar?" I enquired. I wanted to see if the logic applied the other way around.

"No, not at all. I was more turned on watching you become a bi-sexual mega porn star than anything else. The other girl was like a prop for us."

"But another guy wouldn't be a prop?" I checked.

"I know it might sound odd, but it's how I feel. We don't have to have sex with other girls if you feel the same." He made the very reasonable point.

"No, I'm happy for you to be with me when I use another girl as a prop." I grinned at him. "It's good to find out what you like and don't like. It's definitely helping me understand you more. I like it. Let's make sure we get some condoms in case she comes back tomorrow."

"I'm enjoying it too," he nodded. "It's like you're a different person, sexually I mean. It's erotic."

"It's not just sex," I agreed. "The confidence seems to transfer into other areas of my life. I am quite liberated."

"Long may it continue." Paul said as he took me in his arms.

We fell into a doze, which became a sleep. We woke a couple of times, to pull the covers onto us, or get some water. Apart from that we slept soundly, right through until the morning.

Chapter 22 – Sex on A Yacht

When we woke, we showered and dressed, and then walked down onto the seafront. I was wearing a short white dress and sandals and felt I good. The sun and sex seemed to be very good for me. My confidence was sky high. Particularly when remembering how my second interview at the events company had gone. I was smiling a lot, happy to be arm in arm with Paul, on holiday. We passed yachts and boats of all descriptions in the harbour as we strolled along the front. We stopped and had breakfast in a modern looking place. It looked more like a restaurant than a café but was serving fantastic food. We sat outside, for what ended up being a couple of hours, enjoying the food, and several coffees. It felt so good to be abroad, not a care in the world. Holidays automatically give people that feeling. It's strange to only be able to relax and unwind when we've named time as a holiday. Why couldn't this happen during down time at home?

As we gazed out over the sea, I suggested to Paul that we hire a boat for the day.

"Neither of us know how to sail!" Paul attempted to spoil the idea. I don't think he was in the mood for expending much energy. He was relaxing for the first time in a while. I wasn't going to be deterred that easily

"We'll get someone to sail for us, we can relax." I pushed.

"That sounds very expensive." Paul had his eyes closed behind his sunglasses as he talked to me, leaning back in his chair, absorbing the sun.

"If I can get us a trip for free, should we go?" I asked. This was a chance to show Paul some of my newfound confidence. I had told him about the events evening, but I don't think he understood how much I'd put into it. How much braver I had become. He looked at me quizzically for a few seconds, as if wondering whether to ask how I would manage it. Instead, he nodded and went to pay the bill at the bar. Once it was settled, we walked back out onto the front.

All the buildings along the harbour were either restaurants, hotels, or estate agents. Every now and then this pattern was broken by a little boutique. They were selling the usual holiday memorabilia and bric-a-brac. One of these shops had a sign up outside advertising boats for hire. I broke from our saunter and walked into the shop. The boat hire was located at the back of the room, a desk surrounded by postcards and maps. I walked through and approached a middle-aged man. He was sat at the desk, tapping numbers into a calculator.

"Can we hire a boat for the day?" I ask with a smile.

"Do you have sailing qualifications?" He asked, without looking up from his numbers.

"We need the boat for a photo shoot," I continued, ignoring his question. "I have got to supply pictures to my agent by tomorrow, and I thought a boat would be a good location. My photographer will come with me, but I will need someone to sail the boat for us."

"We don't have anyone available," he replied. He was quite sullen, but not rude.

"It's a topless shoot!" I volunteered with a slight smile on my lips.

He didn't say anything. He was still looking down at his calculator and didn't seem interested. I turned to leave. "Perhaps I'm not as attractive as I thought," I pondered as I walked away. My new super confidence having taken a bit of a hit. I moved towards Paul, who was near the door looking at fridge magnets. Before I got back to the main area of the shop, the man called to me.

"I'll take you," he offered. Finally looking up and engaging me as I turned back towards him.

"Free of charge?" I tried my luck. My confidence had returned, as if nothing had ever happened.

He looked at my body, running his eyes up and down me. I could tell that he had started to focus on the opportunity to see me naked. I supposed he didn't have a very interesting life. I bet this was the most unusual thing to happen to him in a long time.

Judging by his demeanour, I don't think sex was a big part of his life either. He put down the calculator and closed the till that was next to him on the counter. He sat back.

"Half price," he offered. I knew I had him now. The more he managed to catch up with the situation, the more he realized that this was a chance he wasn't going to pass up. I leant forward and put my hands on the desk in front of him. My dress was open enough at the neck to show my cleavage, as the material moved away from my body. It was obvious that I wasn't wearing a bra, as my tits fell forward, pushing their way to the opening in the gap of my buttons.

"I'll find someone who'd like to help me, I'm sure. Don't worry." I seized the upper hand and turned to leave.

"Give me a second, I'll need to close up." He relented. "Wait outside and I'll be with you in two minutes."

I grabbed Paul and moved onto the decking outside. As we stood in front of the boats, I handed Paul the camera from my bag. "You're the photographer." I smiled.

"What?" Asked Paul, bewildered again. "I Don't know anything about photography!"

"I suspect my dress and cleavage are closer to the front of the guy's mind than whether you're a real photographer." I suggested. "It's a topless shoot, on his boat." I gave Paul a grin as the guy walked out of the shop. He was carrying a small rucksack and had put on sunglasses.

"Follow me," he requested. He still carried his surly attitude, but never impolite. Maybe that was just how he was, I thought to myself. We walked down a jetty, passing all kinds of boats, and came to a stop next to a beautiful white cruiser. It had blue lines and graphics on its pristine, sharp, projecting hull. It had darkened windows in the cabin towards the back of the boat, below where the controls were situated. There were a set of drop-down stairs that the man had pulled down from the side.

"What's your name?" I asked as I passed him at the bottom of the steps.

"Steve" the man replied. Is no one living in Spain actually Spanish, I pondered.

He followed me up the steps, catching a glimpse of my bum cheeks beneath my short dress. I was starting to feel excited already. Once we were on the deck, I set about exploring. Steve went over to the controls and started to turn the engine on and preparing to set off. I went inside, down the few steps into the main room of the boat. It had a beautiful interior. Small, not much more than two sofas running at right angles. There was a door, which I opened leading into a much bigger bedroom. There was a double bed, and a shower enclosure. I looked back at Paul, who had followed me, and smiled.

I went back up the stairs and shouted to Steve, to be heard above the noise of the engine.

"We're going to get started down here, can you let us know when we are out at sea, and on our own? I want some pictures on the deck as well." Steve nodded. He had the same uninterested expression under his sunglasses that he'd had since I'd first spoken to him.

I went back down and kissed Paul with passion as I entered the cabin. He grabbed my backside under my dress, as I started to undo his jeans. As I dropped to my knees. I pulled my dress over my head and my tits fell free. I could feel Paul's eyes on me. I knelt, wearing only my panties, and pulled his cock from his underpants. I immediately took him into my mouth. I felt a sense of urgency that I hadn't felt for a while. For a couple of minutes, I softly sucked him, using my lips and tongue to stimulate him. After a short time, I stood back up again and smiled. I put his cock back into his underpants. "Let's take some photo's".

Paul picked up the camera as I sat on one of the bench sofas and leaned forward. My elbows on my knees and my hands together in front of me. My tits fell forward underneath me. Paul took several pictures and brought the camera over to me to show me some of the shots. My slender limbs seemed to form elegant angles. Graceful, curved, and smooth. I was pleased. All my work in the gym recently had left me in good shape. Paul then took a picture of me looking straight at the camera, my face serious and seductive. I watched him concentrate as he switched the camera to black and white mode. He then took virtually the same picture again. He leant forward and showed me the camera screen once more. It was an amazing image. I couldn't believe it was me. It had a surreal, old-fashioned look to it. My hair was tussled. I looked seductive. I'd never seen an image of me like that before. I'd never felt like that before. The black and white made me look like a movie star from the nineteen fifties. Sat in a naked pose that all my adoring fans could only ever dream of seeing me enact. Paul took more pictures as I lay back and stretched my arms above my head and behind me. I looked away from the camera and arched my back, trying to get the whole of my body forming one curve. I stood up and walked over to my bag. From it I pulled a white bikini that I'd packed in the morning in case we'd found a nice beach. I put the top on and tied it behind me. Paul constantly took pictures as I was dressing myself and adjusting the straps on my bikini. I then turned away from him and started to slide my panties off my hips with my thumbs. I looked back at the camera as I exposed myself. As the elastic was halfway down my cheeks I bent over further and arched my back again. From my new position I pulled at my panties until they eventually slid down below my bum and fell to the floor. I bent over a little further and moaned as my nakedness was captured by the camera. I felt so amazing. I looked back at Paul.

"Lick me." I demanded.

He put the camera down and moved towards me. I didn't move as he fell to his knees and began to softly lick and kiss my thighs and cheeks from behind. He moved to between my legs, and I gasped. I reached round and grabbed the back of his head with one hand and pulled his face into me. I bent forward with my other hand steadying me on the sofa. His tongue explored every part of me as I began to writhe, more and more. After several minutes of pleasure, I couldn't hold back any longer. An orgasm hit me like lightening firing through my whole body. I held myself up whilst Paul satisfied me until every moment of pleasure had been extracted. I fell forward onto the sofa. I looked back at Paul and smiled.

"I'm feeling horny and dirty," I whispered, breathless from my orgasm, "let's go upstairs."

I stood up and pulled my bikini bottoms back into place. They were tiny, covering my smooth pussy, but hiding nothing of the curves of my bum. I was on show, and I tingled with excitement at the thought. I moved towards the stairs. Paul grabbed the camera and followed. As we emerged into the sunshine the shore was a long way behind us. The blue sea seemed to stretch out forever ahead. I asked Steve to slow down so that we could take some pictures. He nodded and pulled back on the engines. I took a black pair of sunglasses from my bag, put them on, and walked around to the front of the boat. I sat on the hull and leant back against the metal rail that surrounded us. Paul knelt and took a picture of me in the brilliant sunshine. I smiled and enjoyed the light wind dancing over my skin. As the camera continued to click, I got to my feet, and rolled up onto my tip toes. I swung my legs around, exposing my bum to the camera. Only a thin strip of bikini at the top. I let a few seconds pass so that Paul could capture the view. Then I dropped down onto all fours. I looked out to sea as more pictures are taken of me from behind. I reached back with one hand and pulled down one side of my bikini bottoms. The excitement of the situation was making me short of breath. I was lost in the moment. It felt wonderful. I looked back over my shoulder at the camera. I swapped my hands and pulled down the other side of my bikini, so that the material was halfway down the curves of my cheeks. I couldn't hold back any longer. I gave up trying to seduce the camera and reached back to pull the material completely away. The bikini fell down my thighs, exposing my nakedness to the breeze. I was flooded with thrills at the exposed and raunchy nature of my pose. I dropped my head, breathing heavily as the excitement ran through my body. I could feel the camera on me, and Paul's eyes. I knew that Steve would be watching from further back. The outdoors seemed to add to the feeling of exposure, and it was turning me on, so much. I stood up after a minute or two and put my hands on my hips, still looking out to sea. I wanted to try for that movie star look again, silhouetted against the blue sky.

Once I felt we'd put on enough of a pretend photo shoot, I turned and headed back towards the middle of the boat. I knew that Steve would be watching us, and I wanted him to believe our story. I was enjoying the attention of a stranger's eyes. It was a new experience for me to be watched in this way. I was enjoying the sensation. I arrived in front of the raised section of the boat and sat down. My legs together and my knees raised. I smiled at Paul, who had moved back along the boat with me, and then dropped my legs apart. I leant back on one arm and begin to touch myself. The show only lasted for a few moments, but I was as horny as it's possible to be. I stopped touching myself for a moment. I pulled my tits out of my bikini top, leaving the material tied underneath my boobs. I went back to playing with myself. I was breathless and impatient to be naked. I reached around to remove the bikini completely, and the tie at the back of my neck came undone immediately. I was wearing nothing but my sunglasses. I stood up and wandered around the outside of the raised section, to the back of the boat. I stopped beside the control deck.

"I want some action shots," I said to Steve. "Can you take some photos?"

Steve pulled back completely on the engines and the boat came to a drifting quiet state.

"Yeah," he replied. A man of few words, or expressions. It was as if I'd asked him to pass the salt, not take some pictures of me having sex.

I walked out onto the rear deck and took the camera from Paul's hands. I passed it to Steve as he approached and started to direct what I wanted.

"First of all, I want you going down on me, on this seat right here". I beckon Paul over to me. "Take pictures from next to the cabin so that the photo's look out to sea." I ordered Steve.

I sat down and leant back on the rail of the boat and spread my legs. Still wearing my glasses, my hair drifting over my back, ruffled by the wind. I brought one leg up onto the seat and waited. Paul came over and removed his t-shirt before getting onto his knees in front of me. He started to lick me. He had learned exactly what I liked over the years, and it felt wonderful. I moaned and threw my head back, the sea breeze tugging at my hair. The wind was cool enough that I felt it on my naked body, causing tingling excitement, but it wasn't cold. It was cool enough to highlight my nakedness. I looked back at the camera, which was taking constant pictures. I started to build to another climax. Paul moved his tongue across my clitoris, sucking and flicking at me, as I writhed in ecstasy. I felt the excitement of the outdoors, and the thrill of the exhibition that I was putting on for the surly boat captain. It was so much that the orgasm crept up on me sooner than I expected. The usual build-up of sensations happened much faster than normal. I threw my head back and revelled in my second orgasm of the trip. I wanted to learn to do what the girl managed last night. As my body relaxed, I told Paul to fuck me. He pulled down his shorts as he kneeled in front of me. I was so wet that he slid straight inside me, with one gentle push. I gasped as I watched his cock disappear into me. It wasn't the most comfortable position, on the edge of the bench. I pushed him back away from me whilst I turned around. I looked back over my shoulder and watched him while he started to fuck me from behind. My arse cheeks were in his hands as he used them to pull me onto his cock. My tits rocking beneath me. After a while I sensed his excitement start to increase, so I pulled forward.

"I don't want you to cum yet," I said, "I want one picture of me doing anal." I rolled onto my side and pulled my knees towards me. "Careful", I pleaded, "I only want a picture; I don't want you to fuck me." I had never done this before, or even thought about it much, but I was so turned on. For some reason I wanted to try it.

Paul's cock was wet from sex, and very hard. He pushed against me without saying a word. After a few seconds, his cock began to slide into me. It went in more easily than I expected. It wasn't exactly painful, a strange experience. I had thought that it might not fit. I gasped as he edged further and further inside me. I beckoned Steve to move a bit closer and I ordered him to take the photo. It felt like Paul's cock was about halfway into me. "Push it in further", I moaned. I want a picture of you right inside me." Paul kept pushing, it was more painful now, and he moved deeper into me in slow movements. I looked back as he stopped pushing, relieved that it had stopped, and I relaxed. I still had my glasses on. They helped me feel distant from the experience, almost like I was someone else. I started to touch myself. "Stay there", I ordered. I begin to writhe around as I pushed my fingers into myself, giving the most intense feeling as my hips moved. I was still clamped to Paul's cock. I started to moan with pleasure, photo's clicking all the time. As I moved, I could feel Paul getting close to coming again. I pulled away from him. It was a nice feeling as he withdrew from me. I turned around and sat up so that my tits were in front of Paul. He was wanking and immediately begin to cum over me. I continued to play with myself as the cum ran down my chest.

"How do I look?" I asked.

"Incredible" Paul gasped as he relaxed.

"You look outrageous," added Steve. It was by far the most expressive he'd been since we'd met, and an odd turn of phrase, I thought.

"Do you think our camera man has earned a handjob?" I asked Paul, beckoning Steve towards me. Paul nodded and took the camera from Steve as he moved over in front of where I was sat.

Steve took his cock from his beach shorts, and I reached forward and started to wank him. My cum covered tit's bobbed up and down with each stroke of his cock. He was bigger than I expected. He had a nice cock for a man of his age. I looked up at him and smiled. He wasn't going to last long. I was becoming an expert in giving handjobs, and in a matter of only a few minutes he orgasmed. I wasn't prepared for it, but I instinctively moved forward until more cum was clinging to my tits.

"How was that?" I smiled. Steve didn't say anything. He looked a little embarrassed as he pulled his shorts back up. The reality of the situation hitting him after his sexual desires had been fulfilled. He moved back to the controls area, and immediately started the engines up.

Paul took several more pictures of me sat down before I got to my feet and put my hands on my hips. He took more pictures of me stood up. I felt very satisfied. I took his hand and led him back towards the stairs. He continued to photograph me whilst I was in the shower, and then more when I dried myself and got dressed. When I was ready, I picked up my bag and took Paul's hand to go back up on deck. We looked out over the rail as we moved back towards land. "I'm feeling so horny at the moment, let's make the most of our trip." I suggested. Paul smiled and nodded in agreement.

Chapter 23 – I'm A Hotwife!

We walked back along the seafront towards our hotel. We had decided to relax for the afternoon, before going out for dinner later. Once we were back in the room, we looked through the photos from the boat. They were the best ones yet. The blue sky and the sunshine created a perfect backdrop for the pictures. We both agreed that more sexy trips to sunny destinations was a good idea. We went out onto the balcony to sit in the sun and make some plans together. Paul used his laptop to crop some of the best pictures, taking my face out of the shots. He then he sent them over to my Sophie Martinez e-mail account, which I accessed from my phone. I looked through them again and shivered with excitement. I liked the anonymity of the new images. I uploaded them to my account on the porn site, calling the series "going on a sexy boat trip."

I asked Paul to find some porn clips that he liked whilst I went through my swinger app. I accepted and declined the friendship invitations I'd received over the last couple of days. Once I'd been through them, I looked at my list of friends and found an attractive guy who took my fancy.

"Have you found any clips you like yet?" I asked Paul.

"I like this one." He turned his laptop to face me. It was an attractive girl, with a lovely body, curvy, almost perfect. She was in the shower, the camera watching her from outside. I leant forward and skipped on a couple of minutes. She had got out of the shower and was drying herself off. It was very seductive to watch. The camera then followed her into the bedroom where a man was waiting for her. They had sex on the bed in several positions, the camera focussed on her throughout. The shots weren't close ups of her, but she was always centre of the picture. Her boobs and curves displayed beautifully as they had sex.

"I like that. Would you like me to make it for you?" I looked up at him to gauge his reaction.

"Seeing you in that movie would be amazing." Paul seemed to be completely comfortable with our new adventures. I could tell by how relaxed he was that he was being honest. I also knew that he enjoyed seeing me as the object of desire and sexuality. Our sex life over the past couple of weeks was evidence that we were both enjoying ourselves.

"Ok, I've found a guy that I could do that with. What do you think?" I turned my laptop to Paul to show the profile of my friend on swinger app. There were a couple of photos that someone had taken of him that weren't very good. The quality was poor, so you couldn't see much. He had quite a few photos taken in the mirror, showing off his body. There were a few words describing what he wanted. He was looking for no string's fun.

"If you fancy him then go for it." Paul agreed. "He doesn't look like he's into anything weird."

I messaged him and sent a link of the porn clip that Paul had showed me. I asked what he thought we'd look like if we made it together. I messaged about ten other guys, and three couples over the next hour or so. Paul found a couple more clips that he liked, and I used them to gauge people's interest in meeting up.

"Is there anything else you want to do?" I asked Paul. "I'm going to have fun making some more porn for us, but is there anything else you would like to try?" I wanted to keep communicating with him as much as possible. I also wanted to continue to explore my newfound sexual freedom. Making sure that Paul was satisfied and happy would allow me to do that.

"The other day with the woman was fun. We could do that again if you'd like?" Paul looked over from his laptop. "It would be fun to see what else there is to try. Have you had any ideas?"

"There is one couple I've met," I said. "It was whilst you were away last week."

"What are they looking for?" Paul asked.

"A bisexual female. I'm guessing that the wife is having a lot of sex, and she's hoping to bring a good-looking girl home as a treat for her husband."

"Do you like the idea of that?" Paul turned away from the laptop to focus on our conversation.

"I do. I'd rather do it with you, but if I have the opportunity to meet some new people, and experience new things with them. It would be good. The sex would be fun, they're very beautiful. I'll see if I can get you some pictures and videos. Would you be ok with it?"

"No problem at all, it sounds perfect.".

We looked at some of the comments on my new pictures and went into the bedroom to make love. We never went out for dinner. We ordered snacks and drinks from room service. We stayed in our room, talking, and occasionally having sex until we fell asleep.

The next day I woke up at about nine. I left Paul in bed and went out onto the balcony to see what the weather was like. The sky was clear and blue, and the sun was only minutes away from filling the day with warmth. I checked my phone and found that I had a message from the CEO of Zeno. It took me a couple of seconds to place him with the printing company I'd met at the events management trial. He had emailed to offer me a job in a marketing role for Zeno systems. The message was only brief. He asked me to contact his colleague, who was copied in, if I was interested. I was surprised by the message, but not as excited as I would have expected to be. They hadn't been a group of people I had imagined myself working with. It didn't seem as dynamic or fun as the Brightstar team. I decided not to reply straight away, and to give myself time to think about it. The salary they were offering was more than double what I earned at the gym. The money was amazing, but I wanted to make sure my next steps led in the right direction. I didn't want to waste time with any false starts.

Paul had woken up and joined me on the balcony. I showed him the e-mail, and he congratulated me with gusto. It was a chance for him to see that the new confident me was making progress outside of my sex life. After chatting through the opportunity, we dressed and went downstairs for breakfast. Whilst we ate, I looked around the room at the other people staying in the hotel. There weren't many guests there, it was only a third full, at best. There were a few older couples, a group who looked like a large family, and some girls who I assumed were on a hen do.

"What are you looking at?" Paul asked, as he noticed me distracted.

"I was looking to see if there was anyone here who I would want to have sex with," I smiled at him.

He smiled back, in a way that suggested he should have guessed. "Any luck?" He looked around as well.

"None at all," I responded. "There are no attractive people here that I can see.

"It's breakfast time Soph. I don't suppose everyone will be up and about yet. You could see someone at the pool later. Haven't you had enough sex?"

"More than enough," I explained, with a mock tired expression on my face. "It was supposed to be a sexy trip away, and I thought we could do some new stuff. I'm finding that I've been pretty repressed these last few years." I paused for thought for a second. "Probably all my life if I'm honest with myself. Now I'm finding the chance to express myself, I want to enjoy it."

"There's no rush Soph." Paul pointed out.

"I know, but I'm not young anymore, and I want to experience everything. I'm so glad that we've been communicating better. I feel like I will be able to enjoy sex without any feelings of guilt or being a slut. I am so lucky. Those feelings of shame would have stayed with me if I was single and experimenting. The fact that you're ok with me doing it, means I am liberated. It's amazing knowing that I can still have you and have fantasies and fun as well." It had been wonderful that Paul had been present during my first time with a woman. I hadn't expected it. I had planned to gain some experience on my own before I took the risk of involving Paul. That it had happened so naturally, and that we'd both enjoyed it was amazing.

"I understand what you mean. It's a reflection of life generally Soph. Couples who trap each other in any part of their lives become stagnant and resentful. Being a couple means having fun together, but still having other friends. Sex is a logical extension of that. There are so many people who don't allow their partners to have friends. Insecurity and jealousy spoils countless lives."

"How do you manage not to be jealous?" I asked. "I'm not sure I understand."

"I've thought about it quite a bit. Something you said when we first talked made a lot of sense to me. I try and put myself in the other persons shoes. Me wanting to see someone else naked doesn't mean I don't love you. I'll always love you."

"Thank you." I almost felt like I was going to cry. "I feel closer to you than ever. I never thought that sex with other people could possibly make me feel that." I laughed at the absurdity of it.

"Let's go and get our books and have a read by the pool. Perhaps you'll see someone you like the look of." Paul smiled as he got up to leave.

We spent the late morning and the early afternoon beside the pool. I finished an awful romance novel. It got worse and worse. A pathetic woman who wanted a man to sweep her off her feet. He would be brilliant in bed, without any conversation or communication of any kind. I would have enjoyed it more a few months ago, but now I felt like the woman in the story was letting herself down. She didn't need to wait for a man to address her desires and needs. She should have been more in control. Most of these stories are based on a gender stereotype that has been built up over years and years.

I had been surprised by how many people there were engaged on the swinger's app, and the porn sites. It was good to know that the gender stereotypes of the past were being broken down. Now woman, and men, were openly experiencing sexual freedoms. I took a moment to search the web for other evidence that society was progressing in this way. I was shocked to see that most of the results that appeared were on mainstream social media. Facebook was awash with swinging and "lifestyle" groups. Couples looking to meet other couples to push boundaries. To find new avenues of pleasure. Pinterest and Tumblr were full of memes, depicting swinging, cuckolding, and Hotwives. Instagram had thousands of the same topics, presented and discussed in beautiful detail. I Googled each term individually, each time I was amazed by the number of pages dedicated to the topic.

"Everybody is doing it!" I exclaimed, louder than I had expected.

"Sorry?" Paul looked up from his book, a measure of shock in his voice in response to my sudden outburst.

"What we're doing. It's normal."

"You're going to have to back up a couple of steps Soph. I don't know what you're talking about."

I laughed as I realised Paul had joined the conversation in my mind halfway through. "Sorry. I've been looking online, and everyone is having open relationships. There are thousands of people on Instagram, openly discussing it. With pictures of their faces on their profiles. Married couples, young couples, people with children. It's everyone"

Paul gave a nod, as if to show that he'd caught up with me. "I don't think it's everyone, Soph, but it will be a lot of people. The internet has opened up a whole world of choice for people. What was considered unusual in the past, can very quickly become mainstream. The internet has allowed everyone to realise that they're all thinking the same thing. In the past people got their version of normal from three or four television channels."

I felt a surge of power and confidence from my findings. My experiences had been tinged by the thought that I was doing something weird. I had a sudden feeling of empowerment. I was part of the liberated intellectual elite, not a subversive group of outsiders.

"Do they all have solid, loving relationships like ours?" I asked Paul. "With open communication and honesty?" I continued, before he could answer the first part of my question.

"Without doubt." He seemed completely certain. "Jealousy is an emotion that everyone has felt. We all feel it as children. It takes a lot of work and understanding of human nature to think your way beyond it. It's also very brave to have those conversations with a loved one. Their partner may still suffer from jealousy, even if the person raising the subject has progressed beyond it. I suspect all the people you're looking at are very much in love, and very happy." Paul looked back to his book.

I was still shocked. It was quite a lot to process. I had thought that Paul and I were special. That the honesty that we were achieving in our relationship was something hard to attain. A special, or unique bond. It was sobering to realise that many had achieved the same level. Sobering, but very reassuring.

"Are you a cuckold?" I asked as I continued to read about the various types of open relationship that existed.

"No." Paul laughed, almost scoffing at the suggestion.

"Why not?" I hadn't read enough to know what any of the terms meant.

"From what I understand, being a cuckold is about humiliation. I don't want to knock it. I'm sure there are lots of reasons why men desire to be humiliated by their wives, but not me."

"What are we then?" I pushed on. I was surprised he seemed to know so much about this.

"I'm not too worried about what it's called Soph. We're just us. You want to be sexual and fulfil sexual fantasies. I love you, and love seeing you happy, satisfied and fulfilled. That's all that matters. A lot of porn is dedicated to open relationships. From what I have seen the closest thing that describes us would be a hotwife, or Stag and Vixen relationship. I don't know that for sure though, and generic terms are never perfect, are they?"

I Googled the terms and took my time to read a few articles and blog posts. It was fascinating. Paul was right, everything I read about a hotwife relationship described us very well. I read about other forms of open relationship as well. Each one with a slightly different take on the same kind of experience. A lot like the many different forms of monogamous relationships, I pondered. Reading about sex was starting to make me feel frisky again.

I looked around the pool to see who was nearby. There wasn't anybody interesting at all. The pool boy was a boy. There were a few people sunbathing, but all much older than me. I quite liked the idea of an older man, but these guys didn't fit with the image I had in my mind.

We decided to go for a wander into the town to change the scenery. We had a snack and a beer in a bar. It was a beautiful day, but there weren't many people around. We moved further down through the town towards the sea. We sat outside a busier café and ordered another beer.

"It's nice to be in the sun." Paul commented.

"It's lovely." I replied. "I don't think we're going to meet anyone else on our sexy trip, do you?" I was a bit disappointed by how quiet it was.

"Probably not. It's not that kind of a place," Paul observed. "There are places that are more geared up to clubbing and sex. The eighteen thirty type locations, but I don't think they're for us."

"Definitely not," I agreed. "Where do you think is for us?"

"We need to figure out what we want to do a bit more. We were very lucky to meet that girl on the first night here. The boat trip was a great idea, but meeting people by chance won't often work. We could organise things to be exactly what we want. If you meet some people from the website, we could invite people to a holiday destination."

"Like a sex party?" I asked, very intrigued.

"It could be many different things. As long as we had a venue. A house with a pool somewhere nice. We could arrange different things on different days." Paul sipped his beer.

"What sort of things?"

"I'm not sure. We'll have to think about what we want to do. There could be masquerade evenings, swingers' nights, porn shoot days, group sex days. I don't know. You'll find out more about what people would like to do when you meet them."

"Events like that could be way to make a lot of money," I pondered aloud.

"It definitely could, but let's not get ahead of ourselves. We need to get to know some people first and attend some events to see what works and what doesn't. I imagine there's quite a lot to it. Security would be important, and the finances around it would have to be solid. Reputation would count for so much, and we'd have to have enough contacts to make it work."

"You're right," I agreed. "It wouldn't be simple, but it would be great fun. I'll start using the swinger app to get some contacts for us. I'll talk to some of the couples on there and see what other sites they use. I'll also ask what events they go to. I'll send some more messages when we get back to the hotel."

We chatted some more and had another beer in the sunshine. We walked back to the hotel as the evening drew closer and ordered some room service. We spent a couple of hours going through the swinger app. We enjoyed deciding who looked like they would be fun and interesting. I sent ten or twelve messages during the evening. It wasn't quite the trip I'd expected, but it was lovely to spend time together. It was clear that we'd have to put in a bit of effort to things to experience some of the things that I'd like to try. It was going to be fun exploring a new world.

Chapter 24 – Chance Encounter

The next day was our last day in Spain. We lay in bed until quite late, talking about plans for the day, snoozing together, and then having a late breakfast. We made the most of the late morning sunshine relaxing at the pool. I was reading some more awfully written romantic fiction, hoping it would give me some sexy ideas. Paul was reading his phone.

My phone buzzed. It was a welcome distraction from several chapters of the slushy, romantic nonsense. My new book was again focussed on a woman, who was entirely dependent on the whim of a man to find happiness and sexual gratification. It was making me depressed, not sexy. The buzz was an e-mail from Brightstar events. My heart jumped a little at the sight of Dan's name. It was an involuntary reaction, and it didn't last for long. His good looks were obviously impacting my sub conscious more than I had realised. He had contacted me personally, which he had stated he wouldn't do. That had to be a good sign. He thanked me again for my hard work the previous week. He mentioned that I had been picked out for praise specifically by the customer. His e-mail went on to say that he would like to offer me a full-time job. Due to my lack of experience, the role would be as an events coordinator to start with. This would mean that I wouldn't be a full events manager until I gained more project management experience. The role equated to less money. This slight negative element to the message gave a tinge of disappointment to what would otherwise have been euphoric. It was a better option than the Zeno job. It was in exactly the sector that I wanted to work, and it seemed like a good company to gain some experience with. I decided to see what Paul thought.

"I've been offered two jobs now." I said, breezily. Paul looked up from his phone and took his sunglasses off.

"That's amazing," he exclaimed. "When?"

"I got an e-mail. From the company I had the trial with last week."

"That's wonderful news, congratulations." Paul still seemed a bit shocked.

"Why are you shocked?" I questioned him.

"I'm not shocked at all. I'm impressed. You must have done well at the trial event."

"It did go well. The job offer I received yesterday was as a result of that evening. The offer wasn't very well structured. I think they just liked me and wanted to find a way to offer me a role. It didn't feel very formal."

"That's a good thing in a way," Paul mused, "who offered you the job?"

"It was the CEO." I replied.

"That makes sense," Paul nodded. "Small business owners often recognise good people and want them in their team. The exact job role doesn't matter. Remind me what they offered you exactly?"

"It was a marketing role. There wasn't a lot more detail to it than that. It has a starting salary of forty-five thousand, plus a bonus structure. It's a lot more than I make at the gym."

"It sounds like it'll be a customer relationship management role, like an account manager. Responsible for keeping customers and growing the business with them. If he liked the way you interacted, that would be something he could offer you without knowing your qualifications. What was the other offer?"

"That was from the event management company that I did the trial for. It won't be as an events manager. It'll be an events coordinator, until I have more experience."

"You don't sound so happy about that?" Paul noticed.

"I am. I guess I am disappointed that I wasn't good enough to get the role that they were advertising for."

"I wouldn't see it like that," he offered comfort, whilst sounding factual and formal. "You don't have experience, so they're seeing it as an opportunity to save money. They won't take on a manager as well. You'll be doing pretty much the same job."

"They're only offering thirty-seven thousand for the event coordinator role." I informed him.

"How much was the events manager salary?" Paul asked.

"Forty-three, plus bonuses."

"I think I know the answer, but which company would you prefer to work for?" Paul checked.

"Brightstar." I answered without hesitation. "The only thing holding me back is the lower salary and the fact it's not the job I applied for.

"It seems like you're in a good position then. If it was me, I'd let them know you'd been offered another job at forty-five thousand, but you want to work for them. I'd ask them to increase the starting salary to forty thousand for the events coordinator job. Then commit to increasing your salary and change your job title to events manager after a two-year period. During the two years you will gain the experience required. You could agree to complete project management training, which they would pay for. That way, you get a couple of years with less pressure, and do some industry leading training programs, for free. You'll get the manager's job you want in two years, and have a much-improved CV. From what you've told me, the events company is the better option. I wouldn't worry about the salary too much. You'll meet so many different people, from so many companies in a role like that. You won't be short of opportunities in the future."

"That's a brilliant idea," my mood about the situation changed immediately. "Do you think they will agree to that?"

"I would if I was them. They want you. They want people who are keen to improve. They've got the managers salary and the job role signed off anyway. There won't be anything stopping them. I'd be very pleased to have someone show initiative and show willingness to negotiate."

"Ok," I smiled at my newly found opportunity. "I'll e-mail them back now".

It took a little while to write the e-mail. I got Paul to check through it. He made a couple of changes, and then I sent it off. I relaxed back to my book, with a sense of excitement and anticipation that hadn't been there before. I now really wanted the Brightstar job.

In the afternoon we got showered and changed and went down to the beach. We had a couple of cocktails in one of the seafront bars. I was wearing a white, simple dress with a plunging neckline and a split up the left leg. I liked wearing white on holiday. I tanned easily and white seemed to me to be the right colour for the sunshine filled days. We finished our drinks as the late afternoon sun moved lower in the sky. We decided to go for a walk along the top of the cliffs. We were both a bit tipsy after our drinks. The waves crashed onto the rocks as we walked hand in hand along the grassy path that meandered around the coast. We got to a section of the cliff that jutted out into the sea and stood and looked out over the waves at the sinking sun. A feeling that the end of our holiday was approaching was hanging over us both.

A car pulled up into the viewing point car park, a little way back from the edge of the cliff. A couple of lads got out of the car. We continued to look out over the ocean and waited for them to go, so that we could be alone again. The lads came over to the edge of the cliff and looked down to the sea. They were in their early twenties, tanned and athletic looking. They were speaking Spanish and seemed to be talking about something below. They dressed like surfers, perhaps looking for waves, or places to paddle out. Whilst they were talking, I noticed them keep looking over at me, trying to catch a glimpse of my body in my tight dress. I had noticed people being attracted to me these past few weeks. My confidence was allowing me to understand what was happening, rather than not recognising it, as had been the case in the past. In the past I would have thought that people were looking negatively at my clothes, rather than positively at my body. The old me would not have noticed the lads looking at me. I had missed out on so much. It was fun to be desired. I wonder how many women miss out on that. A lot, I imagined. I didn't look back towards them again. I enjoyed the feeling of their eyes on me.

After a few minutes I took Paul's hand and we continued along the cliff top path. As we passed the two lads, I took a deep breath, reached out and grabbed one of them by the hand. I smiled at the other, who was a few yards away at the edge of the cliff and motioned with a movement of my head for him to follow us. Paul looked surprised but didn't say anything. He had allowed me to take the lead in each of the situations that I had engineered on the trip. It was a good feeling to be trusted in that way.

    I led the three of them in silence down away from the high point of the path. We followed a break in the line of the cliff, moving lower as we progressed along it. After a few moments I saw a smaller path that forked off low to the right, doubling back on the main path. It wandered further down towards the sea. I let go of the hand I was holding and set off down the little track. The three men followed me, and as we curved around the cliff, we began to move out of sight of the car park at the top. Whilst I walked, I started to untie the strap of my dress at the back of my neck, taking my time so that everyone behind would see me do it. We came to a wide ledge on the cliff, grass covered, with a view out to sea. It had no view of the cliff top above. I let the top half of your dress fall away, and with one arm I reached across and covered my tits with my forearm and hand. My arm was showing the shape of the lower half of my boobs, but not exposing them. I looked down and made sure my nipples were covered. I turned around and walked back towards Paul. I pulled his head towards me and kissed him. I took his phone out and put it in his hand with a knowing smile. I then turned and walked towards one of the Spanish lads who was staring at me intently. They both looked awestruck, as if something other worldly was happening to them. Neither of them had said a word since I had begun to lead them away from the clifftop. I let go of my tits as I walked towards him and took his hand. I put his it on my chest and I closed my eyes as he began to touch me. After a few moments I pulled his head towards my chest, and he started to lick and suck at one of my nipples. I beckoned over the other lad, and he moved towards me. I thrust my tongue into his mouth and groaned with pleasure. After a few more seconds I backed away from both of them and took a few steps towards the cliff. I sat down on rocky ledge, which made a good seat, and start to pull up my skirt, slowly and deliberately. In a few seconds my legs were exposed, and I was able to move my thighs apart more, having freed them from the dress. I motioned with my hand for the lads to follow me over to where I was sitting. As they got closer, I pulled one of them towards me by the hand, and he dropped to his knees in front of me. He pulled my panties to one side and started to lick me. He was quite good at it for someone who seemed young, perhaps twenty-three I guessed. He gently breathed and licked between my legs for a while, before increasing the intensity. I moaned at the unexpected pleasure and grabbed hold of the other lad. He fell forward to his knees, and I pulled his face to my chest. He began to lick and suck at my tits. I looked over at Paul, who was filming with his phone from a few meters away. I beckoned him closer as I was being pleasured all over. As Paul got closer, I shuddered into an intense orgasm. The young man was actually very good at oral sex. I fumbled at the trousers of the guy who had been playing with my tits, as he stood up to my side. He helped me by pulling his trousers halfway down and I begin to stroke his cock. A couple of minutes passed, with a cock in my hand, as my pussy continued to be being pleasured intensely. I felt dirty, and sexy. After a few more minutes, without warning, I stood up. The lads shuffled back, surprised by my sudden movement. I felt in total control, and I loved it. I moved towards the lad who had been going down on me. I helped him to his feet and kissed him as I started to undo the buttons of his jeans. The lad could hardly control himself as he freed himself into my hands. I pulled the other lad in behind me, and as l bent over, I pushed his head down towards my bum. Let's see if he's as good at oral as his friend, I thought to myself.

    I leant further forward and took the desperate guy in my mouth. His friend pulled my panties halfway down my thighs and began to lick at me from behind. Paul watched as the lad began to lick and kiss and suck at me, slowly moving lower until he is licking deep between my cheeks. I stopped what I was doing and yelped with pleasure as he tongued my most intimate parts, momentarily forgetting about the cock that I had in front of me. As I took him back into my mouth I began to orgasm again. It shook through my whole body. I again ignored the cock that was in front of my face and lost myself in the moments of orgasm. I stifled a scream as I came to a huge climax. It usually takes me a while to orgasm, but as usual, the excitement of my new experiences, made me crash into my second bout of ecstasy within a few minutes. As my body relaxed, I stood up and moved back across the grass bank. I picked up my bag and sat back on the rock that I had been sitting on before. I beckoned the lads forward and motioned for the one on the right to approach me. I took a condom from my bag and gave it to him to put it on. As he did so he took off his jeans from round his ankles and moved to between my legs. I was so wet that he was able to plunge straight into me as he lay down on top of me. I had been desperate to be fucked for the past ten minutes and I had waited, but now I couldn't wait any longer. The lad sensed my desire and fucked me hard. As I was laid back on the rock, my tits bounced forwards and back, as he thrust into me. The other lad had moved next to my face. I moaned as I was fucked harder and harder, the cock moved closer to me, and I took it in my mouth. I recognised that the guy on top of me was getting close to orgasm, so I pushed him back. He pulled out of me. I wanted to make this last, a bit longer. I stood up took another condom from my bag lying next to me on the grass. I bent over from the waist, showing off my legs and bum in the fading sunlight. The lads still couldn't take their eyes off me, and I turned around with the second condom. I give Paul and the recording phone a knowing smile as I walked back across the bank. I was going to put on a quite a show. I would hopefully get the fucking of my life whilst doing it.

    I fell to my knees and started to caress and lick the balls of lad who didn't have a condom yet. His eyes were on stalks as he watched me run my tongue up and down his shaft, looking up at him as I did it. His friend was stood to my right. I glanced over at him. He was watching me intently. I carried on licking and flicking at the balls in front of me with my tongue as I took the condom from its wrapper. I began to roll it down over his cock, being careful and delicate with my fingers. All the time licking and kissing his balls. I was getting better at putting condoms on, but still I took my time. After he was protected, I stood up and put my foot up on the rock to the side of him. I smiled as he faced me. He moved forward, grabbed my tits, and penetrated me hard. I put my arms around his shoulders as he fucked me, stood together in an erotic embrace. I looked around momentarily to make sure the other lad was still wearing his condom. I turned back to the guy who was fucking me. My tits bounced and brushed against his chest as he kept on driving into me. I had wrapped my non standing leg around him and was pulling him into me, still with my arms around his neck. He began to lift me as he fucked me harder and harder. He was very athletic. I could feel the strength in his movements. I lifted my standing leg off the floor and wrapped it around his waist. I was bouncing up and down on his cock, suspended around his waist. After a short time, I became aware of the second guy standing behind me. I felt his hands on my cheeks and I his breath on my neck as he started to wank his condom covered cock next to my bum. It was his turn again.

    I lowered my legs and dropped to the floor, kissing the lad who had held me up for so long. I put my hands on the rock to my right and bent over and ready for more penetration. The second lad came closer and pushed himself into me. I rocked back against him, slowly at first, in rhythm with his thrusts. There was little movement needed now as the sex was so overwhelming that I struggling to catch my breath. I looked over to see Paul, still using his phone to capture us. I imagined the view from the lens. The setting sun in the background, my naked body and my two athletic lovers tending to my desires. I orgasmed for a third time, thrilled by my thoughts. A huge pulsating joy throughout my entire body. The illicit pleasure of being taken by two men in turn heightening the sensation to a level that I didn't think was possible. As my body shook and quivered, I slid forward, off the cock that had pleasured me, and moved onto the grass. I lay down on my side, and presented myself, inviting the lad who had not had much time to fuck me to be inside me again. I was almost spent and wanted everyone to climax right now. As the guy lay down and moved in beside me, he pushed his cock back into me from behind. I beckoned the other lad to kneel in front of me, and I pulled the condom off his cock and started to wank him close to my chest. In no time at all he exploded all over me. I loved seeing the cum splash onto my tits. I licked at the tip of his cock as his ejaculation finished. He pulled away and sat down. I looked back at the remaining lad who was now driving harder and harder into me. I watched him and started to feel like there was a chance that I could orgasm again, but the sight of me with cum splashed all over my chest was too much for him. I pulled away from him rolling over and into a sitting position. He pulled the condom from himself as he rose to his knees and instantly burst all over my tits. There was more of it than there was from his friend. I leant back on my elbows, illuminated in the last of the light. Streams of cum ran down over my chest and onto my stomach. My dress around my middle was grass stained and covered in cum. This was exactly what I wanted. Exactly what I'd seen porn stars look like on the internet. I knew that I could be that sexy. I had wanted to drive men wild for so long and get what I wanted from sexual encounters. It felt amazing. My legs fell apart as I relaxed, completely satisfied. The lads had pulled up their trousers and were leaving, still without saying a word. They looked back at me as they walked away, naked and cum soaked. I smiled at them as I watched them go. I asked Paul to come closer. I didn't want to move. I promised him that I'd fuck him as soon as we get back to the hotel and shower, but right now I wanted him to cum. He had been left out, and he must have been driven wild taking the video of me with two men. I sat up on my arms and pushed my tits so that they were jutting forward towards him. He moved over me and wanked as I watched. He came in no time, floods of seamen rushing onto my face. I didn't flinch, I held out my tongue and moaned as he orgasmed. I stayed still, enjoying the moment. Paul sat down on the grass and then collapsed onto his back. I laughed out loud.

"Quick, I want a picture," I remembered. I didn't ever want to forget this moment. I wanted to see what I looked like. Paul jumped up and picked up his phone. He moved in front of me and took a few shots of me sitting down. Then I stood up and posed for the camera, holing my tits, and showing off me cum covered body. After he'd taken a few pictures, I got a tissue from my bag. I cleaned some of the cum from my face, but there was too much of it for one tissue, and I didn't have a second. I pulled up the dress and tied it behind my neck, the hotel wasn't far away, I would get a shower as soon as we got back. I had a quick look at the photos on Pauls' phone. My hair was dishevelled, I looked sexy and dirty and erotic. I had never felt more desired and sexual. Paul took my hand and we walked back up the cliff and along the front towards the hotel. I was soaked in cum, which thrilled me. The sex I had experienced still clinging to my tits and body.

"Did you enjoy that?" I asked him.

"That was amazing. Even more fun than being with the woman in many ways?"

"How come?" I pushed for more detail.

"Seeing you with that level of sexuality was breath taking. Your power over those guys, the control and sensuality you displayed. Seeing you enjoy yourself that much. It was perfectly erotic."

"You didn't mind being there?" I remembered how he hadn't wanted to be the same as other guys who were being used as props. It hadn't occurred to me when I had taken the man by the hand at the top of the cliff. I hoped that I hadn't overlooked something important.

"No." His response was decisive, with a shake of his head. "I didn't feel how I thought I would, at all. I enjoyed watching you and taking pictures of you. I wouldn't mind watching you or taking pictures of you doing anything. I still think I'd rather not be involved, but I enjoyed being there. It was thrilling. I can't explain how much." I put my arm around him and pulled him closer to me. I didn't kiss him, aware that I was still covered in quite a lot of cum. I was glad that I had been able to finish our holiday in a sexual way. I had acted instinctively, and it had paid off. I deserved to be lucky, I thought.

The next morning, we moved through the airport quite quickly. It wasn't a busy morning. I didn't suppose Wednesdays were a popular day for flying, for business or pleasure. Whilst we were having a coffee and waiting for our gate to be announced, I got an e-mail back from Brightstar. Dan agreed to the conditions I'd set out in my e-mail to him, and he formally offered me the job on those terms. I showed it to Paul, and he gave me a huge embrace.

"Well done," he smiled. "That's exactly the right place to start your career. It's exactly what you wanted, isn't it?"

"It really is. I'm so happy. I'm looking forward to getting started. It'll be great to be a part of a team as well."

"Brilliant." Paul carried on smiling and hugged me again.

"I have loved the gym, but it was always a stop gap. It had started to become very boring. I'm glad I'm making the move into a career. I was worried I never would."

As we sat in there in the airport lounge, I had a realisation. My newfound freedom had changed my life. I don't think I would have been in this position if Paul and I hadn't started talking more openly. I don't think I would have had the confidence to control the interview like I had, or to take my opportunity at the trial evening with both hands. I was no longer the boring old me. I wasn't timid, or submissive anymore. I wasn't going to be stuck in the gym anymore. I was happily married. I had a great sex life. I had a career, the career I'd always wanted. I had a flutter of excitement at the thought of it. I hadn't broken anything to get here. That was the best part. I'd been honest with myself, and with Paul. I had enhanced everything that I already had. I thought about the number of people who go through divorces, and all the associated pain, to get away from where they don't want to be. It's easy to run from what you don't want, it's much harder to know what you do want. When you know that, it turns out you might not need to run at all. If you're with the right person, you have to go out and get what you both want, together.

"My new project management skills might help with our sex parties," I smiled at Paul.

"I'm sure they will. I'd never thought of that." Paul laughed.

"Thanks for your help with the job. That e-mail we sent back was perfect. I don't think I'd have thought to do that on my own."

"It's easy when you're looking from the perspective of the employer," Paul assured me. "You'll recruit people during your career, and you'll realise how much power good candidates hold. Good people are very hard to find. You're going to be very valuable to that company, don't ever forget that. Make sure you keep a good understanding of your own worth."

"Good advice," I nodded, as I considered the power of that sentiment.

"There are so many people in the world who are so full of themselves. So confident in abilities that they don't have. It's such a shame when people as talented as you, are missed because someone is louder or pushier. People who have no doubts, are idiots." Paul assured me. He spoke with a tone and confidence that was convincing.

"I'd never seen it that way. That is true." I drifted into my thoughts as we looked out of the windows at a plane pulling into a gate. I was looking forward to seeing Dan again. I was looking forward to him flirting with me, and me flirting back, but doing nothing about it. I was looking forward to keeping him interested in me for a long time, and him never getting me. So many women are scorned for sleeping their way to the top. If a guy sleeps with women at work, it isn't regarded in the same way at all. Often times he's applauded. Why should men get to use their charm and abuse their power and not us? Can anyone name a man who has been accused of shagging their way to the top? Good looking men get on quicker in life, that's a simple fact. I'm going to do the same. I'm not going to sleep with anyone at work, but I am going to use what I have to get what I want, in exactly the same way that tall, good-looking men do.

As my thoughts flowed through my mind, I realised how relaxed I was. I didn't feel any pressure, about anything. I didn't feel the pressure of the new job, which I'm sure I would have worried about in the past. Paul and I would always be alright, and if the job didn't work out, I was sure I could get another one. I didn't feel the pressure of trying to work out what wasn't right in my life. Everything seemed calm. I leant back further in my chair and enjoyed the sensation of peace.

As the plane started to board, I turned my phone off and reached into my bag for the Sophie Martinez phone. I checked my messages. Thirty-two new messages from beautiful people who wanted to meet me. My stomach fluttered as I turned the phone off. I couldn't wait to continue my adventures.

Chapter 25 – My Ultimate Fantasy Fulfilled

Jess was stood in the middle of the room as I opened the door. She was laughing with a couple of the guys. That girl could put anyone at ease in any situation. I'm sure she could make even the tensest experience feel relaxed. I'd asked her not to dress in anything too sexy, but she still looked stunning. She was wearing cut off jean shorts and little t-shirt. I'm sure everyone in the room wanted to fuck her. It was important that I made my presence felt. This was my fantasy. I saw Nathan fiddle with the camera as he saw me make my entrance. I assumed that he had started recording. I promised myself that would be the last time I would think about the camera today. "Here we go," I thought, and smiled.

I swung my hips, more than I ever normally would, as I moved from the doorway towards Jess. I felt the eyes in the room turn and focus on me as the guys noticed that I had entered. As I reached Jess, I took her hand and pulled her towards me. She came naturally into my embrace, and I kissed her. Our tongues danced together as I put one hand on the side of her face. I ran my other hand over her body and down onto her bum. I felt the gaze of everybody in the room fall onto us. We continued to kiss in complete silence. After a few seconds, I stepped back and smiled at her. Her hand was intertwined with mine, and she lifted my arm, as if to show me off.

"You all know Sophie." Jess beamed her beautiful smile. "Today you are going to treat her like a princess. Between you, you'll fulfil her every desire. Do what I say, and you'll have the time of your lives." She took me over towards the bed in the centre of the room and ushered me to sit down. I was wearing a black mini dress, with black underwear, stockings, and suspenders. I had high heels, make up, and I'd had my hair done that morning. I felt a million dollars. I wasn't nervous at all. I felt sexy and confident. I was going to experience and enjoy every moment of pleasure that was about to present itself to me.

Jess went over to the two guys sat closest to me, took them by the hands, and they got to their feet. I looked around the room and smiled. There were six guys in total. I'd slept with them all, more than once over the last few months. Each guy smiled back, all feeling that they knew me more intimately than the others. I hadn't invited Paul, or Jess' husband, Rob. This was an experience entirely for me. The guys that were in the room were all good blokes. The thing that they had in common was that I thought that they were hot. I was very attracted to each of them. The first two that Jess had picked out were brought over to the bed.

"Strip to your underpants for her." Jess ordered. They both immediately did as they were told. Jess picked up their clothes and moved them into piles next to the wardrobe. I looked at the gorgeous bodies in front of me, sat back on the bed and lent back on my straight arms, breathing a gentle contented sigh. Both men were bulging hard, straining the fabric of their underpants as they stood and waited.

"Sit down with her and give her a kiss to say hello." Jess gave them their next instruction. They sat one either side of me. I turned to my right with a warm smile, before enjoying a deep, erotic kiss. My hand ran over his chest and stomach as the kiss lasted several seconds. My hand continued further until it found a resting place on top of his boxer shorts, where I knew his beautiful cock was hiding. He was as hard as I'd ever known him. Our kiss stopped and I stroked his cock through his shorts. I looked at him and winked. He smiled back at me. I turned to my left, letting go of my first toy, initiating an equally sensual kiss with the second of my lovers. My hands ran over the hard, gym toned physique sat next to me. I again touched what was soon to be mine. He was as hard as the first, and he panted through our kiss at the thrill of my touch. When I pulled back, Jess asked the guys to sit back on the chairs at the edge of the room. The experience was repeated with the next two gorgeous men.

I felt very conscious, aware of each moment as I watched the guy's strip for me. I felt alert and tremendously excited. My senses weren't dulled by nerves, or alcohol, or uncertainty. I engaged passionately in each erotic kiss. Taking the time to explore the array of bodies around me, letting each guy know that I wanted him to be there. I wanted each guy to know that they were a specific turn on for me. After a short, but heady and exhilarating period of time, the guys were sat back in their chairs. They all waited their next instruction, only wearing their underpants. I looked around the room. All eyes were on me. I shivered with excitement.

"Ok, lie back on the bed Soph. Can you guys make your way over to the bed. Three of you stand at each side?" Jess moved them into the places she wanted them. I lay back, supported by my elbows, so I could see all six guys surround me, wondering what was coming next.

"Take off her dress. Be careful, and gentle." Came the instruction from Jess. I watched as hands found their way to my body, caressing the skin of my legs and arms. The guys at my head end touched my breasts through my dress, as the material of the hem started to move up my thighs. The dress slid up and exposed my panties. They were very skimpy. Hands glided over my inner thighs, brushing over the material on the front of my G string. The view of the men focussed on me was heightening my sensations. Hands continued to search out different areas of my body, as more skin became exposed. I sat up, in order that the dress could finally be removed over my head. I lay back down, and the hands continued to touch every exposed part of me.

"Ok, step back again." Jess had moved closer to the bed and interjected. "It's time for Sophie to unwrap her gifts." The guys stood, three along each side of the bed, as they had been before my dress had been removed. I sat up, in the middle of the bed. I looked to Jess for instruction. "I think everyone wants to see your tits Soph!" Jess grinned. "Including me!" She followed up. "Show us, and then take your time to undress your toys." She moved back from the bed again, leaving me as the centre of attention. I moved from sitting, to my knees. My stockinged legs feeling lovely against each other as I moved into my new position. As I kneeled on the bed, I could see myself in the mirror on the far side of the room. My bra was pushing my cleavage up in front of me, and the suspenders for the stockings were framing the curve of my hips. The garters at the top of the stockings gently pinching the flesh of my inner thigh, creating a beautiful gap between my legs. I Turned around, slowly. Partly to look at each of the guys, and partly to let them look at me. I also wanted to see the rest of me in the mirror. I saw my bum framed beautifully by the suspenders. The curved lines at the top of my G string adding to the effect. I loved it. I decided that I was going to keep my stockings on throughout this experience. Nudity was nothing compared to how erotic I felt in lingerie. I turned away from the mirror, remembering that this moment was being captured on film for me to look back at. A shiver ran through me as I thought of showing Paul what I was about to do. I looked around at the guys again and unhooked my bra at the back. I slipped my arm underneath the material of the cups and covered the front of my tits. I took the bra off completely with my other hand and threw it away from the bed. I stayed there for a few seconds, deciding who to approach first. I picked at random and moved on my knees towards the guy at the head of the bed on my right. I got close to him and kissed him. I released my arm from my tits and felt the softness of my breasts push into his hard chest. I kissed him harder. I realised how turned on I was, as I gripped him with my arms, thrusting my tongue into his mouth, and running my hands over the muscles of his back. He held me for a few moments, and then brought his hands round to my front, looking for my boobs. I withdrew from my kiss and leant back, my hands holding his shoulders. His eyes moved down to my chest, and he sighed, before taking my tits in his hands. His mouth followed straight away, sucking, and licking my nipples, in a hurried, but sensual massage. I threw my head back, engulfed in pleasure. My long straight hair falling freely as the sensation in my chest increased in its intensity. I brought my head back up, and ran my hands from his neck, down over his chest, lingering on his flat, tight stomach, before moving down and onto his erection. It was straining at the material of his underpants. I kissed him again, before running my tongue down from his mouth, over his neck and onto his chest. I played with his torso with my hands, lips, and tongue, as I moved my knees back, and bent over onto all fours. I could feel the eyes of the other guys on me, as my face came to rest millimetres from the front of his shorts. My hips were pushed up. I tried to imagine the image of me in the stockings and suspenders that the other men were seeing. My tits free beneath me, as I took the waistband of his boxers in my hands and pulled it down. I gasped with excitement as he sprang from the material as I pulled the shorts down over his thighs. I put my hand gently on his cock and admired it. He was so incredibly hard. It was almost solid. I looked up at him and smiled, as he looked back at me. I placed the end of it in my mouth and engulfed it with my lips and tongue. I stayed there for a few seconds, still looking at him. Watching as he sighed with pleasure. I applied a tiny bit more pressure to him as I brought my lips back and withdrew my mouth. He gasped aloud. I covered my tits with my arm again as I knelt upright. I took his cheek in my hand and kissed him again.

    I moved to my left and began to repeat the experience with the next guy. I was starting to get lost in the sensations of the kissing and touching. The shivers which took over my whole body as my tits were touched, was almost orgasmic. The slightest touch between my legs and I would have climaxed. By the time I had completed the foreplay with the third guy at the foot end of the bed, I couldn't contain myself. After I had exposed his cock, and taken him in my mouth, the same as I had the other two guys, I turned on the bed, and lay on my back in front of him. "Lick me." I ordered, pulling the material of my panties to one side. He dropped to his knees and plunged his face between my legs. I gripped the covers of the bed, as the extasy that had built up in my whole body, began to explode immediately through the centre of me. He could sense my urgency, his tongue was frantic as I writhed on the bed, holding tighter and tighter to the sheets. The orgasm pulsed and span through my entire body and mind. I threw my head back and moaned as the pleasure overtook me completely. My legs pulled him towards me, wrapped around his back, as I dragged his mouth onto me, harder and faster. As the sensations started to ebb, I let go of the covers and grabbed his head with both hands. I felt my body relaxing into the bed. My breathing changed to deep, heavy sighs, as I recovered my senses. He had sensed the change in me and had reduced the pressure and speed of his stimulation. The gentle rolling of his lips and tongue were extracting the last moments of joy from my body. I smiled as I sat up onto my elbows, and let out a small laugh, amazed by what I had experienced. "Thank you." He had stood up, and I looked up at him as I spoke. His cock erect. His underpants clinging to the tops of his thighs. As I got back up to my knees, I pushed his underpants to the floor. "None of you will be needing these anymore." I looked across at the other two on the same side of the bed, who promptly removed their shorts. The three of them stood naked in front of me.

I made my way to the head of the bed again, making sure to cover my tits with my arm as I moved. The guys on the other side of the bed were going to experience exactly the same thing. Although everyone has seen me naked before, I had learned that the exposure of my tits to men was a huge turn on. The longer it was delayed, the more they wanted to see and touch them. I perhaps took slightly longer with the guys on the other side. My orgasm had reduced my desperate need for satisfaction. I took my time to kiss and be touched, enjoying each moment. Savouring the pleasure. I wanted to build back up to the feeling that I had before, and truly immerse myself in the same experience again. It didn't take long before I was starting to feel charged with electricity once more. By the time I got to the third, and last guy, my kissing had become as intense as it was at the beginning. I pulled his head into my tits, increasing the pressure of the stimulation. I became ever more turned on by the continuous touch of lips and tongues on my nipples.

After I released the final guy from my mouth, I moved back onto the centre of the bed. I sighed with pleasure, taking a moment to rest my senses and gather my thoughts. Jess moved close to the foot of the bed. "Ok, can you all come and stand next to me?" The guys walked to the end of the bed and gathered around her.

"Ok gorgeous," Jess addressed me. "It's time for you to get on all fours." I moved to the left edge of the bed and got on all fours. I moved my hair round to the far side of my neck, away from the view of the men, so that it was out of the way. I could see the naked group of guys waiting at the end of the bed, staring at me intently. "You can take her panties down!" Jess nodded to the guy stood closest to the side of the bed where I had positioned myself. He came round behind me, and I gasped at his touch. He pulled the fragments of the material of my G string down over the cheeks of my bum. He left them halfway up my thighs. It felt amazing, as I was exposed and ready to be used. I didn't understand why, but I felt dirtier knowing that my panties had been pulled down, rather than removed completely.

"Thank you." I heard Jess say. "Now, everyone needs to get a condom. You're first!" I didn't see who Jess had pointed at. I heard the guys moving around at the end of the bed. After a few moments I saw one of them move down the side and position himself behind me. I looked back at him and tried to smile. My smile was masked by the pleasure that had completely taken over the expression on my face. I looked back at the audience of guys, naked, about to watch me get fucked.

"I want you to fuck her. Slow at first, speeding up, and then as hard as you can. You can go for as long as you like, but do not cum." Jess was very sincere in her last instruction. "If you feel like you're going to cum, pull out and stop. That's when the next guy can start" She looked around to check understanding, and everyone nodded.

The guy behind me placed one hand on my bum and moved his cock into position. He began to push into me, and I was so turned on, he sank into me without any trouble. I moaned as he entered me, big and completely erect. His other hand moved onto my other cheek, and he slowly started to push into me with rhythmic strokes. The slow penetration didn't last for long, which I was quite glad about. He started to drive harder and harder into me on his thrusts. Before long he was banging and slapping against my legs as he fucked me. I instinctively grabbed the bed covers as his hands moved onto my hips, pulling me towards him. The strength of his arms making each stroke feel harder and deeper. I noticed in my peripheral vison, another guy moving around to the side of the bed. Jess could sense that the guy fucking me was moving towards orgasm, as his speed and effort increased. He groaned as he came to a stop, plunged deep into me, pulling me onto him. He withdrew, and I gasped as we separated. I sensed him move to one side behind me, and new hands gripping my hips as the next guy moved into position. I didn't look back. It was a strange, and erotic feeling not knowing who was behind me. I felt him push into me. He was bigger, and the new condom slowed the penetration slightly. It didn't take long before he forced his whole length into me, immediately dragging my hips towards him and pulling us together as our sex began. After a couple of slow stokes, he built-up speed and began penetrating me as hard as the first guy had finished. It felt like a continuation of the same sexual experience. There were subtle differences in the way it felt. There was also the deliciously erotic knowledge that it was a new partner.

    I listened to the sounds of our sex as I rocked back and forth on the bed. My tits moved beneath me as the sounds of him hitting my legs with his thighs and hips became loud. The sensation of being fucked hard, pulsing through my entire body. I looked across at the group of guys at the end of the bed. I struggled to focus, as my head moved due to the fast and deep penetration behind me. I worked out who was fucking me from seeing the remaining guys watching me. It was one of my favourites behind me. Handsome, athletic, and powerful. The thought of him fucking me, as well as the incredible feeling of being on show, brought me to my second climax.

    "Don't stop." I yelled, as I pushed my hips back onto his cock. He continued to slam into me, taking my breath away with the power of his thrusts. I shuddered through the first waves of my orgasm. The noises of our bodies colliding, and the sensations of the penetration, all combining in sexual harmony. The knowledge that I was being watched as I enjoyed one of the most sexual experiences I could imagine. I gripped the sheets and put the side of my face down into the bed, still watching the guys, who were watching me. The sensations continued to flow through me. I stopped pushing back as the orgasm came to a huge climax. My eyes closed as I revelled in the sensation. I heard the guy behind me exhale as he pushed into me and stop. I moved slightly from side to side, pushing back on his cock, extracting every last feeling from my orgasm. After a few seconds, he slowly pulled out of me.

    "Do you want a break?" Asked Jess, from beside me.

"No." I smiled. My face still half buried in the bed.

"You heard her." Jess moved away. "You're next!"

I lifted myself back up onto all fours as someone new entered me. I realised again that I didn't know who it was. I closed my eyes and enjoyed the sensation and excitement of not knowing for a few minutes. Ater a while I would look at the guys at the end of the bed again, to work out who was fucking me. He didn't last long before he pulled out, and he was replaced by the biggest cock in the group. I felt it immediately stretch me, and I knew who it was without checking. My feelings started to rise again, as he immediately got up to full speed. It was breath taking being fucked that hard by such a big thing. I had started to feel like I was going to cum again when he slowed and removed himself. It must have been difficult for the guys who had watched the show to this point. I didn't blame them for not lasting very long. The fifth guy was smaller, but the sensations continued to grow as he pushed into me as hard as he could. I was about ready to orgasm for a third time, when he pulled out and moved back. From the noise he made I assumed that he had been quite close to cuming as well. The last guy stepped in behind me, and I started to orgasm as soon as he penetrated me. The increased friction of a new cock, combined with what felt like a ribbed condom, pushed me back into an orgasmic state. It felt different to the last one. It seemed to last longer but wasn't quite as intense. I yelped for him to fuck me harder as I rocked on the bed, panting as the erotic sensations flowed through me again.

He slowed and pulled out after it was obvious that I had finished. I collapsed face down on the bed, and then rolled onto my side to look at the group of men.

Jess walked to the head of the bed, a huge smile on her face. "How was that?" She enquired.

"Incredible!" Was all I could utter. My body was tingling and limp as the feelings of pleasure lingered within me. Jess moved some pillows around and told me to sit up against the head of the bed. I moved over, and sat at the side of the bed, my back against the pillows which were propped up against the headboard. I was almost in a sitting position, relaxed back onto the pillows. I was exhausted and wondered what was going to happen next.

"Come here." Jess beckoned a guy over, who immediately obeyed her. She positioned him next to me, his still erect cock projecting to the side of me. "Relax," Jess said to me. "I want you to see how turned on you've made these guys." She took his cock in her hand and started to stroke him. I watched as his cock moved as she stroked it. My tits underneath him. My stockings and suspenders still in place as my legs relaxed into a spread position on the bed. Her wanking started to increase in speed. I looked up at her, she was staring intently at the cock in her grip, focussing on it completely. I looked across at the guy, who was staring at my body. He caught my glance and looked back at me. He reached down and fondled my tits for a moment, before standing back straight upright as he began to cum. Jess didn't change her rhythm, as cum erupted from him, jumping into the air before falling onto my tits. Some of it went so far it missed me and hit the pillows on the far side of the bed. Jess slowly brought her motion to a stop, and they guy moved back. Immediately Jess looked around for the next one. The next guy moved into position over me, and Jess started to touch him. Within seven or eight movements, he ejaculated. He moaned as cum flowed over me, running across my chest, and covering most of my tits. I gasped at the amount of it. I was so turned on by how excited he was by the sight of my body.

  As Jess began the job of satisfying the third guy, I started to touch myself. I was transfixed, watching her wank him. I felt more at the centre of attention than I had before. Even though I wasn't being touched by anyone else. The guy that Jesses was wanking was focussed on me. I looked across at the other guys, and they were enjoying the show as well. Even the two that had already cum. I moved my gaze back to the cock in front of me and continued to touch myself. I could see him very quickly get to the point of orgasm. After the third jet of cum had hit my body, I looked down at my sex drenched tits. It must have been quite an image. I looked up at the camera for the first time since we had started. I broke the promise to myself to make sure it was capturing me in this position. I wanted to know if I looked as good as I felt. I felt used, and dirty, but in a way that was exactly what I wanted. The object of desire and attention. The sexual creature that these men wanted to experience.

Jess brought the fourth guy forward and told one of the remaining two who hadn't cum to put a condom on. She started gently stroking the new cock. The guy she had given the instructions to appeared at her side.

"Move over this way slightly, babe." She motioned to me with her eyes, and I slid my hips around so that I was over the edge of the bed. Jess moved up towards the head of the bed as she continued to wank the guy who was standing over me. I made eye contact with him as his breathing increased in urgency. I continued to touch myself as the guy being wanked started to tense up, as his body prepared for orgasm.

"Fuck her." I heard Jess say, and the guy moved in beside her. He leant down picked my thighs up and pulled me towards him. He immediately penetrated me. As I felt him slide inside me, I continued to touch myself. The sensations of the penetration becoming more electric by the second. I looked up at the beautiful man fucking me and I started to play myself with more urgency. I glanced across at the image of Jess wanking the guy with the big cock, holding him over my tits. As he watched me getting fucked. The touch of Jess was too much for him. I received my fourth explosion of cum across my body. I took in a deep breath, watching the guy fucking me, as cum splashed onto me from an incredibly excited voyeur. It was an overwhelming sexual moment. I gasped and moaned with pleasure. Jess could see that I would soon climax, and hurriedly brought in the fifth guy to stand over me. I barely noticed her quicker motion, as she brought him to orgasm in what seemed like only a few seconds. Watching the fifth guy cuming across my tits, whilst being fucked harder and harder, was more than I could handle. My fingers were the final help in bringing me to my fourth, earth shattering climax of the afternoon. Jess had stepped back, taking the last of the guys with her. Cum splashed and rolled across my chest and onto my stomach. The guy fucking me pulled my thighs towards him, and continued to penetrate me, faster and harder. My orgasm continued to run through me for what seemed like an extraordinary amount of time. The sensation less intense that the first times, but it seemed like that allowed me to enjoy it more. I absorbed the feeling for longer. I took a moment to contemplate the sight of my dishevelled body, and the handsome, muscular frame still fucking me, as fast as he could. As I shuddered to a relaxed state on the bed, he pulled out of me, and pulled the condom off. I continued to touch myself, the final throws of my orgasm sending shivers of relief through me. I looked down as he took his cock, and wanked himself, looking at me, as I lay there, covered in cum. He ejaculated in a matter of seconds. His sperm sprayed across me, missing my stomach, and reaching my chest and my face. It kept coming, as my fingers came to rest between my legs, rivulets of cum continued to land on me. As his massive explosion came to rest, he moved back. I looked down at myself. I had certainly earned a very visual demonstration of the desire and passion that the guys had built up for me through the experience. I felt the cum still running over my boobs, as I saw Nathan move in closer. The lens of the camera was searching over my entire body, taking in every inch of the image of sex that I had become. I stood up, becoming even more aware of how covered I was. I felt liquid run down over my body and down my legs. I touched my chest with my hands, feeling the sex that had landed on me. I held my tits for the camera and smiled. Enormously satisfied, and proud that I'd also satisfied six, attractive men.

"Who wants to help her wash off in the shower?" Jess turned to the guys as she asked. There was a general nod of heads and a couple of raised hands. "You choose." Smiled Jess.

I took two guys by the hand. My favourite two and led them towards the bathroom.

Jess turned to the remaining four men. "You guys can go if you want or stay and watch! Me and the cameraman are going to have some fun."

I looked back as I was about to enter the bathroom, and Jess had pulled Nathan into a kiss. None of the guys were leaving, as some pulled on their boxers and sat down on the chairs. Keen to watch Jess take her clothes off and perform for them. They are in for quite a treat with those two, I thought to myself. Something told me that the afternoons fun wasn't over quite yet.

Connect with Danielle Aimie

Thank you for reading my book. If you enjoyed it, won't you please take a moment to leave me a review at your favourite retailer,

Get in touch by either sending me a personal message via e-mail or follow/message me on [Instagram, @danielleaimie](). [Twitter]() or [Pintrest]() Find all my contacts and new books on my website https://danielleaimie.com/books.html

Thanks!

Danielle Aimie